MW00979398

A SHERLOCK HOLMES TRILOGY

A SHERLOCK HOLMES TRILOGY

▼

Allen Heiss

Writers Club Press
San Jose New York Lincoln Shanghai

A Sherlock Holmes Trilogy

All Rights Reserved © 2000 by Allen J. Heiss

No part of this book may be reproduced or transmitted
in any form or by any means, graphic, electronic, or mechanical,
including photocopying, recording, taping, or by any information
storage retrieval system, without the permission
in writing from the publisher.

Writers Club Press
an imprint of iUniverse.com, Inc.

For information address:
iUniverse.com, Inc.
5220 S 16th, Ste. 200
Lincoln, NE 68512
www.iuniverse.com

ISBN: 0-595-15155-8

Printed in the United States of America

A PASTICHE
DEDICATED TO ALL SHERLOCKIANS

and to Vicki, whose encouragement
and assistance made this book possible.

As many authors have stated, no book can be written
without the help of others. I would like to acknowledge
and thank the following:

Victoria Rubel
Jennifer Jones
Dorothy Heiss
Ronald Mendelsohn
Connie Saunders
Michael Guest

CONTENTS

▼

FOREWORD

▼

After more years than I care to remember, actually a lifetime, for that matter, I have read and reread the Sherlock Holmes stories, plus countless pastiches. I have watched almost all the motion pictures and have listened to many, many radio broadcasts over the years; such is their appeal.

I began to wonder why this appeal was so universal. No other fictional character has caught the imagination for so long in such a global manner as Holmes. This indeed is a mystery in itself. How would Holmes deduce his immense popularity? For one thing, I am sure he would agree that Watson and he represented the embodiment of all that was Victorian and Edwardian England. Our little views into the snug comfort of Baker St. next to the fire with crying winds in the chimney and rain lashing at the window panes. Or dashing down fog-laden gas lit London streets in a hansom cab. Yes, he would concur he gave us a wonderful view of a time when England was at the zenith of her power and prestige.

With all this in mind, I have always felt that Sherlock Holmes, taken out of the context of that background, was something akin to the sacrilegious. Surely, to remove him from the Victorian and Edwardian atmosphere was to invariably weaken his character. Yet countless productions have done just that over many years.

It was at the tender age of thirteen when Cousin Bob, four years my senior, introduced me to Sherlock Holmes. Together we listened to the radio at our grandmother's house, to the incomparable Basil Rathbone as Holmes and Nigel Bruce as Watson, in "The Hound of the Baskervilles." How I waited for those Sunday evening broadcasts, and eventually hear the thrilling conclusion. I became an addict then and there.

I purchased my first complete volume of Sherlock Holmes stories at sixteen. As I read, questions arose, such as, what in the world was a gasogene? What did a boiling retort produce? What kind of ammunition was a Boxer cartridge? On and on went the questions, and over time and study they were slowly answered, almost like being Sherlock Holmes himself.

I still have that first volume, and it brings back fond memories of youth. In that volume there was a wonderful memorial by Christopher Morley. "Those of us who in earliest boyhood gave our hearts to Conan Doyle and have had from him so many hours of good refreshment find our affection unshakable."

There is something about Holmes that reaches deep into the psyche. He was self-reliant, self-confident and self-employed. A wonderful ideal, but I'm afraid quite difficult in the real world. As Conan Doyle put it in his foreword for "The Casebook of Sherlock Holmes":

"I thank you for your past constancy, and can but hope that some return has been made in the shape of that distraction from the worries of life and stimulating change of thought which can only be found in the fairy kingdom of Romance."

The study of Holmes has taken me to far away places such as England, France and Switzerland. I can well remember my English friend taking a picture of me, deerstalker on head and pipe in mouth, at the cliffs of Poldhu Bay, Cornwall ("The Case of the Devil's Foot.") With a great pathetic smile, he snapped my picture and I could not help thinking that he thought we were crazy Americans.

In "The Sign of the Four" I read and adapted the maxim, "When you have eliminated the impossible, whatever remains, however improbable, must be the truth." It has served me well and has very seldom failed me throughout the years. However, when one begins to write stories about Holmes, all this logic goes out the window and we are faced with Conan Doyle's "fairy kingdom of Romance," which is to say intuitive imagination. Of course any attempt to follow in Conan Doyle's footsteps is what show business people refer to as "a hard act to follow." But then again as Sherlock has stated, "We can but try."

With that thought in mind, it is my sincere hope that these three stories will give a renewed thrill to all past readers of the canon, and for the new reader, the encouragement to explore the original stories in all their fascinating avenues of mystery and interest.

Allen J. Heiss
Montgomery Highlands
Salem, Wisconsin

BOOK ONE

THE SATYR OF STONEHENGE

Author's Note

▼

"Here also I find an account of the Addleton tragedy and
the singular contents of the ancient British Borrow."

From *The Golden Pince-Nez*

Besides being intriguing, it is great fun to speculate on the suggested but
untold stories of *The Canon*. Having made several trips to England over
the years, I became fascinated with Stonehenge on Salisbury Plain in the
county of Wiltshire.

I can well remember the first time I entered the Sarsen Circle. It was a
time just before it was made inaccessible to the general public. I lost nothing of that breathtaking moment, when the eye first catches sight of the
thirty-foot trilithons at sunset.

Needless to say, the immense mystery of this prehistoric monument
caught my imagination. What a tantalizing location for a Sherlock Holmes
mystery.

CHAPTER ONE

▼

BAKER STREET AND BEYOND

As I reviewed my notes for the year 1884, still early in my association with Sherlock Holmes, my attention was drawn to the nefarious affair, which took place at Stonehenge on Salisbury Plain.

It was the third week in October on a damp, cloudy morning as I entered our sitting room. My senses rebelled. Holmes was seated at his chemical table absorbed in a chemical investigation. A large retort boiling furiously in front of him gave off malodorous fumes. As he looked up and caught my wry expression, he lay down his pipette and graduate. He then began a disquisition on the merits of coal tar derivatives.

"The potential of coal tar distillation is immeasurable. Why, the alkaloid products and aniline dyes alone are boundless."

I sat down to Mrs. Hudson's poached eggs with little enthusiasm.

"Really, Holmes, I can't say which is worse, this foul atmosphere or your chemical dissertation."

"As you well know, my dear Watson, my professional activities have been rather quiet of late; indeed, upon reflection, I am convinced the London criminal has become a rather dull fellow. Hence, these experiments."

"Will you be at this all day?"

"More or less," said he laconically.

As I looked around our rooms bathed in a chemical haze, I could see there was no point in pressing the matter. I resolved then and there to spend the day elsewhere.

I had awakened that morning feeling somewhat rheumatic, which, more than likely, was due to the recurring after-affects of my Afghanistan experience. I considered for a moment that perhaps a Turkish bath at Neville's on Northumberland Avenue would be a welcome relief. As it is also a cleanser of the system, I felt I could rid myself of these noxious fumes. I should add that at this time, Holmes was not a devotee of the baths.

With my breakfast only half eaten, I left Holmes perched at his chemical table like some huge bird of prey.

It was just after one o'clock when I finished dressing and left the drying room. Feeling much refreshed, I leisurely walked in the direction of Regent Circus to the Criterion Bar.

I was seated at a table near the bar when suddenly I heard my name called out.

"Watson, old man." I turned and saw Stamford at the far side of the bar. I must admit it was a pleasant surprise to hear one's name called out in this immense sea of unknown faces.

"Well, Watson," said he, as he strolled over. "I see you're still smoking that Ships mixture."

"Yes, and it has gone a bit sour for me. I really need a change."

"You must try some of my Arcadia. It will be a pleasant change."

"That is very kind of you. Won't you join me for a glass of claret?"

"With pleasure, and by the way, how goes the Baker Street diggings with Holmes?"

"I am, for one thing, constantly exasperated by his lack of consideration." I went on to relate my morning annoyance, much to Stamford's amusement. "Furthermore, 'Elementary, Watson!' is a remark I frequently hear from Holmes, but in truth I find nothing elementary, only complexities, when Holmes is deducing aloud.

"Believe me, at times it is extremely difficult to share lodgings with Holmes. If you don't believe me, you should come to see for yourself."

"Heavens, no. I have always had a severe feeling of inferiority in his presence."

"Yes, he does affect most people in that way. However, I have nothing but profound admiration for his methods of detection. One could write volumes about his analytical deductions."

"Speaking of volumes, I never dreamed you had literary talents, Watson. I must admit to being deeply interested in your published narratives. How did you get started writing about Holmes?"

"Well, as I have stated in my book 'A Study In Scarlet', I had time on my hands while recuperating from my war experience. I made something of a hobby out of him. However, not much time passed when I became more or less mindful that I must record as many events as possible about his amazing powers of deduction. We have something akin to a fragile working partnership."

"In what way is it fragile?"

"Well, most of the time he is appalled by my so called romanticizing of his activities."

"What does he want?"

"Well-nigh a textbook discourse. Yet, on the other hand, he is pragmatic enough to realize my narratives promote an increase in his clientele."

"I certainly would imagine so," mused Stamford.

"For my part, I not only enjoy recording Holmes extraordinary faculties, but the revenue received from the stories is enough to give me hope of purchasing a small west end practice in the future."

"I see, but what about all the chemical tests you complain about?"

"I did a little investigation work myself, and after a few discrete inquiries, I ascertained that Holmes occasionally does chemical research for Burroughs' Chemical, Ltd."

"Does he need this extra income?"

"Oh, I doubt that, even with his sporadic consulting schedule. I imagine that he was sought after by Burroughs because of his experience with coal tar derivatives," I said, not knowing at all if this was the case.

"Well, well, he seems quite extraordinary."

"Extraordinary is an understatement," I remarked, feeling the sting of guilt at having already exposed a hidden side of Holmes to the inquisitive Stamford. I therefore refrained from discussing my alarm at Holmes' use of a 7% solution of cocaine from time to time. I swallowed my words, hoping that Stamford could not read my expression. As a doctor and as a friend, which I consider myself to be, I had admonished Holmes about the consequences that such activities could eventually produce.

Rather, I simply stated, "Some days he seems to be in a frenzy of activity, then for a period of time he is as dead as the proverbial dodo. Generally, he laments that his mind is like a great machine tearing itself apart because of a dismal lack of work for which it was built."

Stamford reflected for some moments. "Perhaps some other diversion would be helpful. He could take up the game of chess. I play now and then, and it is stimulating to the intellect. Undoubtedly, Holmes would be a master at the game."

I neither agreed nor disagreed with this premise, as Stamford did not realize how difficult it was to take personal liberties with Holmes, especially concerning his private pastimes.

Our conversation turned to more mundane subjects, such as conditions at Charing Cross Hospital and recent government scandals, in particular, the Alfred Dreyfus case in France.

The afternoon had passed quickly, and it was time to leave. We parted with the cordial exchanges of meeting more often in the future. I decided to walk back to our rooms. Most of the day the weather had been cold, damp and misty.

The hour was near five o'clock as I turned the corner at Oxford Street into Baker Street. As I arrived at the front door of 221B, I felt a gust of wind. Above me the dark sky was threatening rain. I entered, relit my pipe and mounted the stairs to our rooms.

My first impression, as I entered our rooms, was that thankfully the fumes of the morning had disappeared. Holmes was seated in his favorite armchair near the fire with what appeared to be an ancient manuscript in his lap. I walked over to the end table next to his chair and knocked the ashes from my pipe into the ashtray. I was about to comment on our improved atmosphere, when he looked up suddenly.

"Well, Watson, how is Stamford getting on these days?"

"Holmes, this is intolerable! Have you had those unsightly urchins, your so-called Irregulars following me today?" I demanded with some asperity.

Holmes smiled. "By no means, my dear boy. I have not left these rooms or sent anyone to follow you."

"Well then, how on earth could you know I was with Stamford?"

"I simply observe, then deduce."

"And what did you deduce?" I cried.

"Come, come, Watson. It is much too elementary to bear repeating," he said, still smiling.

"Nevertheless, I should like to know," I persisted.

"Very well, if you insist."

"I do."

"One minute from now you will exclaim how simple and obvious it all is."

"I will do no such thing!"

"We shall see. First, when the good doctor comes in from the inclement weather puffing away on his pipe and his tobacco has not the usual aroma of Ships, I take notice. Second, when he taps the ash out in the ashtray, and I perceive the distinct ash of Syrian Latakia, the main ingredient of the Arcadia mixture and the only tobacco Stamford has ever smoked, it behooves me to reason you met him today and received the Arcadia mixture from him."

I reflected a moment and replied perfunctorily, "Well, it is obvious as you state it."

Holmes expression fell. "Yes, yes, your usual response when all is made clear."

"Holmes, you surely would have been burnt at the stake in the last century for something akin to witchcraft."

"Not at all," he objected. "I simply observe and deduce."

At that moment, Mrs. Hudson knocked at our door with our evening meal.

CHAPTER TWO

▼

LESTRADE'S DILEMMA

Our light dinner long past, I lay down my latest treatise on medical research and looked at my pocket watch, considering retiring for the night. Holmes had settled down again with his manuscript and was still concentrating on some small passage. Occasionally, he spoke aloud to no one in particular, regarding some abstruse expression.

I rose from my chair to stretch my legs and walked over to our bow window. As I looked down the length of Baker Street, I could see that the late autumn storm had gained in strength. The early mist had turned into a driving rain. One could feel the insignificance of mankind in the midst of these powerful elemental forces. Baker Street had become a muddy morass bordered by sidewalks glistening under the street lamps. Few cabs were about on Oxford Street, but through the descending deluge, I saw a pair of blurred carriage lamps turn down Baker Street. I turned to Holmes.

"A hansom cab is stopping here! Who can it be, out on such a night?"

"Well, Watson, it must be of capital importance to bring Lestrade out."

"How do you know it's Lestrade?"

"I received a wire from him this afternoon."

As I looked out again, the familiar figure of Inspector Lestrade emerged from the cab.

"Be a good chap," said Holmes, "and let the inspector in. All decent people will be in bed by now."

Lestrade, wet and glistening in the gaslight, looked rather spent. Holmes came forward.

"Inspector, the Doctor has a tonic for such a night as this. Let me have your wet things while Watson makes a whiskey and soda. Now, my good Inspector, you look a bit worn. Have a cigar. Pull up to the fire."

"Well, Mr. Holmes, I have had a difficult day."

"Hmmm, so I gather from your telegram this afternoon. My curiosity has been aroused."

"The whole district around Salisbury Plain is in terror, mortal terror."

"Perhaps, Inspector, you should start from the beginning, as we know nothing of these events."

"Very well, Mr. Holmes." As the little detective began to speak, all his bulldog self-confidence was absent. He took a long drink of the whiskey and soda and settled down to his narrative. "Last week, on Tuesday morning, the Yard received a wire from Inspector Henslow of Salisbury asking for assistance. I was sent down to lend a hand. By and large, I was disappointed by what I encountered." Lestrade drew a folded newspaper clipping from his pocket and handed it to Holmes. Holmes gave it a cursory glance and handed it to me.

"Would you be so kind, Doctor?"

I began to read: "'Early in October, the lanes and commons of Salisbury Plain suddenly became places of dread. A bizarre figure, said by the local inhabitants to be possessed of supernatural powers, was stalking and frightening the villagers by night, and effortlessly avoiding capture by the police. Numerous witnesses testified that the apparition appeared to have a strange limping gait when running, and stranger yet, small horns protruding from its temples.

"'A Miss Dunbar, a young woman of 18 who lives at Amesbury, went to visit her sick aunt at a nearby farm. On her way, she encountered the apparition near the vicinity of Stonehenge. She described it as having 'the most hideous appearance.' She made a hasty retreat to her home, screaming all the way. Miss Dunbar later testified that it was the devil himself roaming the plain. Several others have described similar nocturnal encounters as they came near the locality of Stonehenge.

"'This mysterious intruder has the residents of Salisbury Plain so disturbed by these forays, that the local magistrate approved the formation of a vigilante committee to hunt down the interloper. All efforts have failed to capture the apparition.

"'Inspector Henslow, of the Salisbury Constabulary, is seeking assistance from Scotland Yard.'"

Holmes had listened intently, but now was slipping into a lethargic attitude with disappointment clouding his features.

"A curious account, to say the least. It appears the Western news article has quoted fragments of distorted superstitions and beliefs. I can see no way in which I would be of service, since it is actually out of my providence. As I have stated in the past, I confine my investigations to this world only. What say you, Watson? How does all of this strike you?"

"It sounds like a series of Guy Fawkes pranks," I answered, laughing.

"There you have it, Inspector. I concur."

"Yes, Mr. Holmes, that was my impression also," admitted Lestrade. He took another sip of his whiskey and soda and continued. "However, all that was last week. This week we have a dead body on our hands, found lying on the altar stone in the center of the Stonehenge circle."

Holmes' lethargic attitude vanished as he riveted to attention. Unconsciously, I stiffened with this new development. What had been nothing more than a curiosity a moment before, now took on dimensions of the bizarre.

"This is most gratifying —er, rather, this casts an entirely different light on the matter. Pray, continue, Lestrade."

"I was called out around four o'clock this morning. The Yard had received a telegram from Salisbury about three-thirty. I caught the first milk train at five and was in Salisbury by six-forty. Inspector Henslow met me at the station and we immediately went out by dogcart to Stonehenge, approximately ten miles from town. This is open country, Mr. Holmes, and right in the middle there are these piled up stones, some as high as thirty feet, with cross beams. Very strange place. The whole general layout seemed to be a broken circle with a central stone, which looked like an altar. It was here we found the body, horribly beaten to death. Around the altar stone were the hoof prints of a goat."

Holmes interjected, "If memory serves me, that is sheep and goat country. It wouldn't be unnatural to see cloven hoof prints anywhere in the area."

"But these prints, Mr. Holmes, were unusually large, such as a Shire horse might make. Believe me, it gave me a queer feeling to look at them. As you have stated, this is sheep and goat grazing land, but these hoof prints were wholly unnatural."

Holmes considered for a moment. "What do you make of those hoof prints?"

"What do I make of them? Neither heads nor tails, Mr. Holmes."

"What about boot prints?"

"There were none outside of those made by the constables' who removed the body, and those of the shepherd boy who found the body."

"Most singular," pondered Holmes.

"Lestrade continued, "The body proved to be a Mr. Farnsworth, a local farmer. I roped off the area around the altar stone and posted two constables on guard. Inspector Henslow and I then went off to the Farnsworth Farm, adjacent to the village of Amesbury. Of course, the family was distraught, and frankly, Mr. Holmes, I gained no factual information about this horrible deed, but I did get fairy tales of such a nature that I'm hesitant to repeat them."

"Never mind, Lestrade. Go on with your story."

"Well, it seems that this family, which tends their livestock in the district around Stonehenge, has been hearing strange pipes playing across the moors and the plain late at night."

"What kind of pipes?"

"They wondered about that also. About three miles distant lives Professor Conyers, an archeologist, who had taken up residence in the district about one year ago. He was consulted and was most helpful to the family members by giving readily of his knowledge. It seems these were the same as the pipes of Pan."

"This brings us to the Greeks and their mythology," reflected Holmes.

"So I have heard, but I must say, I was disappointed. I had heard a long time ago that Stonehenge was once a ritual site for the Druids. I was going to check every man, woman and child for possible sympathy to the long-lost pagan religion."

Holmes was leaning back in his chair, eyes closed and finger tips touching. I could see that some infinitesimal point had been touched and the chain of reasoning had begun.

Lestrade continued, "From that time onward, these pipes were heard more frequently. However, at that hour few people are out and about, but some who travel to Salisbury to labor, come across the plain from nearby villages. It seems these people, according to Inspector Henslow, have not only heard the pipes, but have seen some form of an apparition likened to a satyr—half man, half goat."

Holmes fell silent. I could see his mind was in deep concentration again.

"Well, Mr. Holmes, at any rate, the conclusion is that the entire countryside is up in arms and I haven't got any facts; only fairy tales. Inspector Henslow is out of his depth, and I stand a chance to lose a promotion if I cannot find the culprit who committed this murder and is terrorizing the countryside."

With this, Lestrade finished his whiskey and soda and made a clean break of it.

"If you could come down with me tomorrow, I would be deeply indebted. I know we at the Yard have been impatient with your theories in the past, but you have assisted me on several cases. I have appreciated that."

Holmes got up and reflected for a moment. "By all means, Lestrade, the case has curious points and I would be remiss if I did not lend a hand, but you know my methods. I must have a free hand until my data is complete. Is that agreed?"

"Agreed, Mr. Holmes!"

"Watson, be a good chap and check the Bradshaw for London to Salisbury."

Reading down the column, I found the earliest train was at seven in the morning out of Waterloo.

"Very good, Watson. Lestrade, bring a four-wheeler at six and we'll have breakfast here before we leave."

"Thank you, Mr. Holmes, and good night." I turned off the hallway gas when I heard the front door close, and turned to Holmes.

"Well, Holmes, what do you make of it?"

"This is contrary to human experience, where facts must always be sorted out from a mass of confusing and irrelevant information. There is an unfortunate tendency for some rural people to exaggerate the extent of any stimulus they receive. Their testimony then becomes unreliable as to describe any event which may or may not have taken place."

"Could this have religious connotations, as Lestrade pointed out?"

"One must have data. It is a capital mistake to theorize before one has all the facts. However, there are points of great interest and, as I see it, there are three separate lines of inquiry to engage our attention."

"Our?" I inquired.

"By all means, Doctor, if you can spare the time. Your assistance will be invaluable."

"I would be happy to accompany you if I can be of any use."

"Then it is settled," said he. "By the way," he added, "be sure to bring along your service revolver."

"Do you believe the killer will strike again?"

"It has been wisely said, forewarned is forearmed." With that we retired for the night.

CHAPTER THREE

▼

SALISBURY AND STONEHENGE

We went with Lestrade the following morning. The storm of yesterday had passed, but the weather remained cold and cloudy. Our cab took us to Waterloo Station and within a short time, we were rapidly moving through the county of Wiltshire. The beauty of the countryside's cathedral towns and villages was marred by the somber, lead grey sky.

Holmes was occupied with a large-scale ordnance map of Salisbury Plain. Lestrade, still distraught from yesterday, was napping. I, for one, could not concentrate on the medical book before me. Thoughts of the mystery of Stonehenge and this horrible murder made the trip of under two hours seem much longer.

When we arrived in Salisbury, Inspector Henslow was waiting at the station for us. It began to rain. Lestrade introduced Holmes and myself.

"Mr. Holmes, I want you to know how pleased I am that you are taking the time to assist us in this case. Please call upon me or my men for any assistance you may need."

"That's very kind of you Inspector. I trust Lestrade has told you of my particular methods?"

"We are aware of your methods, Mr. Holmes, by your friend here, Dr. Watson, and also we have a young constable who is forever singing your praises."

"Indeed," commented Holmes dryly. "I suppose that is inevitable when one has a biographer." I made no comment. "However, I reiterate that I must form my own conclusions on my own terms and pass them along when I feel it is appropriate."

"Yes, yes Mr. Holmes. That is no problem, as long as we get results. The countryside is terrified."

We mounted a four-wheeler for our journey and from just about any vantage point one could see the four hundred four foot high cathedral tower and spire. My mind went back to the thirteenth century when the idea was first conceived to build the largest tower and spire in Europe, taking a total of thirty-eight years to complete.

Very quickly we were away from the bustle of the town's center and into the tranquility of the cathedral close. Ancient, beautiful houses overlooked the green, from the center of which rose the glorious spire of the cathedral.

Holmes, sitting opposite me, observed, "Is it not remarkable, Watson, that there was a time when mankind excelled over his limitations and created all this?" I concurred.

There was no doubt that Inspector Henslow was proud of his historic town. During the drive he gave a thumbnail history from the time of the Romans to the present. He finished with, "The very road we are riding on was once a Roman road."

Holmes listened with keen interest. "I had no knowledge that the Romans penetrated this far northeast," said he.

"That's right, Mr. Holmes, they were all around here at one time."

Soon we were out of the town driving through the Wiltshire countryside.

"Has it been raining very long, Inspector?" I inquired.

"Well, Doctor, it has been raining intermittently since five o'clock this morning. However, this countryside is another question."

Holmes looked out at the dreary landscape. "This may be a complete waste of time. This rain will create a sea of mud."

At this, Lestrade sunk further into his seat.

We passed through the tiny hamlet of Amesbury. Its small white walled cottages with contrasting Tudor woodwork of red, black or light blue gave a touch of brightness to the monotony of the plain. Inspector Henslow informed us the hamlets in the area were known as Celtic Clachons in ancient times. As we passed the last distant isolated farms perched on the nearby hills, we suddenly saw the famous stones, standing stark on the windy plain of Salisbury.

"The place of the hanging stones," said Inspector Henslow, "which has defied the winds and rains of four thousand years."

We were about a half-mile away and from this distance it was impossible to realize their actual size. They seemed to be clustered in a small space, which gave the appearance of a mass of natural rocks. The road dipped abruptly and Stonehenge disappeared from view. When it reappeared after a short rise, we were only two hundred yards from the main circular colonnade.

We left our carriage and began to walk. Apparently it had been raining torrents before we arrived and the rush of water scoured the path up to Stonehenge.

Once inside the circle, having passed through a gateway formed by two pillars, our attention was arrested by the immense size of the uprights.

Inspector Henslow saw our amazement. "These uprights, which are about fifteen feet high, are called sarsens, and the stone blocks lying across them are lintels. The sarsens average about fifty tons each, and the lintels around four to five." Several that were still standing gave an impression of great order.

"Far out there, Mr. Holmes, is what is called the tooth stone."

Suddenly the inspector caught himself, "But alas, we are not here for a guided tour. We are investigating a death. I am afraid I get carried away, Mr. Holmes."

"Not at all, Inspector. I find what you say most interesting."

At that moment a young constable came up and smartly saluted Inspector Henslow. "This is Constable Saunders, one of our brightest on the force."

The young constable looked at Holmes with admiration and awe.

"If you gentlemen will step this way."

We followed as the young man led us through blocks of stones, tilted or lying on the ground, some on top of another. We approached what seemed to be an altar stone. Above it was mounted a very large tarpaulin sitting on four wooden poles.

Holmes' expression brightened. "Who ordered this cover?"

Constable Saunders stepped forward. "I brought this with me when I came on duty, Mr. Holmes. You see, sir, the weather on Salisbury Plain is remarkably changeable. It is not rare to see three or four periods of rain alternating with sunshine in a single day, and Mr. Holmes, we are aware of your methods and my first concern was to preserve, if necessary, these curious hoof prints."

"Capitol!" cried Holmes. "Here is a colleague, indeed. I tell you, gentlemen," and he looked directly at Lestrade, "If I am any judge at all, this young man will go far on the force."

"I told you he was a bright lad," chimed in Inspector Henslow.

"Thank you, Mr. Holmes, and might I add that my fiancé has experienced seeing this apparition. Would you care to hear her statement this evening?"

"By all means," replied Holmes who was already inspecting the strange hoof prints with his lens. "Please give your address to Dr. Watson and we will have a word with her this evening. This whole case would be impossible without the preservation of these prints. Look, Watson, what do you make of them?"

As I knelt to look, Lestrade also bent over. "I see nothing but these gigantic goat prints which are all muddled together."

"And you, Lestrade?"

"Well, Mr. Holmes, this is the second time that I have viewed them, and I can state nothing more than what Dr. Watson has said."

Holmes looked from one to the other of us, his eyes twinkling. "And yet, as I said before, the whole case hinges on these prints."

I looked again, but saw nothing different. Surely his observation read much more into the prints than what we all saw. Holmes' demeanor was that of a hunting hound with its first smell of the game.

The morning was wearing on. Holmes had examined several of the sarsens within the circle, then branched out to the outside area and viewed what Inspector Henslow called the Aubrey Holes. As I watched Holmes, standing beside the altar stone, I thought not only were we presented with a bizarre death, but the stones themselves presented a baffling mystery. I looked out on Salisbury Plain and felt as if London were a thousand miles away. A shepherd tending his flock was the only sign of life out on the lonely, grassy expanse. The heavy sky overhead seemed to accentuate the solitude around the monument. Holmes came back from the outer perimeter with the two inspectors. As we walked back toward our carriage, he took me aside.

"Watson, did you see the inscription?"

"What inscription?"

"The inscription with the hilted dagger below it, in a vertical position with its tip pointing down, with two crossed axes. It was high up on the second upright when we entered the circle."

"No, Holmes, I did not. What does it mean? Has it any bearing on the case?"

"It may mean everything or nothing, but it is the second significant link in the chain I have observed out here." With that he would say no more.

Our trip back to town was uneventful. We pulled up to the White Hart Hotel on St. John's Street. The Georgian facade and pillared portico were a welcome sight after traversing the primitive area of Stonehenge. We took rooms and met the two inspectors for lunch in the main dining room.

CHAPTER FOUR

▼

PEOPLE OF THE DRAMA

Holmes and I were seated across from Lestrade and Henslow near one of the large, mullioned windows on the main floor of the hotel dining room, and we were afforded a good view of the glistening street beyond. Inside, the warmth of polished brass and velvet, and the mixed aromas of smoked trout and old wood enveloped us. Quite frankly, I was grateful for the respite from our excursions in the foul weather, and I basked in the comfort of a stomach full of roast beef and a pipe full of Stamford's recommended Arcadia mixture.

Lestrade looked somewhat distraught as he finished the last of his Yorkshire pudding. "Mr. Holmes, I must catch the afternoon train back to London. Can you shed any light on this matter?"

"In the past, my dear Lestrade, I have found the rural public unobservant and, generally speaking, deliberately evasive with regard to anything that strikes a note of fear into their hearts. In addition, I'm afraid it's too early in the game for definite conclusions, but as I have told Dr. Watson in London, one of the three lines of inquiry I am making has been satisfactorily resolved, thanks to Constable Saunders. When I have all my facts, you can be sure I will wire you to join us. And now, Inspector Henslow, I would be deeply obliged if you could introduce us to Professor Conyers after lunch."

Despite my reluctance, we all four rose to leave the cozy ambience of the dining room.

Once outside, the cold, wet wind struck me full in the face, and I wrapped my ascot close around my neck. We made our farewells to Lestrade, whereupon Holmes, Inspector Henslow and I started back on the road to Amesbury.

Halfway there we came to a fork in the road. Our carriage veered to the left under the instructions of the Inspector.

"We are passing the Farnsworth farm, Mr. Holmes," said he.

Holmes glanced in the direction the Inspector indicated. "I should like to pay a short visit when we return."

"Well, the funeral is not until tomorrow, so in all probability we will find them at home."

Our drive continued for another fifteen minutes or so, until we reached two ancient columns on which were inscribed barely visible shields, indicating the entryway to Netherhamton Farm. The lane was poorly kept and our carriage had some difficulty making its way. Large beech trees lined the lane, until around a short bend, we had a full view of the farmhouse. It was a large rambling building, very old in the center, with a newer wing. Its Tudor chimney was lichen-spotted and the tall, pitched roof was made of slate. The entire impression was of drabness and neglect.

We climbed the ancient doorstep and knocked. A manservant of considerable size who appeared to be very powerful opened the door. Our attention was caught by the gigantic face on him, the jaw and brow of which were heavily boned and had a coarseness of features which resembled a throwback to primitive man.

"Who shall I say is calling?" His unexpectedly low pitched voice and perfectly articulated King's English was absolutely incongruous to his appearance.

At that moment Professor Conyers entered the hallway. "Show these gentlemen into the study, Emil."

We entered a very large room with a ceiling of heavy oaken beams. An odor of age pervaded the whole room. Along three of the walls, from the floor to the ceiling, were shelves filled with Neolithic artifacts. Pots, vases, bronze axes and tools of every description were displayed.

Professor Conyers followed us in. The Inspector introduced Holmes and myself.

"I have heard many reports of your work, Mr. Holmes. How may I be of service to you?"

Holmes turned his attention from a large bronze dagger that was hanging on the wall. "We are led to believe you have made it known to some of your neighbors that the sound of pipes heard across the moor and plain were the pipes of Pan. How did you know that?"

"I have heard them, Mr. Holmes, more than once."

Holmes looked keenly. "There can be no mistake?"

"None."

"How do you account for these strange occurrences?"

"I cannot, Mr. Holmes, outside of the fact that I discussed my theories of how Stonehenge was built." Professor Conyers' large-framed body became animated, his large forehead was thrust forward and his reddish beard almost bristled as he got into his subject. "I believe that the Mycenaeans of the Mediterranean region almost four thousand years ago were responsible for designing Stonehenge. There were great trade routes by land and sea. Commerce meant wealth, wealth meant power. Anyone sailing to this land was either a raider or a trader.

"My studies lead me to believe an architect from Myceanae designed the sarsen circle by looping a long twine rope around a central stake and revolving it to form a large circle. This then indicated where the uprights were to be set. When the circle was complete, a large stone was placed two hundred and fifty-six feet from the center of the circle. By drawing a line from the center of the circle to this outer stone, the longest day of the year was determined by the rising sun. This outer stone is known today as the tooth stone, or the heel stone."

Holmes appeared to be completely attentive to the professor, but I could see his eyes were taking in everything. "You then believe that the carved dagger on the entrance upright is the Mycenaean signature of the architect?"

The professor looked sharply at Holmes. "You are an astute observer, Mr. Holmes. Even the great archaeologists Stukeley and Petrie have not managed to find that." He spoke unconcernedly, but his small bright eyes glanced suspiciously at Holmes. He then caught himself, and smiling, said, "Really, you have missed your calling, Mr. Holmes."

Holmes waved away the compliment. "Observation is my business, Professor. I perceive you are an enthusiast in your line of thought, Sir, as I am in mine. But one last question, Professor. What do you make of this alleged satyr seen about the district?"

"I make nothing of it. I have not seen it, and truthfully, I do not believe it exists. These country folk are a superstitious lot. Anything they cannot understand is the work of the devil."

Holmes picked up a large bronze axe head and said, "Inspector Henslow tells me you spend a great deal of time excavating around Stonehenge. Are these artifacts some of your findings?" With that he waved his hand at the shelf-lined walls.

"Oh yes, but they are of little value. Mostly we find pottery, which helps us to define a time period."

"Well, thank you, Professor. We will trouble you no more."

"But it's no trouble at all, Mr. Holmes. I am glad to have had the opportunity to meet you. Emil will show you out." With that, the grotesque servant led us to the hall and out.

Inside the carriage Holmes asked, "Watson, don't you find it curious that a man who spends all his time and energy digging up Stone Age pottery and weapons could only speak of a Mycenaean designer or architect of Stonehenge?"

"I don't know about that," said I, "but that manservant was the most extraordinary creature I have ever seen."

Inspector Henslow turned towards us. "I did not know the professor had a manservant like that either. However, I have not been up to the house for at least six months. I have met the professor at the local inn at Salisbury on occasion, and I have never heard the name 'Emil.'"

Our carriage was turning into the Farnsworth Farm lane. The last of the fall flowers lined the driveway, and the general area was in good order and well kept. The farmhouse was old, but nowhere near the age of Netherhamton Farm.

A tall, slender young man opened the door at our knock. He was dressed in the plain attire of the farming community, but was clean and well groomed. Only his red-rimmed eyes betrayed the grief and worry he was apparently suffering. Inspector Henslow, at his elbow, quietly introduced us to the lad, and we learned he was Farnsworth's son, Tom. We were shown into the family living room, which seemed at first glance to be completely filled with large women in black. The atmosphere was forlorn. The casket of Jack Farnsworth was at the far left, with its lid closed. We followed the young man and edged past the crowd, which we learned later was primarily family members in attendance.

Young Tom hesitated at the far threshold and said, "Mother, these gentlemen have come to pay their respects and ask you a few questions."

The Inspector stepped forward to the widow and introduced Holmes and myself from London.

Jack Farnsworth's wife struggled up from an armchair, a short unwieldy woman, in whose face the features seemed half submerged in layers of fat, but the expression of pain in her red rimmed eyes made me feel compassion, and I felt as one who chances upon a scene of torture.

She stared at us with plain distrust and said, "You are very kind, but my husband is dead," in a toneless voice which indicated the emotional agonies she was experiencing.

Holmes stepped forward. "Please forgive us, madam, for disturbing you at a time like this, but it is imperative that we speak with you. We are here to see that justice is done."

"Justice," she repeated slowly. "What justice can be done against the devil? Aye, it was that devil out on the plain. We have heard his devilish pipes out there at night. I begged him not to go out that late, Mr. Holmes, and now look at him. All cold and still." She began to sob uncontrollably.

Holmes, when he wished, could be masterful in his dealings with the opposite sex. In a nearly mesmerizing way he pierced her agony. "We want to destroy this devil. We must know why your husband went out at that hour and—"

At that moment young Tom stepped forward. "Begging your pardon, Mr. Holmes. Perhaps I can help you better than my poor mother. Please come with me." We retired to an adjoining room.

"We have been losing sheep, Mr. Holmes. My father had suspicions, but did not confide in me. When the numbers of lost sheep increased in the last two days, he was determined to find the culprit and report the situation to the constabulary."

"At what hour did your father go out last night?"

"It was around ten o'clock, sir."

Holmes reflected for a moment. "The post mortem should give us a reasonable estimate for the hour of death. If I am not mistaken, your father did not have too long a vigilance before tragedy overtook him."

"If only he would have listened to my mother. She begged him not to go. She was so fearful of the so-called apparition and the sound of those pipes."

"And yourself? Were you fearful of this devil?"

"I can't say that I was, Mr. Holmes. I simply do not believe in things like that, but the older folk round about here all believe in things like that."

"It's important that I examine the boundary lines of your property," said Holmes.

"Well, sir, it is about three hundred acres, and you'd best follow me so I can show you exactly."

We all moved out of the house to the back gate entrance and on into the adjoining field. To the left were the sheep pens. Young Tom went to the demarcation stone and began walking to the north.

"Are we heading toward Stonehenge?" asked Holmes.

"Yes, sir. It's about one quarter mile from that demarcation stone."

"So I thought," said Holmes.

We had gone some distance when we encountered several excavated holes. Holmes looked keenly. "I see Professor Conyers has been digging here recently."

"In the beginning, the professor said he was going to dig only a few and then cover them up, but as you can see, there are many holes, and only a few are covered up."

"Yes, yes, so I see." Holmes knelt down and closely studied the excavated site. I walked forward and had just come over a rise, when Stonehenge appeared. It had a completely different appearance from this vantage point.

Holmes called to me, "I have seen enough." We turned to go back.

Inspector Henslow looked for a long moment at the London specialist. "Mr. Holmes, you seem to have come to some conclusion. Can you shed any light on this unfortunate incident?"

At times Holmes could be as taciturn as a Red Indian. "As I have said to Lestrade earlier at lunch, it is early in the game, Inspector." With that he would say no more.

Leaving the main road from Amesbury, we turned down Highbury Street, then turned right on Wilton Road to the Police Station. Holmes assured the Inspector that he would be summoned at the first ray of light in the case.

CHAPTER FIVE

▼

THE SATYR

Back at the White Hart Hotel, we ordered an early light dinner. When we had finished and were sitting over coffee and cigars, Holmes looked keenly at me.

"Well, Doctor, can you stand a few more visits tonight?"

"After that excellent dinner I can stand anything."

"You may have to."

"What do you mean?"

"I propose that we return to Stonehenge tonight after we talk to Constable Saunders and Miss Montgomery."

It was just fifteen minutes past five when we left the hotel as the cathedral bells pealed the quarter hour. We walked south on St. John's Street, which led into Exeter Street, then to the bridge across the River Avon. As I looked down the river at the lingering glow of the western sky, Holmes' deerstalker was silhouetted against the last rays.

"Here's Britford Lane," said I.

We turned left and walked until Number 387 came into view. We were standing in front of a humble dwelling that appeared to be a boarding house. The gaslights were on, as it was now dark outside.

When we entered his rooms, young Saunders asked us to be seated.

"It was great foresight you displayed this morning," said Holmes.

"Well, sir, we have great admiration for your methods, as Dr. Watson has made some of your cases known."

"I see," said Holmes. "Tell me, what are your impressions of these pipes and a spectral satyr in the vicinity of Stonehenge?"

"Sir, I simply cannot believe in ghosts, and the truth of the matter is I have neither seen nor heard these things."

Holmes' expression showed disappointment.

"But my fiancée, Miss Helen Montgomery has."

"How is that?" inquired Holmes.

"Well, she lives in Warminster and teaches school in Salisbury. She takes the Devizes Road to Warminster each evening, and passes by Stonehenge on her way home. On some occasions she has stayed late with her ailing aunt. It was at one of these times that she heard and saw the satyr."

"Where may she be reached?" asked Holmes.

"At Old Meadows Walk. I have asked her to stay at her aunt's home in town here until this mystery is cleared up."

"That was a wise precaution," said Holmes.

Having accepted Saunders' offer to bring us to Miss Montgomery, we summoned a cab. The three of us arrived at Old Meadows Walk in a very short period of time.

"Helen, this is Mr. Holmes and Dr. Watson from London. Mr. Holmes would like you to tell him what you know about the creature and the strange music you've heard."

Standing before us was a charming young woman whose intelligence shone forth from the very keen expression in her eyes.

"Mr. Holmes, I have heard the notes of these infernal pipes drifting on the wind on my way home at night. I am not an emotional person and I wondered who would do such a thing and why. My curiosity got the better of me late one night after leaving my aunt, so I left my dogcart on the road and headed toward this unusual sound.

"As I caught my breath at the top of the first rise, I saw this apparition about a hundred yards away. For a moment I was near faint at the sight of it, but intuitively I felt it was more alarmed at my presence than I was of it. I gathered up my courage and shouted, 'Who are you? What do you want?' whereupon it turned and ran in a strange fashion."

"In what fashion did it run?"

"I momentarily was horrified at this sight, but again regained my courage, and looking intently, I realized that its movements were very unnatural, as if running were very painful and awkward. As it approached a rise, it fell and immediately regained itself and disappeared. No longer seeing it, I returned to my dogcart and hurried home. I arose two hours earlier than usual the following morning and drove to approximately the same spot. I again got out and climbed the rise just as the sun was rising. When I reached the top, I went forward about one hundred yards to the place where I thought I saw the thing. I looked on the ground, but saw nothing. I circled the area and then I saw them, gigantic cloven hoof prints in the soft soil. I was completely at a loss as to how to explain them."

"Capital!" cried Holmes, who had his fingertips together as if in deep meditation. "Now, Miss Montgomery, this is of utmost importance. Carefully describe this apparition."

"It was a moonlit night and I saw two white lambs wool legs and a grizzled head on which appeared short horns."

"Bravo, Miss Montgomery. Your testimony so far has been the most thorough and enlightening. I might add, I sincerely admire your cool-headed pluck in dealing with something so outré."

"Well, Mr. Holmes, this is an enlightened scientific age, and I am sure there is some explanation for all these happenings."

"Precisely, Miss Montgomery, precisely."

"Furthermore, Terence has put me more at ease this evening."

"How is that, Miss Montgomery?" inquired Holmes.

Constable Saunders interjected, "I told her of the human footprints intermingled with the hoof prints around the altar stone."

"Most excellent, Constable, so you caught that."

"Yes, sir."

"I can assure you that I am going to recommend you to your superiors," said Holmes, who now had a new degree of respect in his voice.

"That's very kind of you, sir. If that happens, Helen and I may be able to get married much sooner than we planned."

"You may very well do that," said Holmes. "Thank you very much, Miss Montgomery. Your narrative was very informative. At least we know we are not dealing with nocturnal ghosts."

We left the young couple and walked back to the hotel to pick up a dogcart. The forlorn October day was dissolving into a clammy fog that blurred the streetlights and the carriage lanterns. Surely this would turn into rain later.

"Well, Holmes, so much for your earlier proclamation about rural people and their fears."

"There are exceptions, Watson, and Miss Montgomery is a rare one. What she has revealed to us has substantiated the second hypothesis which I have formed about this case."

"And what is that?" I questioned.

"All in good time, my dear Doctor."

We arrived at the hotel and entered the bar room, as it was still too early to return to Stonehenge.

I had just settled back gratefully into the lushness of the velvet seat, when a young man in hotel uniform approached our small table, looking quizzically from Holmes to myself.

"Telegram from London to Mr. Sherlock Holmes."

Holmes rose and followed the boy out to the lobby. I sipped my cognac and stared out the rain-spattered window while I waited. The dark, dripping shapes moving along the street were in stark contrast to the reflection of a lively fire in the hearth on the other side of the room. As I silently expressed my gratitude for being on the dry side of the window, Holmes returned.

"Would you be so good, Doctor, to go upstairs and bring your service revolver back down with you? We are dealing with human agencies here."

With a sigh, I left my half finished drink to do as he bade. When I rejoined him, the grim set was gone from his face, and he seemed preoccupied, almost pleasantly distracted.

Holmes could detach himself at will from the problem at hand, and now began a long dissertation on Von Bulow's conducting abilities and his interpretation of Wagner. My mind constantly returned to the problem at hand, as I was reminded of it by the weight of my service revolver in my coat pocket.

I looked around the bar, which was quite empty at this hour, when suddenly young Tom Farnsworth was standing in front of us.

"They told me at the front desk that I could find you here, Mr. Holmes."

"Sit down, young man."

"I just wanted to tell you that Mr. Bailey came to our house today to pay his respects, and said my father had suspicions as to why his sheep had gone missing and who was to blame."

Holmes leaned forward. "Did he say who he suspected?"

"Mr. Bailey wasn't quite sure, but he thought he heard, 'That blaggard Professor.' He knew my father would stop at nothing until he had restitution."

"Well, well," said Holmes. "So the professor has not told us the entire story. Thank you for coming, Tom. Please repeat our condolences to your family."

As young Tom rose to leave, I turned to Holmes and said, "My suspicions of Professor Conyers are becoming very strong. What in the world is the man up to?"

"You mean, what are his motives, don't you?"

"Yes, it's all so vague. A man has been killed for no reason at all."

"Don't be too sure of that, Watson. I suspect deep waters here. This man is clever, very clever."

"But for what purpose?" said I.

Holmes relit his pipe and stared at the ornate bar with its mirror reflecting his image back to me.

"Yes, for what end? That is the question."

Once again, we set out for Stonehenge, this time in a dogcart Holmes had acquired from the hotel. While heading north on the Amesbury Road, the rain stopped, as it had many times that day. Here and there, moonlight penetrated the racing clouds, which gave momentary views of the landscape.

"Watson, I believe it is necessary to make a roundabout trip to avoid being conspicuous. We will head in the general direction of Beacon Hill, which, according to my ordnance map, is high ground. That can be to our advantage."

The trip took less than a half hour. After a short walk, we found ourselves looking down at Salisbury Plain, with all its hills and depressions. The horizon stretched impossibly long, broken only by the isolated monument. After walking down the hill for a quarter of an hour or so, we came to the outer perimeter of the Farnsworth Farm.

Suddenly we were both alert. The sound of the pipes of Pan came floating down with the wind.

Disconcerted, I whispered to Holmes, "From what direction is it coming?"

"Southwest, I believe," he whispered back.

We both moved forward in crouched positions. Another hundred yards ahead the sound was much louder. I brought out my revolver just as the cold light of the moon broke through the clouds.

There was the satyr! Momentarily the sheer terror of facing this anomaly froze both of us, and, I must confess, struck a chill in my heart. But it saw us as we saw it, and immediately it broke into a run.

"Fire, Watson! Fire!"

My shots penetrated the wind-swept plain. I was running hard, ever watching the creature just ahead of us. The sight contradicted everything I had ever learned of nature and reality.

Suddenly, without warning, I was face down with all the breath knocked out of me. I lay there and ached all over, but could not detect anything broken.

I heard Holmes calling to me, "Watson, Watson, are you all right?"

Apparently I had pitched forward and fallen into one of the excavated holes, which I had failed to see in my dogged pursuit of the satyr. Holmes was at my side with great fear and concern on his face.

"Watson, for God's sake, are you all right?" His deep concern revealed a part of his nature I rarely saw.

"Yes, I believe so. Nothing is broken," said I.

With great relief, he began to chuckle.

"I fail to see anything amusing," said I, with some asperity.

"If you could but see yourself, covered with this white chalk mud," said Holmes, "you could give the so-called satyr a run for his money. Watson, remain here for a short while. I'll check the general direction he took." With that, Holmes left me.

I was now feeling the effects of the strain of the day, and was glad to rest. A short time later, he returned.

"Impossible to track it," said he. "It appears it's dropped into a hollow and vanished into the night. However, I must admit, Watson, it was a remarkable phenomenon."

It was hard for me to imagine after this confrontation how profoundly it unsettled my skepticism. I admit it was not without great inner struggle that I gradually accepted the evidence of this unearthly creature. Convictions established over as many years as mine are not easily given up without a struggle.

Having found great relief in a hot bath, a glass of whiskey and my pipe, I sat smoking while Holmes paced back and forth in our hotel room. The great cathedral struck eleven. I took out my watch to wind it for the night. It had stopped completely.

"Confound it," said I. "My watch has stopped. I must have damaged it in that wretched fall I took tonight."

Holmes stopped pacing and came over to my chair. He picked up my watch and he looked closely at the stopped hands. Suddenly he exclaimed, "That's it, Watson!"

"That's what?" I asked.

"It's an immense clock."

"No, it's just a small pocket watch that's been in my family for many years."

"No, no, Watson. I perceive Stonehenge as an immense clock." Holmes turned toward the fireplace and looked at the glowing embers. Suddenly, as if making up his mind, he said, "I must return to London."

"When will we leave?"

"No, Watson. You must stay, and this is what you must do: First, you must take the dogcart in the morning to Stonehenge where you will await the arrival of Professor Conyers. He surely will be excavating. When you encounter him, you must tell him I have returned to London to fulfill a case that has been pending. Also, that I see little hope of solving the Farnsworth case. Tell him I cannot cope with ethereal beings that can withstand bullets and disappear before one's eyes."

"Very well," said I, "but what do you mean by saying Stonehenge is a giant clock?"

"I promise all will be made clear shortly, Doctor, but first I must speak to Sir Edmund Kersey at the British Museum, and make several other inquiries."

CHAPTER SIX

▼

A DAY ON THE PLAIN

The fresh beauty of the following morning did much to erase from my mind the grim impression of the night before. Holmes had left before I had awakened. I ate a solitary breakfast and felt quite restored. I reviewed Holmes' instructions. They were quite explicit.

It was a pleasant ride to Stonehenge, and I posted myself in such a way as to take in as much of Salisbury Plain as possible. As I looked out into the bright sunlight, I observed that the Plain is a series of depressions and broad plateaus. According to Holmes' ordnance survey map, which I held in my hand, the roads across this strange plain were seldom level and formed an uninterrupted series of rises and descents. The depressions and valleys disappear, and seems to give the illusion of flatness and may explain why the region is called a plain. It is understandable how one could disappear at night with little effort especially if one was intimately familiar with the terrain.

About an hour later, two small figures near the horizon caught my attention. I presumed this was Professor Conyers and his manservant because it appeared they were headed toward the Farnsworth property adjacent to the monument. As I headed southwest in their direction, I noticed the whole region around Salisbury Plain was well cultivated despite the thinness of the soil over a layer of hard chalk.

After a thirty-minute walk I climbed the highest rise nearby and observed the professor and his manservant excavating a new hole about four hundred yards away.

As I approached, he looked up at me in mild annoyance.

"Well, Doctor, what brings you out here? Is Mr. Holmes with you?"

"No, Mr. Holmes has returned to London and I thought I'd stay on for a day or so to enjoy the fresh Wiltshire air."

A fleeting trace of triumph crossed his face. I went on in regard to Holmes' despair about the case, and it seemed Professor Conyers became more relieved and civil as I talked. From the side of the pit, Emil's ungainly face and expression revealed total vexation as he cast glances in my direction.

"Well, I can't blame Mr. Holmes. It really is extraordinary how superstitious the peasants are about here." The professor's mood was now becoming expansive and he spoke with a smile on his chalk-covered face. "You know, Doctor, how these old folk—mind you, we're talking about the people who lived four thousand years ago—had the ability to erect these stones. They can be found all over Europe, but there is nothing quite like Stonehenge anywhere else in the world. See that demarcation in the ground over there? It's quite faint, but that was once a roadway to the River Avon. Imagine, they transported those trilithons by primitive barge."

"You mean those stones in the sarsen circle?" I asked.

He looked directly at me. "I am referring to the large megalithic stones, Doctor. They are about twenty-five feet high and are arranged in a horseshoe configuration with the altar stone at its center."

"I see," said I. "The spot where the Farnsworth murder took place." With this, the professor glanced in the direction to which I was referring, then sharply back to me. It now seemed apparent that he wished to terminate our conversation, and I, too, wished to move along, having completed Holmes' instructions. As I excused myself, Emil gave one last ominous look in my direction. His simian features, made all the worse by the chalk, were contorted by hatred.

I turned in the direction of my dogcart. It was a pleasant walk. No sooner had I reached the dogcart when the sun disappeared and threatening clouds came rolling in over the plain. This was followed by rain, which came in sheets. Constable Saunders' statement that the weather was remarkably changeable was, in the least, an understatement.

Amesbury had one inn in which I took refuge. The gas lamps were lit and cast shafts of light through the pints of ale that glowed in the hands of the few villagers sitting near the bar. As I sat down by the fire, the friendly voice of Inspector Henslow called out.

"Why, Dr. Watson, you're soaked to the skin! What brings you to these parts?"

I stammered some excuse about wanting to visit and study Stonehenge again.

"Well, sir, that's all well and good, but you'd best dress for the weather when you go out there."

"Yes, so I have learned."

"By the way, Doctor, we heard Mr. Holmes had left for London very early this morning. Has he abandoned the case? All of us would be sorely disappointed if he did."

I was filling my pipe with Stamford's mixture as the Inspector was speaking. As I struck a match, I said, "By no means. He will return by late train tonight." The Inspector looked relieved.

The pub's owner brought two glasses of whiskey, and the Inspector saluted me with his glass. "Here's to your health, Doctor."

"Thank you, but tell me, how did you know about Mr. Holmes' departure?"

"Well, sir, we have our methods also."

"Well, then, how is it you're here in Amesbury?"

"I knew Jack Farnsworth well and the funeral was today."

"I see," I said. "What are your views in this case?"

"Well, for one thing, we believe the murder took place elsewhere and the body was later placed on the altar stone."

"For what purpose?" I asked. The Inspector looked for a long moment. I waited, puffing on my pipe.

Turning fully in his chair to face me, he leaned closer and said, "I believe, to strike fear in the hearts of the residents of this area. The Inspector leaned back and took a cigar from his pocket. He lit it and said, "What does Mr. Holmes think, Doctor?"

"I really could not say," said I. "but one thing I do know: Once he forms his conclusions, he is seldom wrong." I sipped my whiskey and asked myself why in the world strange things are seen and heard and murder committed in this remote corner of the country. I expressed these thoughts to the Inspector, but he could shed no light upon the matter.

CHAPTER SEVEN

▼

SETTING THE TRAP

It was nine-thirty that evening when Holmes entered our rooms at the White Hart. He looked drawn and tired, but his eyes were bright. He sat down by the fire and looked at the flames in the hearth. "It's been a long and exhausting day, Watson, but we have our man."

"Do you mean Professor Conyers?"

"Yes, Watson."

"Do you have means to prove his guilt?" I asked.

"Ah, that is the question. I have several lines of inquiry going forth, and have every reason to believe we will have our man."

"But Holmes, what possible motive could he have?"

"The stakes are high, very high," said he. "We must proceed with great caution." With this, he began to enumerate the steps that must be taken. "First, tomorrow we will take the train back to London; however, we will get off at Bath and take the next train back through Salisbury to Warminster. We will see Inspector Henslow before we leave in order to inform him I have given up the case."

"Why is that?" I asked.

"Because he meets with the professor from time to time, and he must convey disappointment to him. We, in turn, must wait in Warminster for the proper moment."

All this was beyond my understanding, but I could see Holmes had his conclusions formulated.

As I finished my last pipe for the evening, the cathedral bells struck eleven o'clock. The rain was still lightly beating on the windowpanes. Holmes had already retired. I reflected on the strange events of the last two days, and on the professor who was at the bottom of it all. What strange flaw of character could convert this highly educated man to a life of crime? Holmes had remarked the stakes were high, but what stakes could there be? I tried to retrace the steps that Holmes had taken. His remark that Stonehenge was an immense clock must have been the pivotal point of his deductions. I retired more confused than I was before his return that evening.

The morning light shone through our window as I completed my breakfast. Holmes' short note on the breakfast table explained his absence. He had gone out early to send several telegrams and left instructions for me to meet him at nine o'clock that morning at the Wilton Road Police Station.

I arrived a few minutes before nine and was shown into the Inspector's office. Holmes was standing by the window as I entered.

"Good morning, Inspector," said I.

"I can't really say it's a good morning, Doctor. Your friend, Mr. Holmes, informs me the case is hopeless." I was at a loss as to how to respond, when Holmes interjected.

"Inspector, I did not say it was 'hopeless.' I indicated that the case is ethereal, and for all we know, Farnsworth may have fallen into one of those holes and some shepherd may have placed him on the stone out of respect for the dead."

Henslow's face fell. "Can you honestly believe that, Mr. Holmes?"

"Well, it is within the realm of possibilities. In the final conclusion, Inspector, I believe it was accidental."

"But, Mr. Holmes, what of those hoof prints?"

"I would strongly suspect some prankster." With that, Holmes turned to the door. "Come, Watson. We should most certainly tour the Salisbury Cathedral before we leave this charming town. I am really very sorry we could not be of more service, Inspector."

As I said goodbye, the Inspector sank in his chair, a perfect picture of disillusionment.

"Honestly, Holmes, I felt extremely sorry for the Inspector."

"Yes, Watson, I'm quite certain we have convinced him. He probably thinks I am the most overrated detective in the whole of England, and something of a dilettante to boot."

It was a very cold but pleasant walk, and we were not very far from the constabulary, when we caught our first view of the cathedral in its entirety. Its vast age and beauty left a profound impression on my mind. Once again, Holmes demonstrated his ability to detach from the immediate problem, and he devoted all his attention to the cathedral with intense interest and animation.

"Just think of it, Watson," he said as we viewed the huge clock works of the chimes and bells "The ingenuity of medieval man."

"Holmes, why are we here?" I asked. "Were we not going to Warminster?"

"I expect some important telegrams before we leave, and if I'm not mistaken, we will have some CC"

Before he could finish his sentence, the cathedral bells began to peal as the immense gears went into motion. With the eleven powerful strokes finished, he continued, "I was about to say, 'Some time for lunch before we leave.'"

We arrived in Warminster early in the evening, having spent some time in Bath waiting for our connections from London. The local inn, the King's Arms, was comfortable, but certainly not as luxurious as the White Hart.

Holmes once again laid out his ordnance map. "You see, Watson, we now are approximately fifteen miles west of Stonehenge." The light of the gas lamp played over his long fingers as he indicated the two points. He continued, "we must leave an hour before dawn in order to be in the correct position to view how far the sun rises from the heel stone."

"Is that important?" I asked.

"It is paramount to this whole case, and therefore, I suggest we retire early."

Early the next morning, our dogcart took us halfway back to Salisbury on the main road. Holmes pulled up the horse. "We must walk the rest of the way," said he. The rising quarter moon gave enough light to negotiate the terrain.

"Watson, at what hour did you observe the professor starting yesterday?"

"Well, I was without my watch, but I estimate it was near nine-thirty."

"We must do our work quickly and move out of the area before full light takes place. We cannot afford to be seen by anyone, or all is lost."

Holmes kept up a brisk pace and in a short time we spotted the faint silhouette of the monument in the distance.

"We must go faster!" he cried, and with that he doubled the pace, which I found difficult to match. Another half hour later, quite winded, we rose from a depression, and Stonehenge lay before us. The sun's eastern glow was quickly expanding.

Holmes stationed himself at the center of the circle on the main axis while I watched. The first pinpoint of light came into view upon the horizon. Holmes gauged the distance from it to the heel stone and walked toward the sarsen circle. He dug his heel into the ground to indicate which upright corresponded with the sun. He then sat on a rock, brought out a notebook and pencil, and began making notes. After that, he indicated for me to come. We walked out as far as the Aubrey holes, where he stopped and consulted his notes. Then he picked up a large rock and placed it in line with one of the uprights in the sarsen circle. We went another hundred paces and stopped. Holmes seemed satisfied.

On my right, I noticed the professor's excavations. We were on the Farnsworth property.

"Watson, have you noticed how methodically the professor digs his holes? They are spaced approximately five feet apart in a semicircle, which corresponds with the sarsen circle, only much further out. Curious, is it not?"

"Well, as you mentioned, he must have some method to his madness," said I.

Holmes looked about quickly. "We must leave now, for the light is growing stronger."

Our predawn walk had exhausted me, and upon our return to Warminster, I lay down on the sofa and was fast asleep before I knew it. The nearby church bells awakened me at two o'clock. Holmes was seated at the table with several charts before him.

"Did you have a good nap, Doctor?"

"Yes, and I'm famished."

"Well, we shall have an early dinner, then," said he. I was peering over his shoulder, looking at his charts. They appeared to be diagrams of Stonehenge. Holmes turned and looked up at my perplexed expression.

"Believe me, Doctor, all will be made clear tomorrow night! In the meantime, we could not employ our time more profitably than by visiting a small museum, which I understand has an excellent collection of Neolithic artifacts."

CHAPTER EIGHT

▼

CLOSING THE NETS

The following day was wild and tempestuous. Holmes and I sat together in silence, he engaged with a powerful lens, deciphering the remains of some ancient document, and I, looking out the window, speculating on what I could do to occupy myself until the evening. As if in answer to my thoughts, Holmes looked up.

"Plan, if you will, doctor, an early lunch, as I am expecting Inspectors Henslow and Lestrade at two o'clock this afternoon, and would appreciate your meeting Sir Edmund Kersey at the station at one-thirty. I have retained the sitting room downstairs and we shall all meet there."

"In the meantime," said I, "a breath of air should help my constitution."

"Very well," said he, "but by all means, keep yourself inconspicuous, Watson. Stay away from the center of town until you go to the station, then take a circumlocutious route back here."

I discovered a small bookshop on the outskirts of town that was open. I browsed for an hour or so, then purchased a small monograph by Henry Ward Beecher. I then walked to the adjacent countryside. As I looked at the interminable Salisbury Plain from this eastern position, it lay unbroken to the farthest horizon. The wind had increased since I started my walk, and I had difficulty lighting my pipe as I turned to go back. Large waves of mist and fog were gathering strength. Tonight would be a trial, I thought, if this continued.

Holmes had the instincts of a great artist who needed his dramatic moment. In the meantime, his associates suffered in ignorance until the final grand moment. This conclave taking place at one o'clock was a complete surprise to me, I reflected, as I finished a light lunch at a country inn just outside the town, and mulled over the day's events.

Circumventing the main roads, I came to the railway station, making sure I was as inconspicuous as possible. I approached the lone figure on the platform. "Sir Edmund, my name is Dr. Watson. Mr. Holmes has sent me to meet you."

Standing on the station platform was a surprisingly youngish man, who revealed an extent of stodginess ill suited to his youth. He peered at me through thick spectacles. A perpetual look of inquiry was written over his features.

"That's very kind of you, Doctor. I can't tell you how much I am looking forward to seeing Mr. Holmes' theory proven correct."

"He has spoken to you about a theory?"

"Yes, yes, of course. That is why I am here."

I said no more, but felt myself to be the most long-suffering of individuals.

As we entered the sitting room of the King's Arms, Inspector Henslow was speaking. "Yes, Mr. Holmes, Professor Conyers seemed in high spirits when I told him you had abandoned the case. I met him at the White Hart Hotel bar, as we were wont to do from time to time."

Holmes looked up. "Sir Edmund, thank you for coming."

"Not at all, Mr. Holmes," said he. "Nothing in the world could keep me away."

"This is Inspector Henslow from Salisbury and Inspector Lestrade from London." When introductions were finished, everyone sat down.

Inspector Henslow continued, "When I received your message this morning, Mr. Holmes, I truly knew your methods were unorthodox, but I can't tell you how overjoyed I was to receive it. I might add that constable Saunders seemed quite relieved to be on firm ground again."

"Thank you," said Holmes, "but all these precautions have been of the utmost importance. Inspector Lestrade, what can you report to us?"

"Well, Mr. Holmes, your suspicions were correct. We made inquiries and finally traced to a public school in Berwick-On-Tweed. He is not a professor at all—just a school teacher whose main subject is anthropology."

Holmes pondered for a moment. "Archeology must be a personal line of pursuit."

"That I would not know about," said Lestrade. "But I do know there was a very large scandal in scholastic circles, in regard to Conyers taking bribes for passing grades from some of the rich, aristocratic students in the school."

Holmes glanced in my direction. "There is your character flaw, Doctor. Now, gentlemen, I would like to propose this plan of action." It was amazing to see Holmes, whose demeanor was generally laconic suddenly galvanized into action, that of a general instructing his troops for battle.

Holmes was pointing to his large ordnance map and addressing Inspector Henslow. "You and your men must station yourselves on the Farnsworth property far enough away to be unobserved by Conyers and his manservant when they arrive at their digging site."

Henslow looked closely and nodded his approval. "Our party, Sir Edmund, Inspector Lestrade, Watson and myself, will be situated within the sarsen circle. At my signal from this dark lantern, we shall all move in on Conyers. We must be in these positions just after dark —it is quite essential that none of us are detected. Is all that clear?"

Henslow said with resolve, "It will be done as you say, Mr. Holmes."

"Lestrade, I trust that you have your weapon?"

"Mr. Holmes, as long as I have my trousers on, I can assure you I have my revolver."

"And you, Watson?"

"I shall have it with me."

"Excellent. Now, Sir Edmund, I would advise that you stay well in the rear until you are able to make verification."

"I understand, Mr. Holmes."

"In conclusion, gentlemen, we have no way to determine how long we may have to wait tonight, so in consideration of the weather, I would advise warm clothing."

We arrived just after dark and took our station within the sarsen circle. We were crouching behind a large trilithon that had fallen over in some past age. Holmes was keenly observing the western horizon. The day's bad weather had not subsided. If anything, it had grown worse. Great gusts of wind raced through the uprights, chilling all of us to the bone. Even though it was not raining, the mist that blew down on us felt like rain after a few hours.

"Holmes," I whispered, "will he come?"

"He must," said he.

I turned to Lestrade to inquire as to the hour.

"It's just half past eleven, doctor." His bulldog tenacity had not failed him. I sat there, cold and stiff, longingly thinking of the Northumberland Turkish bath. Sir Edmund looked rather numbed, but a definite determination played over his features.

Holmes grew impatient. "Where is he? He must feel secure; he must come —he must!" As if in answer, a faint glow of light was visible on the plain before us.

Holmes reacted like a hunter who has his prey in his sights. "It's him, Watson! He's moving in the direction of the Farnsworth property…just a little further." At that moment, Holmes opened his dark lantern and flashed a signal through the dark expanse to Inspector Henslow.

"Now!" cried Holmes. "Now!" We were all upon our feet, staggering after him on our stiffened limbs, while he, with an outburst of nervous energy, was running swiftly over the plain.

"Richard Conyers, it is my duty to arrest you for the willful murder of Mr. Jack Farnsworth." Inspector Henslow's words came to me just as I caught sight of him with Holmes and several constables standing and looking down the entrance of a tomb-like enclosure. Lestrade was beside me, gun in hand, and Sir Edmund was still out in the darkness.

A lantern by the entrance illuminated Conyers' face glaring up at us. Frustration, awe and hatred played over his features. He started to climb out of the pit. "I have never killed anyone."

"I must warn you that your words will be taken down and they may be used in evidence either for or against you."

"It was my manservant that did it. I am innocent!"

At that moment we heard a stifled howl of dire protest. Emil clambered out, raging and swearing oaths at Conyers.

"Constable, restrain that man!" cried Henslow.

Emil, sensing the game was up, lurched forward, knocking down those in his way, and, with amazing speed, took off into the darkness. Lestrade, gun in hand, fired three shots before he disappeared. Henslow assigned four men to stand guard while Lestrade and Constable Saunders took off in pursuit of Emil.

Henslow and two constables took charge of their prisoner. As they passed us, Conyers stopped and turned his malignant eyes upon my friend. "I have much to thank you for. Perhaps I'll pay my debts someday."

Holmes looked keenly at him. "I imagine that for some few years you will find your time very fully occupied," said he. "By the way, did Emil use special shoes to create hoof prints, or was it a slip on arrangement? You won't tell? Dear me, how very unkind of you!"

"Oh, there you are, Sir Edmund. You missed a little excitement," said Holmes, as the archeologist came puffing out of the darkness.

"I fell down," said he, "and I am quite miserable. I heard shots, also."

"Yes, yes, it is all over now," said Holmes. "I suggest you take this lantern and inspect the cairn. Perhaps it will rejuvenate your spirits."

Reluctantly, Sir Edmund took the lantern held out to him by Holmes and slowly climbed down to the entrance. The wind and mist rolling over the plain had not diminished. It was several moments before the archeologist reappeared. There was a look of dazed amazement on his face.

"Mr. Holmes," said he, "this may be the greatest historical find in all of England. It may take months to catalog and review."

"If that is the case, Sir Edmund, I suggest we all return tomorrow morning for a more complete inspection."

"Yes, Mr. Holmes, I must wire London for additional help. I can't tell you how gratified I am to have had the opportunity to be here. It's an absolutely spectacular find."

Holmes turned to me. "Now, Watson, you and I had best leave. Emil may be headed for Netherhamton Farm. If that is so, we must be prepared. It's a thousand to one chance our finding him there, but we can leave no stone unturned."

The front door of the old farmhouse was locked. I fired two shots from my service revolver to smash it open. We rushed in and hurried from room to room. Holmes had lit a lamp and we went to the second floor. We could see no sign of the man we were chasing until we reached the last bedroom. Here, piled in the corner of the closet, was a pair of trousers with lamb's wool sewn on the upper half. A skullcap with grizzled hair and horns was lying next to the trousers. But the most fantastic item was in Holmes' hands: something that looked like a pair of Dutch wooden shoes with straps to fit over one's boots. They were carved to resemble large cloven hooves.

"Well, Watson, so much for the satyr. It appears Emil has come and gone, as is attested to by these empty dresser drawers." Holmes came to attention, took my arm, and putting his finger to his lips, beckoned me to stand in back of the closet door with him. Apparently, he had heard something downstairs. The next instant Lestrade and Constable Saunders burst into the room.

Holmes laughed as we stepped forward. "Well, Lestrade, I wondered how long it would take you to get here. For a moment I half thought Emil had returned."

Blowing and puffing, Lestrade said, "That wretched creature gave us the slip. The cunning devil weaved a trail up one rise and down another for a quarter mile before we lost all sign of him. I judged I'd best get back here as fast as I could. If it were not for this constable here, I could still be out there on the plain."

"The term 'plain' is not exactly correct, as you have discovered tonight, Lestrade. One who knows his way out there can evade anyone who is unfamiliar."

Constable Saunders admitted sheepishly, "I was familiar up to a point, Mr. Holmes, but the possibilities of his direction were innumerable."

"It's quite understandable, Constable, but it is of no importance, since our bird has flown the coop. We can pick up Emil when we want him," concluded Holmes.

"That's right, Mr. Holmes. I shall alert every constabulary in the district. I shall have him under arrest by morning."

"I hardly think so, Inspector."

"What do you mean, Mr. Holmes?"

"I mean I believe your time would be spent more profitably if you were to return to London."

"Return to London?" he repeated. "I shall do no such thing. We will get our man more than likely at the nearest rail station."

"I think not, Lestrade. He has enough provisions with him to last a few days. After that, I am sure he will gravitate back to London. You are aware, I am sure, that Emil is a rather well known French citizen. No, you were not? Tut, tut. Well then, I suppose you also do not know that he has made quite a name for himself in France. Not that either? Well, well."

Lestrade looked at Holmes with his ferret like appearance accentuated. "Look, Mr. Holmes, I agree that your methods gave some results tonight, but it takes a good deal more footwork to get the full results."

"I grant you all that, Inspector, but I repeat: You would do better in London."

"Your theories are fine, Mr. Holmes, but we at the yard must apply practical measures."

"My dear Inspector, nothing could be more practical." Holmes removed a slip of paper from his pocket and handed it to Lestrade. "I am reasonably certain that if you supply your men with a description of Emil Gasconeux, and place them at the address I have just given you, you will have him under lock and key within a few days."

"What address?" I asked, perplexed.

"It is simply Emil's last known employment, the Lyceum Gymnasium, near the East India docks."

A degree of annoyance crossed Lestrade's face. "See here, Mr. Holmes, how would you know Emil would be at this address?"

"Dear me, you mean you did not notice his ears? No? Tut, tut."

"Hang it all! What have his ears to do with all this?"

Holmes regarded Lestrade with a mixture of disdain and amusement. "It's quite elementary, Inspector. If you had observed more closely, you would have noticed Emil's ears are cauliflowered, which strongly suggests the profession of a boxer. You really must pay more attention to details." With that, Holmes turned to me. "Come, Watson. It has been an exhausting night, as I am sure you will concur."

As I followed Holmes out of the room, I noticed that all this was not lost on Constable Saunders, who had watched and listened with keen admiration.

CHAPTER NINE

▼

THE GOLDEN QUEEN

The mist and fog-laden night had been followed by a glorious morning. Holmes and I walked along the broad plain toward the tomb. Sir Edmund and Inspector Henslow were at the tomb's entrance. The constables who were on guard for the night were being relieved.

"Good morning, gentlemen," said Sir Edmund. "We have been waiting for you."

"Where is Inspector Lestrade?" asked Henslow.

"He has returned to London," said Holmes. "I'm quite sure he wants to wrap up this case and have Emil under lock and key."

"Will he find him there?" asked Henslow.

"In all probability," said Holmes.

Henslow reflected a moment. "It was a bit of bad luck that we lost him out here last night."

"So it was," responded Holmes. "Now, Sir Edmund, let us see what the tomb has held in secret for so long."

We all entered the cramped quarters. The lamps were lit and their rays fell on a sight I shall never forget. We were in a rectangular chamber that had been walled and roofed with oak beams. A skeleton lay on a five-foot sheet of gold C actually a funeral bed. Gold jewelry was strewn over the remains. A gold necklace on the skeleton, Sir Edmund informed us, was an important status symbol of a Celtic queen. The hilt of the queen's dagger had been plated with gold, and she wore a gold armband. A delicate band of gold adorned what once must have been a leather belt. Together with these ceremonial articles, her followers had offered many personal items for her afterlife.

Holmes was extremely impressed, as all of us were.

"Sir Edmund, there appears to be quite a substantial amount of gold. What value would you place upon it?"

The archeologist pondered a moment, then said, "Incalculable, Mr. Holmes, simply incalculable. Its historical value alone is immeasurable at this moment. It will take months to excavate, study and catalog. After this closer inspection I shall have to return to London to consult my associates and form a team of archaeologists. I really must say, this has exceeded all my expectations. I can't tell you how gratified I am for this extraordinary opportunity."

Holmes turned to Inspector Henslow, whose face was filled with awe. "Inspector, I would suggest doubling the guards in the interim until Sir Edmund returns."

"By all means, Mr. Holmes. I'm sorry to say that I am almost struck dumb by the fact that all this gold will be our responsibility."

"Tut, tut," said Holmes. "I can't think of anyone more qualified than yourself and Constable Saunders."

As we climbed back out into the sunshine, Constable Saunders stepped forward. "Begging your pardon, Mr. Holmes, seeing things have been tidied up here, I would imagine you will be returning to London shortly."

"That is correct, Constable," answered Holmes.

"I wonder if you would be so kind as to give me a general idea of your basic working method."

Holmes regarded the young constable with a degree of kindness that was somewhat rare in my friend's character.

"My method begins with a statement of the problem. I then endeavor to gather relevant data, which subsequently requires the formulation of a hypothesis to be tested. If this hypothesis proves correct and conforms to the existing facts, the result is a working theory, or conclusion to this testing. However, one must never let the theory become fact until every avenue has been explored, and one feels sufficiently comfortable with everything laid before oneself."

It was late in the afternoon when we boarded our train back to London. Sir Edmund elected to join Holmes and me.

"You know, Mr. Holmes, my curiosity was aroused when you inquired about that Celtic inscription on our first meeting at the British Museum, especially since you were the second person to make such an inquiry in the past year. The first person, Conyers, who did not use that name when I met him earlier, had asked me over and over what I thought the inscription meant after I translated it for him. Naturally, I had no idea as to its exact meaning. That is, not until you suggested it may have been a tomb site of a Celtic queen. With that reference point, I spent days in the archives of antiquity. This is what I uncovered:

"Stonehenge stands in the midst of an enormous cemetery. There are fifty such sites known, and Conyers uncovered God knows how many more. It's safe to say there could be as many as three hundred or more within a possible two mile radius."

Holmes was very attentive to Sir Edmund's statement as he continued.

"The first phase of Stonehenge was built by a pastoral band called the 'Windmill Hill People' around 2900 B.C. The giant stones we see today, were raised around 2000 BC by the Wessex Warriors, a fighting people ancestral to the Celts. These warriors exemplify a Homeric lifestyle with their raiding, pillaging and feuding. Revenge, booty and women were the motivating factors. And so it was when the Romans came onto the scene much later. It is this period of time that interests us." Sir Edmund reflected for a moment or so.

"Pray, continue," said Holmes.

"Well, Mr. Holmes, it's a long story, but I will endeavor to digest it for you and Dr. Watson." As Sir Edmund warmed to his subject, my first impression when we met at the station was completely altered. Here before me was a dedicated scientist in the realm he loved.

The archeologist continued, "As I studied museum manuscripts, the long wars of Julius Caesar against the Celts began to unfold. Caesar constantly pushed the Celtic hordes westward until they were forced to flee across the channel onto the shores of England. Of course, there were Celtic people in England as far back as five centuries before Christ. However, this was a huge migration. Caesar, not satisfied, mounted new legions and invaded England in 55 B.C. and again in 53 B.C. It seems the Roman philosophy was that if the Celts were unconquerable, then they must be annihilated. These wars continued into the fourth century A.D., until, by the year 410, all official connection between Britain and the Roman Empire was terminated.

"My research brought me to the Roman historian Ammianus Marcelinus, who recorded his impressions of the Celts and an unusual story of a king and queen. First, he states that the Celtic men were fair-headed, blue eyed and of great stature—magnificent physical specimens. In war, their assaults showed absolute, reckless courage. The whole race was madly fond of war. The Romans, having themselves given up human sacrifice, (though they still massacred captive men, women and children) expressed shock at these wild haired barbarians that wore pants, not togas as civilised people did, and made great sport out of headhunting. But if we think these men rough, Marcelinus tells us of the gentler sex. A Celtic woman fighting beside her man was a match for a whole troop of Romans.

Steely-eyed, she swelled her neck, gnashed her teeth, flexed her huge biceps and rained blows and kicks as from a catapult.

"In the year 54 A.D. such a man and woman were fighting side by side against the Roman incursion in and around the vicinity of Stonehenge. This was King Vercingetorix and his queen, Boudicca. They were vastly outnumbered, and in a freak battle situation, the king was captured alive. This was generally unheard of, as Celtic warriors had no fear of death. They believed in a greater life after death. This king was sent to Rome chained like a wild beast, and six years later he was dragged out of his cell and paraded through the forum in great triumph. He was then strangled.

"When Queen Boudicca received news of the king's death, her wrath was overwhelming. She gathered her troops from far and wide and made war on the Roman legions. In her war chariot, with her troops at their side, she drove the Romans all the way back to Londinium (the Roman London) and burned the city to the ground. This took place in 60 A.D. Later, when she died, she was honored as a daughter of the goddess of war. Gentlemen, it's Queen Boudicca that we uncovered today, and who still lies in her tomb at Stonehenge."

"Sir Edmund," said I, "beyond the fact we have actually seen the queen's tomb, don't you feel these descriptions sound rather far-fetched?"

"Not in the least, Doctor. These documents are far from tales, spun out of thin air. On the contrary, as the historian Marcelinus pointed out, it very closely conforms to Celtic patterns. I could give you many more examples, but I see we are arriving at Waterloo Station."

Holmes stirred from his corner of our compartment. "Your profound dissertation," said he, "has been most enlightening and informative. I fear we must bid you farewell, but by all means, please keep us informed of your progress."

"Yes, of course, Mr. Holmes."

The train came to a sudden halt. With our light baggage in hand, we hailed a hansom cab just outside the station. I could already detect a degree of depression taking hold of my friend. As far as he was concerned, the case was finished. Suddenly, he brightened.

"Watson, if we hurry we can still make the second act of Das Rheingold at the Covent Garden. Are you familiar with Teutonic mythology? No? Well, let me tell you, this is Wagner at the zenith of his powers. He has set forth in symbolic form, the whole cosmos of ideas on man and God, nature and society." Holmes was carried away by the prospect of a musical evening.

When we arrived at Baker Street, Mrs. Hudson handed each of us a message. Holmes tore his open and read it quickly.

"It's from Inspector Putois in Lyon. He wishes me to come over immediately." So much for Das Rheingold and the sonorous tone of the Flügelhorn.

My note was from Stamford suggesting a lunch at my convenience.

"Are you leaving immediately?" I asked.

"Yes, Watson."

"Can I be of assistance?"

"No, I think not, my boy, but in any event, if the need arises, I shall most certainly summon you."

CHAPTER TEN

▼

IN RETROSPECT

The first week of November had come and gone. There was a light snow on Baker Street, which was unusual this early in the season. The drab slate roofs silhouetted against a monotonous gray sky did nothing to lift my spirits.

The week had been wearisome for me and my main activity was putting my notes, regarding what I called *The Satyr of Stonehenge* in order. My thoughts continually went back to Stonehenge and how Holmes had arrived at these conclusions about the case. I had discussed most of the details over lunch with Stamford. He was as mystified as I was. Holmes' allusion to the sarsen Circle as a tremendous clock strained our minds. We wondered how this theory related to the overall solution.

The London Times mentioned the Salisbury Plain murder in several articles during the previous week. In one account it reported the energetic cooperation between the Metropolitan Police and its country counterparts in Salisbury. The account ended with, "Through the brilliant detective work of Inspector Lestrade of Scotland Yard, both suspects have been apprehended and are now in custody."

Far back on the last few pages was a single account of a spectacular discovery of an ancient Celtic queen's tomb. "Sir Edmund Kersey," it said, "Chief Archeologist of the British Museum, has stated the burial chamber revealed vast amounts of gold artifacts. However, he feels the historical significance of this discovery near the vicinity of Stonehenge in Wiltshire County is of incalculable value." In all this, there was no mention of my friend's name. I began to question his often-repeated "art for art's sake" philosophy.

On Tuesday afternoon I received a wire from Holmes stating that he would return to England by the boat train and would reach London by eleven o'clock that night.

Just after ten o'clock I heard a cab pull up to our front door and thought perhaps Holmes was arriving earlier than anticipated. Therefore, the knock on our door was a surprise.

"Come in," said I. Inspector Lestrade hesitated at the doorway then came into the room.

"Why, Inspector, what are you doing here?" I asked in mild surprise.

"I received a telegram from Mr. Holmes to meet him here at eleven o'clock."

"Well, then, take off your coat and help yourself to a glass of brandy. The decanter is on the sideboard."

"Thank you, Doctor. A wee nip should take the chill out of my bones." As he sat down with glass in hand, he hesitated for a long moment. Then, no longer able to contain himself, said, "You know, Doctor, I don't mind telling you, as unorthodox as Mr. Holmes is in his theories and methods, and worse yet, his constant holding of vital information to the very last moment for some fanciful, dramatic effect, I am nonetheless compelled to admit my respect and admiration." The little detective, who was generally cocksure of everything, was genuinely humble.

"I suggest you tell him that yourself,' said I.

"Ah, Lestrade, you received my message," Holmes said as he entered our rooms.

"Yes, Mr. Holmes. I was about to tell Dr. Watson we have Emil in custody and charged with murder."

"Excellent!" said Holmes as he sat down in his favourite chair by the fire. There were signs of exhaustion on his face when he turned to me and said, "Watson, I do believe I shall accept your kind invitation of the past and join you in the benefits of a Turkish bath. Is tomorrow morning convenient for you?"

"By all means," said I, as I handed him a glass of brandy.

"Now, Lestrade, what else can you tell us?"

"You were right, Mr. Holmes, about the gymnasium. We traced him down to the East India dock area. Rough district, you know. My agents located him at the Lyceum Gymnasium, and I went down and personally made the arrest. Put up quite a ruckus until I clapped my revolver to his temple. I shall never forget his expression —it was inhuman, and I am glad to say he is under lock and key.

"When we confronted Conyers with Emil's testimony, he quickly saw how their conflicting stories would eventually condemn both of them for murder. Sensing the hopelessness of the situation, Conyers confessed everything.

"It appears Farnsworth found them slaughtering a sheep that had broken its legs in Conyers' excavation hole, and told them he was going to report them to the constabulary. Of course, all this would put an end to Conyers' excavating. Emil, sensing the possibility of losing the riches Conyers promised him, rushed forward and struck Farnsworth to the ground. Finding that Farnsworth was dead, Conyers very coolly conceived the plan of laying the body on the altar stone and instructed Emil to drag the body there with his hoof print clogs over his boots.

"Conyers will serve time as an accessory to murder, plus an attempted felony on Crown property. Emil will swing for his fatal blow to Farnsworth." Having finished his statement, the little detective rose to leave.

"Inspector, haven't you forgotten something?" I asked.

He paused for a moment, then said, "Oh yes, so I have, Doctor. My promotion has been posted, and I owe it to you, Mr. Holmes. We think your methods are a little queer down at the Yard, but you are a gentleman and have played the game very fairly with me, and I want you to know I appreciate it."

Holmes considered Lestrade standing there and said, "The work is reward in itself, but I must tell you the official force, in very large measure, lacks imagination which, believe me, Lestrade, is a key factor in the art of detection. However, I should be remiss if I did not add there is no finer force in the world than Scotland Yard for courage and bulldog determination."

After Lestrade left, Holmes lit his last pipe for the night.

"You know, Watson," said he, "Lestrade is basically a good fellow, just misdirected. A review of the history of crime would do a world of good for his career. Without that history of crime, my sojourn in France would have been impossible. It was a difficult case I just completed in Lyon, and was made worse by a certain French dialect, which constantly hampered my progress. I'll give you all the details in the near future." I could see the strain of the last few days on his features and decided not to bring up the subject of Stonehenge until the next day.

As I have said earlier in this narrative, there is an establishment for Turkish baths on Northumberland Avenue. It is on the upper floor in an isolated corner in the drying room that Holmes and I smoked in silence.

Suddenly he said, "I must say, Watson, I have been missing something by not participating in these baths."

It was in this atmosphere of lassitude that I first sensed the impervious nature of Holmes take on a mellowness. I answered him, saying, "We doctors call this an alternative to medicine, a fresh starting point, a cleanser of the system."

"Yes, I quite agree," said he.

This being such a conducive environment, I ventured to inquire about the finer points of his reasoning in regard to the Stonehenge affair. "You know, Holmes," I said, "I still can't understand how an intelligent fellow like Conyers could have gone so wrong."

"I'll tell you this much, Watson, life at best is a gamble. There are no legal shortcuts to wealth. Greed has undone many throughout history. Conyers was just another example."

"Perhaps you could enlighten me as to how you arrived at your conclusions."

Holmes relit his pipe and said, "Much has transpired since then, but I shall endeavor to reconstruct the main points." With the air of a professor who lectures his class, he began.

"Before we ever left London, my instincts were alerted to Conyers. It was he who informed the people what kind of pipes were played and by whom. I had mentioned to you three lines of inquiry that could be made. First, I had to establish whether we were dealing with fact or mythology. Second, was the death accidental or willful murder? Third, if murder was committed, then by whom, and for what motive?

"When we arrived in Salisbury, we went directly to Stonehenge. There I ascertained we were dealing with humans, not ethereal ghosts by the boot prints intermixed with huge goat prints. This was established thanks to Constable Saunders. Next, we interviewed Conyers. He directed and diverted our attention to the Mycenaean culture, not the Celtic. On our return to Salisbury, I sent a telegram to Sir Edmund asking for a translation of the Celtic inscription on the sarsen upright.

"Leaving Conyers, we met the Farnsworth family, who informed us of the existing problem of lost sheep.

"Our encounter that same night, in which the satyr appeared and disappeared, proved beyond all doubt that someone was trying to frighten the countryside. Later I received a telegram from Sir Edmund with the translation. It read, 'Queen Boudicca, daughter of the goddess of war.' A second line showed a curved horn, followed by Brythonic letters with two crossed axes at the end.

"I was struck immediately by the word 'queen.' It was now apparent Conyers was looking for the burial chamber of a queen, which in all probability was filled with gold. Back at the White Hart Hotel, I reviewed all my data. My observations answered all three inquiries. All these circumstances, which I learned on the first day in Salisbury, pointed heavily toward Conyers. Establishing Conyers' guilt in a court of law would be another matter.

"Stonehenge itself appeared to me as a huge cryptogram that was waiting to be decoded. It was not until you made the remark about your watch that I began to look at this problem in its historical context. You acted as a catalyst, Watson, when you said the word 'watch,' which made me think, 'Clock: solar clock.' It's fairly common knowledge among scholars and historians that Stonehenge could be a solar guide to a burial location. I then announced my return to London and the British Museum.

"Back in London I spent the day at the British Museum, primarily in the Language Department. Taking the second part of the inscription, which Sir Edmund had kindly transcribed for me, I began to build a hypothesis.

"Thus, using the main axis which runs out to the heel stone as a reference point, I counted from left to right, from one to thirty, the total amount of uprights in the circle. Of course, many of the sarsens are missing or have fallen down, but this is of no consequence, since they are all about four feet apart. Between sarsen number one and number thirty, the main axis points to the summer solstice, June twenty-first, the longest day of the year. Continuing to count to the right, sarsen number two would be July, number three August and number four September. In September we come to the fall equinox, which is the time of harvest, and sunrise is directly east. Counting to the seventh upright, we are at December, and the shortest day of the year. Then, as the sun swings back to rise a little more to the left each day, it finally moves back in line with the upright number four—directly east—and we have the spring equinox, or the time of planting.

"I reasoned that the curved horns symbolically were the horns of harvest; hence, the queen died in the fall of the year. The Brythonic letters between the curved horn and the crossed axes were a fixed arrangement denoting numbers. Sir Edmund assured me this was unique to the Celts at that period. The numbers were six, seven, nineteen, twenty, and three hundred. It was a simple expedient to draw a line between sarsen uprights six and seven through the axis of the circle, the altar stone, and continue through uprights nineteen and twenty in a northwesterly direction.

"I further reasoned the number three hundred designated three hundred paces. My line went well beyond the Aubrey holes that are ninety-eight feet from the altar stone. A pace being roughly equivalent to three feet, one only had to walk nine hundred feet from the altar stone using the uprights as a simple sighting device to fix the exact location of the burial chamber. The crossed axes could be a symbol denoting royalty or signify a threat to anyone tampering with the grave.

"Conyers missed the significance of these symbolic letters denoting numbers, but was clever enough to ascertain the number three hundred meant three hundred paces to the place where the queen lay on Salisbury Plain. He then, by trial and error, began excavating, using the main axis as a reference point, a very arduous and time consuming process.

"Back in Salisbury I made it appear I had abandoned the case. This was necessary to throw Conyers off guard. He then thought he could continue without fear of discovery. Of course, that was a capital mistake on his part.

"In Warminster I reviewed my diagrams of Stonehenge and had to take the risk of ascertaining whether Conyers was near the burial site or if he had passed it. If you remember, Watson, I remarked on his precise five-foot excavations. I have to admit, it was a stroke of good fortune that he was so close to the burial chamber that we did not have to wait weeks or perhaps months for him to locate it.

"The following day I trained a telescope on him from Stonehenge while you were on your way to meet Sir Edmund at the station. Conyers found the burial chamber, but immediately sealed it again, which signified he wished to remove the contents under the cover of darkness.

"I trust you are familiar with the rest of the chain of events?"

I had listened to this extraordinary narrative with rapt attention and admiration. "But Holmes, this is marvelous! You are at the zenith of your powers."

"Really, Watson, you have a tendency to over-dramatize. As cases go, it was quite commonplace. The solution in itself was not complex. The real problem lay in the precise timing of the arrest. As it were, we could still be waiting for Conyers to locate the burial site."

His tone was self-deprecating, but I could see from the tinge of color on his cheeks, my words had affected him, and like all great artists, he valued the compliment.

Holmes continued his discourse, "I already feel the dullness of inactivity. My mind is like a racing engine. I need problems to solve." He went on like this for quite some time.

As I listened to this long complaint and considered his extraordinary gifts, I rebelled at the possibility of his brown Moroccan case being opened when we returned to Baker Street. As a medical man, I had warned Holmes many times of the harmful consequences of cocaine addiction. With this thought in mind and with a look of mild annoyance on my face, I turned to him and said, "Holmes, have you ever considered playing the game of chess?"

BOOK TWO

THE CURIOUS CONNOISSEUR

Author's Note

▼

"Holmes suggested spending some time in one of the Bond Street picture galleries."

From *"The Hound of the Baskervilles"*

Having spent many years dabbling in art as a Sunday painter, I have often wondered why there never was an art mystery in *The Canon*.

The subject of art has been introduced on several occasions but never in depth. We know that Holmes was a distant relative of the French painter Vernet, and Holmes has proclaimed, "Art in the blood is liable to take the strangest forms."

Watson said that Holmes had only the crudest ideas of art, but the detective denied it (*The Hound of the Baskervilles*), and I believe him. He knew all about the value and beauty of a Gruez painting hanging in Professor Moriarty's study.

All in all, I believe we can be assured Holmes was well versed in art history, and was a knowledgeable appreciator.

CHAPTER ONE

▼

BAKER STREET INTERLUDE

The year 1902 in many ways was memorable. My friend Sherlock Holmes was in great demand and his reputation had gained an international level. As I look back now, some twelve years later, and review our active and adventurous days together, a longing pulls at my heart.

The Edwardian era had just commenced, which in retrospect, looked like a golden age considering that at the present moment England and Germany are at war. During the Victorian era of some sixty-five years, an empire had been established and people of many classes were now enjoying its fruition. King Edward was a popular monarch who brought a new liberal spirit to all classes of people here and abroad.

To what extent this liberal spirit took, Holmes and I had no concept until we were engaged in a case involving the highest echelons of society.

As I review my notes, I find it was in the latter part of October 1902 when wind, rain and fog for three consecutive days somewhat entrapped Holmes and myself in our Baker St. rooms.

Holmes was seated at his chemical table and had been engrossed for several hours, but as I glanced up, he pushed a Florence flask aside, turned off the Bunsen burner and turned around on his stool. I, in turn, put down my novel, half expecting him to communicate his well-known diatribe about the London criminal being a dull fellow. Instead, he got up and began to pace back and forth in front of the fire. I had come to know Holmes' moods very well over the many years, so this was nothing new to me. He was as ascetic as ever, however at this time he tried to impose on his private life the kind of order and high polish that he had achieved in his work. I noticed also he had developed a passion for respectability, a well-nigh compulsive need to present himself to the world as a successful gentleman of means. This, in turn, made him lose touch somewhat with an intensity of emotion, which I might say I had seen displayed on many previous cases of the past. Whether this deficiency succeeded in raising the level of his art even higher was difficult to ascertain.

When finally he sat down opposite me, he began to philosophize on the vicissitudes of life.

"To my mind," said he, "I see mankind capable of inflicting every wretchedness possible on his fellows."

"Surely you can't believe this is everyone's objective," I commented as I looked up in bewilderment.

"You forget, Watson, that I have had a very propitious training at St. Bart's. It taught me lessons I have never forgotten and for which I can never be sufficiently grateful. It was there that I saw human nature in the raw—and when Cecil Gaffney sends me a note like this, it most certainly justifies my attitude," he said indignantly.

As he spoke he held up a folded note, which he then tossed over to me. I began to comprehend the true texture of his discourse as I unfolded it and read:

Dear Sir,

I shall be brief and come to the point immediately. Since you failed to recover my painting, I see no possible way I can acknowledge or be held responsible to pay your rather inflated fee. If you find this unsatisfactory, you may contact my solicitors, Brown and Ramsey.

Cecil Gaffney

I could see that this affront to Holmes' professionalism was the catalyst that brought on his seething analysis of humanity.

"Throughout my career, Watson, I have never experienced such a lamentable rebuff. I was engaged to locate Gaffney's painting, which I did at considerable expense. I was not obliged or directed to deliver said painting. I am afraid this will necessitate consulting my solicitors."

"Litigation of this nature is time consuming," said I. "You have had excellent financial success. Would it not be simpler to drop it?"

Holmes picked up his pipe and contemplated it. "No, it's a matter of principal." Holmes, with all his gifts, still had negative aspects to his nature. I sat for some moments after this outburst and considered some of his weaknesses of character, such as a lack of compassion, a dislike of women, a cynical point of view, and a categorical contrariness that showed itself on occasions such as this one.

After several silent moments he suddenly said, "No, Watson, you are mistaken. I do not have a lack of compassion, but I must agree with you, I dislike and mistrust women. As for my cynicism and stubbornness, they are only expressed on rare occasions."

I looked up in flustered astonishment. Holmes had, in the past, played this type of reasoning on me, but as always, I found it disconcerting and a little unnerving when he intruded into my most intimate thoughts.

"How on earth do you know that?" I demanded, trying to regain some composure.

There was a gleam of amusement in his deep-set eyes. "Five minutes from now you will tell me how absurdly simple it was."

"I will do no such thing." I hoped that my indignation would prevent his penetrating eyes from reading my deeper irritation at him for mollifying his own sour mood at my expense.

"Very well," he said lightly. "Knowing your personal habits so well, it was not difficult to follow your very expressive face while in repose."

"I see no connection," I said resentfully, chafing at his patronizing tone.

"My mention of St. Bart's stirred your memory of your own hospital experiences, which was service to your fellow man, whereas mine was in pursuit of knowledge and chemical research; hence, my lack of compassion. You then developed a distant look and turned to the photograph on the mantle of your late wife Mary. The question came to your eyes: How could Holmes dislike women so much? Next, you turned to my casebooks on the shelves next to my chair. Your expression hardened: All these cases; that's what has made Holmes so cynical about life! Whereupon I interjected to agree with one of your reflection, but disagreed with the others."

"Holmes, you never cease to astonish me." Indeed, my amazement had outpaced my pique and I asked, "But how do you explain your agreement and disagreement?"

"Simplicity itself," said he. "My compassion lies with the underdog, the one whom justice passes by, especially the one wronged by society. As far as women are concerned, my distrust is instinctive, such as a man will avoid a carriage while crossing a street to escape being injured.

"Last, but not least, my cynicism and obduracy are provoked only on such rare occasions as the receipt of this annoying note from Cecil Gaffney."

Just as I was about to respond, there was a knock at our door. Billy announced Inspector Stanley Hopkins.

"Well, well. This is a surprise, my dear Hopkins. Come in, come in out of this abominable weather." It was now Chief Inspector Hopkins, upon whose promising career Holmes had more than once shown a very practical interest.

"Come warm yourself by the fire," said Holmes as he hung up his moist mackintosh. "The Doctor has a prescription containing whiskey and soda for such a day as this."

The inspector sat wearily down as I handed him his drink. "Thank you, Doctor. I believe I need this medicine."

"That suggests you have a case," said Holmes.

"Indeed I do, Mr. Holmes. I have just returned from Greenwich…" His words were cut short when his eyes caught sight of Cecil Gaffney's note on the side table. "By all that's wonderful!" he uttered. "Is this sorcery, Mr. Holmes?" Hopkins was staring hard at the note.

"Are you referring to this note from Mr. Cecil Gaffney?" asked Holmes.

"This is the very man I came to see you about. How came you to correspond with him?"

"He was a client. What has happened?"

"He is dead, Mr. Holmes."

We sat in stunned silence for a moment.

"You had best start from the beginning," said Holmes, as he reached for his pipe and tobacco.

Stanley Hopkins took a sip of whiskey and reached for the cigar I extended to him. He had matured over the years, and his intellectual acuity had developed under the helpful guidance of Holmes.

"As you well know, most of my duties are at my desk in administration, but at the moment, we are short handed, and it was no surprise when I was asked by my superiors to handle this case."

"Which was at what hour?" inquired Holmes.

"It was eight forty-five this morning when Sir Charles stepped into my office and laid what facts he had before me. No more than ten minutes earlier the Constabulary at Greenwich informed Scotland Yard that a murder had occurred early this morning. A Mr. Cecil Gaffney, well known art connoisseur, dealer, collector and writer was found dead in his home at 805 Brampton Road.

"I arrived at ten o'clock and began my investigation. A Dr. Westcott, personal friend and physician of the deceased was on hand and waiting for me.

"This is a most shocking affair! For the life of me, I cannot understand such brutality,' he said to me. He was extremely agitated as I spoke with him. According to Dr. Westcott, he was called in at a quarter past eight in the morning by Gaffney's manservant, Matthews. The only other servant is Emily, who does not live in. She had let herself in the kitchen door sharply at seven thirty, as was her habit, with her own key. She claimed there were no visitors yesterday, and left the premises at five that evening. She turned off the servants' bell, knowing it was Matthews' day off, before she left.

"Matthews has been employed by Gaffney for the past ten years, and was reputed to be loyal to his employer and beyond any suspicion or doubt. He spent the day in London and returned to his room and claims he heard nothing unusual all night. However, he did feel it was more quiet than normal.

"At eight the following morning Matthews went to the kitchen to fetch his master's breakfast tray from Emily. When he had no answer to his knocking on the bedroom door, he entered and found the room unoccupied and the bed undisturbed. Somewhat alarmed, he put the breakfast tray down and went to the adjoining study. Again, there was no response to his knocking, whereupon he entered the room, and to his horror found Cecil Gaffney slumped over his desk.

"Thoroughly frightened by what he saw, he followed his first impulse to fetch Dr. Westcott. He returned with the doctor in a few minutes, as he lives nearby.

"I brought my attention and questions back to Dr. Westcott. His first impression was that Cecil Gaffney had suffered massive heart failure.

This was strange to Dr. Westcott, as it was his opinion that Gaffney had only a mild heart condition for which he prescribed small doses of powdered foxglove.

"Upon further observation, he noticed a painting was missing from the wall in back of the desk, and concluded that its disappearance could have been the very element that brought on the severe attack.

"It was decided that the body should be moved to the sofa until the coroner arrived. When Dr. Westcott endeavored, with the help of Matthews, to move the body from the desk, he was horrified to see a letter opener protruding from his chest."

Sherlock Holmes had been listening attentively, puffing on his pipe, when he paused and an intent look of interest came over his face. "Was this letter opener unseen until they moved the body?"

"That's correct, Mr. Holmes."

"What about blood stains?"

Stanley Hopkins consulted his notebook. "The deceased's clothing was stained, as was the blotter upon which he lay. But overall, my impression was that there was not as much blood as one would expect with such a fatal wound."

Holmes was now, I could see, in a state of suppressed nervous excitement.

"Singular, most singular," he reflected. "Pray, continue, Inspector."

"There's really not much more to relate. I concluded my inquiries with Matthews. He described the missing painting and confirmed that the letter opener belonged to Gaffney. I compiled a list of friends and associates, which I have here in my notebook, and I made a separate notation of the last visitor to have spoken to Mr. Gaffney."

"And that was?"

"A Mr. Frank Sutcliffe, an artist of some repute."

"I trust you will be checking his whereabouts."

"I wired Scotland Yard before I left Greenwich and inquiries are presently being made. I then caught the train back to Charing Cross Station and came directly here, as I know how these unusual cases intrigue you."

"And how they sometimes mystify you," smiled Holmes.

"I will certainly admit I found no practical clues at the scene of the crime, but our experts are checking for fingerprints."

Holmes relit his pipe, leaned back in his chair, and became more contemplative. He put the tips of his forefingers together in a precise gesture. "You have made your report extremely clear as far as it goes."

"Can you put forward any theory, Mr. Holmes?"

"I have insufficient data; however, Matthews' statement that the house was more quiet than usual that evening, Dr. Westcott's impression of massive heart failure, and the fact that there was an unusually small quantity of blood are all points for consideration. Tell me, Inspector, do they not suggest something to you?"

"I can't say that they do."

"Dear me, I suppose we shall have to run down to Greenwich with you."

"I certainly would be obliged if you would do so, but tell me, Mr. Holmes, how do these points you describe bear on the case?"

Holmes pointed at Hopkins with his pipe, shaking his head with a pedantic attitude. "You must understand, my dear Hopkins, that the life of an independent investigator is extremely specialized, and by following each case minutely, it is highly probable he will gain experience which will be of great value to him afterward. These points I have enumerated similarities with past cases and therefore warrant our first considerations. Watson, would you be so kind as to consult the Bradshaw for the next train to Greenwich?"

CHAPTER TWO

▼

THE BOROUGH OF GREENWICH

London was huddled in cold and shrouded in fog as we stepped out into Baker St. In spite of the early afternoon hour, it was dark. Leaving Charing Cross Station, our train moved eastward some six miles to the metropolitan borough of Greenwich. I reviewed the Victorian landscape as it passed by and noted it was slowly changing into the twentieth century. Somewhat sadly, I also observed it was losing its antique charm under the pressure of modern industrial development.

"How far is it to Gaffney's house from the station?" inquired Holmes.

"About a twenty minute walk if we walk around Flamsteed Hill," replied Hopkins.

"And if we climb the hill?"

"Oh, perhaps ten minutes."

"Can we see his house from the hill?"

"Yes, and the River Thames also. I understand on a clear day, one can see the dome of St. Paul's in London."

"Then we shall climb the hill," said Holmes.

Some thirty-five minutes and two stops later, we pulled into Greenwich Station, located on the south bank of the Thames. A heavy mist rising from the Thames greeted us as we reached the top of the hill.

"Over to the left, Mr. Holmes, is Gaffney's home, among those other houses." We looked out over the scene. "I understand the meridian longitude zero degree line was established up here," said Hopkins.

"I really would not know since it is not in my province," said Holmes with a deprecating wave of his hand. "But tell me, Inspector; I see a surprising number of steam launches moored at the pier below—is there much traffic?"

"By all means. A great many of these people that live here work in London. It's a timesaving and scenic way to go."

We came down the opposite side of Flamsteed Hill to King William's Walk. A turn to the right would take us to the pier and the steam launches. A turn left would take us to Gaffney's house.

As we turned toward the house, Holmes asked, "Do you know if Cecil Gaffney used these steam launches?"

"I really can't say, but it seems probable that he did."

"As I recall they land at Westminster Bridge."

"Yes, that's correct."

"Watson, I think when we are finished here we will return by the scenic route to Westminster Bridge."

The architecture was a dour impersonation of upper middle class London. Red brick houses with eaves and white painted windowsills frowning on the misty Thames, and gardens with dark green-brown lawns gave a forlorn impression.

The house stood on a slight rise. It was Edwardian in design and rather new. The canted roof had three gables with two chimneys on each side. The two storied building was well kept and surrounded by a white fence.

As we entered the yard, Holmes indicated he wished to inspect the outside windows and grounds first.

"I found nothing, Mr. Holmes," said Stanley Hopkins. "I checked the ground for foot prints and each window for tampering. There was no indication as far as I could ascertain."

Nevertheless Holmes reviewed each window minutely with his lens and the ground below was examined even more closely.

"You were correct in regard to the first floor windows, Inspector," said Holmes. "I see they were not tampered with and no footprints but your own were on the ground. And yet a man has been murdered and a painting stolen. What does that suggest to you?"

Hopkins considered a moment. "The possibility of an inside job."

"Offhand one would have every reason to believe so, but…" As Holmes spoke he moved further from the house, some fifteen feet or so, and began searching the ground, quartering like some huge hound on a trail.

"Hello, hello! What have we here?" We came over to the spot. Holmes was kneeling and closely examining an impression in the garden path. He stood up and reflected a moment. Then, pointing to the house he asked, "Which window is that on the second floor?"

"Why that is Gaffney's study. What have you found, Mr. Holmes?"

"This rectangular impression with scrape marks and footprints coming and going. It suggests something was thrown from the second floor window, then later picked up hastily. Someone came in a circumspect way from the rear of the house, possibly the kitchen. Notice how the prints turn sideways as one would when checking to see if anyone was behind him. Then, moving forward again to this rectangular impression, he snatches up the article, leaving these scrape marks and quickly runs off, indicated by the length of the stride and a lack of heel marks."

"Does this mean there was an outside confederate?" I asked.

"Perhaps, Watson, perhaps. We have done all we can here. Let us go inside."

A constable saluted Inspector Hopkins at the front door as we entered. The hallway was dimly lit by a single small lamp, which stood on a bracket on the wall. The house had an ambience of masculinity, both in the oversize furnishings and the choice of rich color used to adorn the walls, carpets and various decorations artfully placed about. The feminine touch, though lacking, was not missed, as my eyes roved from sculpture to clock to wall hanging, all positioned in a symmetry designed to be both tasteful and comforting. The heavy velvet drapes hanging from windows let in just enough glints of muted light to spotlight the rich, well-kept surroundings. Paintings were hanging everywhere, even as we went up the staircase to the second floor, then along a corridor where a sergeant was standing before a door. Hopkins had a few brief words with him. He then took a key from his pocket, unlocked the door and we all entered.

It was a fairly new room, very dim until Hopkins pulled open a drape. The room was somewhat foul with cigar smoke mixed with the odor of a burnt out fire. Apparently the fire had gone out hours ago, only the smoke remained, hanging like an ethereal shroud over the room. The furniture was upholstered in tastefully subdued colors. The floor was carpeted in an intricately designed oriental pattern. A mantel over the fireplace was lined with small medicine bottles.

Cecil Gaffney's body was lying on the sofa near the fireplace where Dr. Westcott and Matthews laid it. Rigor mortis had set in and the facial features of the corpse were frozen in the agony of extreme pain. Still protruding from his chest was a large letter opener.

Holmes knelt beside the body and studied it closely. He leaned over and smelled the lips of the dead man.

Stanley Hopkins rubbed his chin. "What do you deduce, Mr. Holmes?"

Holmes did not answer, but instead arose and surveyed the mantel over the fireplace with the medicine bottles. He went to the mantel and each bottle was opened and its contents sniffed. He then filled a small envelope with the contents of one of the bottles.

"My dear Hopkins," said Holmes, "this is a complex situation, I grant you, but deduction is not applicable in this instance. We must think in terms of induction. In other words, reasoning from this singular end product (a dead body), to a definitive conclusion, specifically how and why it happened." Holmes moved to the large, ornate desk. An obvious bare spot on the wall in back of the desk signified that a painting had hung there. Scattered on the desk next to the bloodstained blotter were several invoices and statements.

"All these bills of sale are initialed G.B. Would you happen to know who that is, Inspector?"

"I am sorry, Mr. Holmes, but I have not had the opportunity to check those papers."

Moving from the desk, each of the four windows were inspected, when suddenly Holmes stopped and looked closely at the rug.

"There have been several people next to the window."

The Sergeant stepped forward. "Begging your pardon, Mr. Holmes, the Scotland Yard fingerprint gentlemen came through, and…"

"And a thundering herd of buffalo could not have done worse," said Holmes caustically.

"Were any fingerprints found?" inquired Hopkins.

"Their results were inconclusive outside of that of the deceased and the butler Matthews. However, there were several smudges on the window frame where Mr. Holmes is standing."

"This missing painting, Hopkins, does it not strike you as curious that only one painting is taken, in a house full of paintings and other valuable objects?"

"As you put it, yes, but…" A knock on the door interrupted Hopkins. A tall thin figure, curiously large-boned and angular emerged through the door. Peering from left to right as though myopic, he approached Inspector Hopkins.

"If you are finished, Inspector? I would like to have the body removed." Despite his size, the man's voice was thin and reedy, betraying restrained emotion.

Hopkins glanced at Holmes. "Yes, I am quite finished."

"Dr. Westcott, this is Mr. Holmes and Dr. Watson. I am sure he would like a word with you. When you are finished, I'll have Sergeant Wilkens and Constable Peters remove the body."

Dr. Westcott looked warily at Holmes. "How can I be of assistance to you?"

"Tell me, Doctor, what was the general state of Mr. Gaffney's health?"

"He had a mild heart condition."

"What did you prescribe?"

"A normal dosage of powdered fox glove."

"From this bottle?" Holmes held up one of the bottles from the mantel.

"Yes, I prescribed that medicine."

"I see," said Holmes. "I understand that three grams of dried leaf of foxglove may be considered as a minimal fatal dose for a normal adult."

"That is true, but what are you implying, Mr. Holmes?" The thin voice raised even higher in pitch.

"Forgive me, Doctor. Essentially I was thinking out loud, as Dr. Watson will surely attest to."

"I was not only Mr. Gaffney's physician, but also a friend of long standing," Dr. Westcott said somewhat testily. His angular frame stiffened in a posture of defensive indignation. "I prescribed a daily dose of one to two milligrams of powdered foxglove."

"I see, but what, in your professional opinion was the cause of death?"

"My first impression was congestive heart failure, but upon moving the body and discovering the letter opener, I am not at all certain of the cause of death. That is to say, whether the heart failure occurred before the assault, or if it occurred after the letter opener wound was inflicted."

"Dr. Westcott," said I, "as a medical man like yourself, I concur with your finding, but I am sure an autopsy will tell us the cause of death, which in all probability was due to the stab wound."

"That remains to be seen, my dear Watson," interjected Holmes impatiently. "In my limited medical knowledge, I should imagine one or two milligrams to be a conservative dosage," remarked Holmes.

"That is true and this adjusted dosage was administered to prevent nausea and vomiting," replied Dr. Westcott.

Holmes had moved behind the desk and was staring at the empty wall. "Dr. Westcott, do you have any suggestions why someone should take this particular painting?"

"None whatsoever, Mr. Holmes. The squared shoulders rounded somewhat as Wescott's expression softened to one of sorrow and loss. Mr. Gaffney particularly valued this painting, not so much for its monetary value, but rather on a sentimental basis."

"How was that?"

"I believe it was the first painting he acquired in his extensive collection. It was quite valuable, by sheer age, alone. It was one of the Giotto Madonna paintings, from the early fourteenth century. I believe it was the only rendering with a religious theme in his entire collection."

"Mr. Gaffney had a previous intrusion and a painting stolen last month, Doctor. Was that painting of any value?"

"Oh yes, indeed, it was an early Monet oil sketch of the coast of Normandy and was valued at over five hundred pounds."

"Outside of its value, can you explain why it and it alone on that occasion was stolen in a house full of paintings?"

"Again, Mr. Holmes, I have no idea whatsoever, but it does strike me as a curious incident."

"Yes, a very curious incident," reflected Holmes. "How often did you meet with Mr. Gaffney?"

"At least once week for chess and discussing art, as I also am a collector."

"Who is the executor of the estate?"

"I am. You see, Mr. Gaffney had no living relatives. His will states that in the event of his death, I was to receive his art collection in its entirety."

"That is interesting," commented Holmes. "Well, Doctor, we must not keep you any longer. I am sure your original statement to the Inspector will be all that is required of you."

With that, Dr. Westcott turned and bade all of us good day as he left the room. Shortly after that the two constables removed the body.

When the door closed, Stanley Hopkins cried, "I see motivation enough! All these paintings must be worth a fortune!"

Holmes had moved over to the tea table and seemed intrigued by two cigar stubs in an ashtray that he peered at through his lens.

"Well, it is a line of thought to pursue, but I should rather call your attention to the fact that the missing painting was thrown out from that window."

"How does that bear upon the case, Mr. Holmes?"

Holmes looked up. "It may be nothing, then again it may be everything," was his cryptic reply.

"Mr. Holmes, you are way beyond me."

"Well, let me suggest then that the first theft annoyed Cecil Gaffney to the point that he enlisted my services to locate his painting. Once, however, the painting was located, he rejects any responsibility in its regard, even though we have been told of it great value. That alone is suggestive."

"But what does it suggest?" asked a perplexed Stanley Hopkins.

"It suggests a very curious chain of events that eventually led to the second painting being thrown out of the window. It would be premature to hazard any theory, Hopkins, and yet it is quite indicative..." Holmes attitude took on a remote, preoccupied appearance.

"Mr. Holmes, can you be more explicit?"

At the mention of his name, Holmes seemed to wake from the reverie into which he had fallen. "Indications strongly suggest premeditated murder in a most diabolic way. Would you be so kind as to ring for Matthews?"

Holmes would say no more until the manservant stepped in the room. Matthews was visibly shaken and would not look in the direction of the sofa or the desk.

Holmes stepped forward and addressed the servant in an affable way. "We can understand how this household has had a great shock. Will you please be seated over by the window and I will try to be as brief as possible."

Holmes' kindly manner put Matthews at ease and his countenance brightened somewhat.

"Now then, your answers are of the utmost importance, so please consider each one before you answer. Is that clear?"

"Yes sir."

"You have supplied Inspector Hopkins with a list of friends and acquaintances which I have glanced at. Which of these gentlemen were the most frequent visitors?"

Matthews reflected a moment. "Generally speaking, Mr. Gaffney had few visitors. Of course, Dr. Westcott was regular. He came about once a week. generally on Wednesday nights. Now and then Mr. Frank Sutcliffe stopped by. Mr. Gaffney was promoting his portrait work, which he thought very highly of."

"I understand that Mr. Sutcliffe was the last visitor Mr. Gaffney had?"

"That is correct."

"That was Thursday evening?"

"Yes sir."

"Was there anything unusual about their meeting?"

"Well, sir, I can't say for sure, but it sounded as if the master and Mr. Sutcliffe had some sort of altercation. Mr. Sutcliffe left rather early, and slammed the front door when he left."

"I see," said Holmes.

The servant continued, "At least once a month Sir Reginald Dawson came for dinner. That is about all, Mr. Holmes."

"Did Mr. Gaffney have a social life in London?"

"At least once a week during the season he attended Sir Reginald's Art Society, usually on Friday afternoons."

"Were there any occasions when he remained in the city?" inquired Holmes.

"Only when his business partner required his presence for certain decisions."

"What kind of business was he engaged in?"

"Mr. Gaffney was in partnership with Mr. Geoffrey Banner in the buying and selling of fine art. One of my duties was assisting in cataloguing various works."

"Geoffrey Banner …the G.B. initials of the invoices on the desk," remarked Holmes. "What is their business address?"

"No. 6, St. James Street."

"Watson, would you kindly make note of that? Were there any other business activities he participated in?"

Matthews considered a moment. "He was an irregular contributor to the various art periodicals as an art critic."

Holmes went to the tea table and picked up the ashtray. "There are two distinctly different ashes here; one is the ash from a Rajah cigar, the other a very expensive Embassy." Holmes looked back at Matthews. "Did Mr. Gaffney smoke?"

"He always smoked Rajahs."

"I see," said Holmes. "We understand from your earlier statement that Mr. Frank Sutcliffe was the last visitor on Thursday night."

"That is correct."

"Does he smoke Embassy cigars?"

"Mr. Sutcliffe does not smoke at all."

I saw a distinct flicker of vexation and disappointment register on Holmes' face as he replaced the ashtray.

"How many days a week did Mr. Gaffney go to his place of business?"

"Every weekday from Monday through Friday."

"Did he take the train?"

"Mr. Gaffney took the steam launch when weather permitted."

"The painting that was stolen last month, did Mr. Gaffney speak about it?"

"Outside of the fact that Emily and I were instructed to ensure that all doors and windows were secure each evening, no, he never mentioned the incident after that."

"I understand today is your day off. Where do you usually spend it?"

"I generally visit my sister in Deptford, who is an invalid. I do her weekly errands and help out the best I can."

"Were you going there today?"

"Yes sir."

"How came you to serve breakfast to your master this morning."

"It is my custom to do so before leaving for the day."

"Well, Matthews, your statement is all very clear. That will be all for now. Please tell Emily I shall come down shortly to speak with her."

"Begging your pardon, sir, but may I be permitted to leave the premises? I just do not think I could endure staying here another night."

Holmes glanced at Hopkins, who had been following Holmes' questions closely. He said, "Leave an address where you can be reached."

"Thank you, Inspector."

Hopkins was about to make a comment when something caught his attention through the window. Peering out he exclaimed in astonishment, "My God, the pressmen are gathered out in front of the house! How in the world did they get word of this affair so quickly?"

"How, indeed," pondered Holmes. "It is best you go down and speak with them while Watson and I question Emily. We will meet in ten or fifteen minutes and catch the steam launch to Westminster Bridge. By the way, Inspector, I should not go into too many details with the press. There are deep waters here, possibly scandal in high places."

"You have read all that in just this short time?" said an astounded Hopkins.

"Well, there are many other indications, but all will have to be substantiated."

Hopkins left the room more perplexed, I think, than when he first entered. On the first floor Matthews directed us to the kitchen. A very young, buxom and ingenuous girl greeted us with a degree of apprehension on her face.

"Now, Emily, this will take but a moment," said Holmes. "Matthews has indicated that you come each morning and leave each evening."

"That is so," said she.

Holmes quickly put her at ease, and within a few minutes was chatting with her like an old friend.

"That's correct, sir, I let myself in with my own key and I have an extra at home in case of an emergency."

"Where do you keep the extra key?"

"In the cupboard by the side table."

"I see," said Holmes. "I imagine such an attractive young lady like yourself has a young gentleman friend?"

Emily blushed and said, "Yes, sir, I do have a special gentleman..."

"Which is all very natural," interjected Holmes. "Tell me, does he visit you here, Emily?"

"Oh Lord, no, Mr. Holmes. I would never allow such a thing."

"Well, then where do you meet?"

"Peter walks me home to Waltham Street Mondays and Wednesdays when my work is finished for the day."

"Are your lodgings on Waltham Street?"

"Yes and Mrs. Wilkenson, my landlady, is almost like a mother to me. She has always chaperoned us when Peter stops in."

"I see," said Holmes.

"Mrs. Wilkenson thinks Peter is a fine young man."

"Peter who?"

"Why, Peter Shaw, Mr. Holmes."

"How long have you known this Peter Shaw?"

"A little over a month."

Holmes considered this information for several moments, then said, "Thank you, Emily. You have been most enlightening. If you will give your address to Dr. Watson, we shall detain you no longer."

We left the kitchen and met the Inspector coming in the front door. "It's amazing, Mr. Holmes, it seems all the press people were alerted to this case by printed messages."

"Printed messages," repeated Holmes. "I should have expected something of the sort, but printed messages."

"How on earth should you expect a development like that?"

"I should like a few more facts before I go so far as to state a theory, but if you come around to our rooms at five o'clock tomorrow, more than likely I shall be able to enlighten you. In the meantime, we should make every effort to speak with Geoffrey Banner."

CHAPTER THREE

▼

THE CONNOISSEUR'S PARTNER

We had come up the river in the raw grey weather of an early winter and arrived at Westminster Bridge exactly as Big Ben was striking the four o'clock hour. The fog and mist of the day had turned into a gloomy drizzle. It was already dark as Holmes hailed a cab.

"No. 6 St. James Street, and hurry," said he.

As we raced along the London streets, Holmes addressed Hopkins as to how the steam launch took only half the time to arrive in London, as opposed to the morning train ride to Greenwich. Through the fogged windows we saw the blurred gas lamps moving past with the occasional larger glare of a shop front.

It was not too long before we arrived at our destination. As we alighted from the cab, I noticed that a "Closed" sign was being hung in the glass of the door. Holmes stepped forward and vigorously knocked on the door.

"It's after four o'clock. We are closed," came a voice from within.

Hopkins stepped forward and shouted, "This is Scotland Yard business. Please open the door immediately!"

The latch fell and the door opened upon a balding young man peering out at us.

"Please come in, gentlemen. I assume you are here in connection with the tragic death of Mr. Cecil Gaffney."

We stepped into a fair-sized art gallery with paintings everywhere. Hopkins glared at this rather studious and dreadfully earnest-looking young man.

"And how would you know about this since it only came to light early this morning?"

"Why, from the message I received."

Holmes stepped forward. "This is Inspector Hopkins of Scotland Yard, and I am Sherlock Holmes. This is my associate, Dr. Watson. May I see that message?"

"Of course, but please step upstairs to my study where we can be more comfortable."

Geoffrey Banner had a small flat above the shop. The building was one of a few dating from the mid-1600's, full of switch-back floors and low-slung beams. The study was on the second landing. We all sat down in a partially paneled library containing innumerable books that pertained mostly to art subjects.

"At what hour did this message arrive?" asked Holmes.

"It arrived at ten o'clock this morning."

"You did nothing?"

"At first I thought it was some sort of prank. Later in the afternoon I had second thoughts, and wired Matthews. He sent this wire confirming the fact." Geoffrey Banner held up a telegram. "There was really nothing I could do, Mr. Holmes. I can tell you it was a dreadful shock."

Holmes had been looking closely at the message. He passed it to me. It read:

"Cecil Gaffney has been murdered in Greenwich."

"This message has been printed by hand in letters such as found in a printer's shop," mused Holmes. "The italic Roman is predominant."

"It is the same message the pressmen received," said Hopkins as he glanced at the paper. Holmes fell silent. Inspector Hopkins pursued his line of inquiry. "For how long have you been associated with Mr. Gaffney?"

"For the past ten years."

"Can you tell us anything about Mr. Gaffney that may help us in this investigation?"

Geoffrey Banner considered for a few moments, as if deciding where to start.

"I met him some ten years ago. We were both attending a special art exhibition at the National Gallery. He was working at the time as a free-lance art critic for the Sunday Times. One could not miss his tall lean figure and rather sardonic grin. His peculiar offering of two fingers for a handshake was well known everywhere in the art world. He cultivated public opinion by making the fullest possible use of the press.

"We found that we had many common interests in art, and when he learned of my expertise in art restoration and knowledge of art forgery, he proposed a business partnership He knew instinctively what the art-buying public wanted, and I am proud to say we were the first in England to introduce and promote the works of Edgar Degas."

Hopkins finished taking his notes and asked, "Now then, in the event of Mr. Gaffney's death, or your own, how would this art gallery be legally settled?"

"If either of us died, this establishment would revert to the survivor. In case we both died, it was to be sold and the proceeds were to go to charity."

"I see," said the Inspector. "Therefore, Mr. Banner, you have much to gain under these circumstances."

"That is true. Does that make me a suspect?" Geoffrey Banner looked incredulously at the Inspector.

The room fell silent. Outside, the rain was falling quietly against the buildings.

"Naturally it would, if you cannot account and verify your whereabouts on the night of the murder."

"Well, Inspector, that is simplicity itself, as I was a guest that evening at Sir Reginald's Art Society, which can be easily verified. I met Mr. Gaffney just as he was leaving."

"What time was that?

"Just around four o'clock."

"Was he alone?"

"Yes, he was."

Hopkins made several more notes. "That fact shall have to be corroborated."

"I understand, Inspector."

Hopkins appeared to be finished with his questions. Holmes, who had been listening attentively, brought out his pipe.

"Do you mind smoke, Mr. Banner?"

"Not at all. I indulge myself."

"Excellent! I find smoking most conducive to the reasoning processes." Holmes had straightened up in his chair, leaned back in an attitude of complete relaxation. "I am sure you are cognizant of the theft of Mr. Gaffney's painting last month."

"Yes I am, and it is strange that you refer to it."

"Why is that?" asked Holmes.

Hopkins interjected, "I find it strange, Mr. Holmes, that you constantly go back to those stolen paintings."

"It is not strange, Inspector. All the threads of this complex investigation go back to those paintings. I would venture to say they are pivotal."

Geoffrey Banner looked from the Inspector back to Holmes.

"I only thought it strange because in our ten year association, it was the first time Mr. Gaffney purchased a painting that proved to be a forgery."

Holmes looked keenly at the young man. "You are referring to the Monet Normandy Coast scene?"

"Yes, that was the painting. He had brought it to the shop and asked my opinion and appraisal of it. After a thorough examination, I declared it was not an original. Mr. Gaffney was extremely annoyed and agitated when I told him."

"Where did he buy the painting?"

"In Paris."

"And who was the dealer?"

"It was purchased from a private party whose name he did not give me. It had been authenticated by an independent expert."

"I see," said Holmes reflectively. He seemed to read a great deal more into this information than either I or Inspector Hopkins.

"We understand Mr. Gaffney was promoting a young artist by the name of Frank Sutcliffe, who, incidentally, was the last person to visit the Gaffney house. Do you know him?" inquired Holmes.

"Yes, of course. Mr. Gaffney and I met him at Sir Reginald's Art Society a few years ago."

"What was your impression of him?"

"I did not know him on intimate terms, but the tendency of men close to Frank Sutcliffe was to go through three stages of ratiocination: One, to observe his activities with utter fascination; two, to attempt to analyze and understand him; and three to finally throw up their hands and admit the impossibility of such understanding. This came about because he was a mass of contradictions, supremely inconsistent, ever in conflict with himself."

"That is an extremely interesting viewpoint," said Holmes, but we understand Sutcliffe is a painter of distinction."

"Yes, that he is, when he so chooses. When the work fit is upon him, he'll spend weeks at sittings and will only execute a portrait after laborious travail."

Holmes directed his attention to Hopkins. "Inspector, I believe Mr. Sutcliffe's statement will be most interesting." Turning back to Geoffrey Banner he said, "If my theory proves to be correct, I am quite sure I shall seek your expertise in the near future."

"I am at your service, Mr. Holmes."

"One last point, Mr. Banner. Can you recall if Mr. Gaffney had any enemies?"

"As far as I know he did not."

Holmes got up to leave. Hopkins and I did likewise.

"Inspector, do you have any more questions for Mr. Banner?"

"No, I have all I need for now."

"Then I believe we are finished. Oh, incidentally, I should like to keep this printed message for chemical tests, if you don't mind." Holmes was already carefully folding the note to place in his pocket. Geoffrey Banner nodded his head in acknowledgment.

We stepped out into St. James Street. The inclement weather had not subsided. After bidding good evening to Inspector Hopkins at Scotland Yard, we proceeded back to Baker Street.

A cheery fire greeted us as we entered our rooms, and Mrs. Hudson's cold dinner laid out on the sideboard was a welcome sight after a long day.

We ate in silence. Outside the storm was still raging and the rain lashed continually against the windows. When Holmes was finished, he went to his chemical table and sat down to work. Very quickly, he became lost in his chemical analyses.

After some time I heard him mumble to no one in particular, "Definitely printer's ink."

I sat for a time smoking by the smoldering fire and turned over in my mind the curious incidents that had occurred and the strange experiences that might lie before us. Why, for example, was Holmes so interested in the housemaid's gentleman friend? Additionally, why was he putting so much emphasis on the two stolen paintings? Those were just two of the many intriguing questions raised by the investigation. Finally I went to my bedroom and undressed. Turning out the lamp, I lay down, and after long tossing, I fell into a fitful sleep

CHAPTER FOUR

▼

THE NATIONAL GALLERY

Sunday, November the second dawned damp and grey. I came down to breakfast rather late, and noticed Holmes had already finished and had gone out. There were two notes lying on the table addressed to me. The first one was from Holmes. It read:

> *If convenient, meet me at the*
> *National Gallery at one o'clock. If*
> *inconvenient, come all the same.*

Holmes often had an enigmatic manner about him.

The other note was from my old friend Colonel Hayter, asking me to join him for lunch on the following day, Monday. I had not seen the Colonel since last year, when I visited him in Reigate. I quickly jotted down a note of acceptance and rang for Billy.

"You rang, sir?"

"Yes, come in Billy. I have a note I want delivered to the Dukes Hotel at St. James Place. Do you know where that is?"

"Oh, yes sir. I have studied all the streets of London."

"You have?" I said, somewhat surprised.

"Yes, sir. Mr. Holmes said it could be invaluable to me someday."

"I see. By the way, at what hour did Mr. Holmes leave this morning?"

"Mrs. Hudson said she heard the front door open and close just before six this morning."

"Well, thank you Billy." I handed him two pence.

As he closed the door, I went over to the window and looked out onto Baker Street. It was one of those dismal early November days, with west winds driving low lying clouds across the slate coloured roofs. The prospect of going out was not very appealing. Nevertheless, I finished my breakfast, and having read the Sunday Times, which gave a great deal of space to the Greenwich murder, I prepared to meet Holmes.

It was nearly one when my cab pulled up to the National Gallery in Trafalgar Square. As I entered, I did not see Holmes immediately. However, two figures came toward me from the far end of a side gallery. I then recognized Holmes walking and conversing in a very animated way with a tall middle-aged gentleman.

"Ah, Watson! There you are," said he. "Let me introduce Sir Clifford Dawes, the chief director of the National Gallery."

Introductions followed, and I sensed a very dedicated and knowledgeable man had been giving Holmes a dissertation on Art History.

"And so you see, Mr. Holmes, the history of painting in Paris looks somewhat similar to fifteenth century Florence, and seventeenth century Rome. These, too, have had their successive waves of revolution, each generation trying to sweep away yet more of the conventions in which the official art of the academies had become entrenched."

We had been moving through the halls and galleries, when Sir Clifford stopped in front of a medium-sized canvas.

"Regard this painting, gentlemen. It is by the French artist Claude Monet, the leader of the Impressionists. What brilliance of colour, especially in the play of light and shade. Simply pure genius."

Holmes looked closely at the painting. "I concur," he said. "It is, without a doubt, the wave of the future."

"And you, Dr. Watson?" asked Sir Clifford.

"I can't say that I agree. All these little dabs of pigment—all these short comma-like brush strokes. A child could do better! It's apparent these fellows have failed to master elementary draughtsmanship. As for me, I would take that Gainsborough over there; without a doubt, a masterpiece!"

"But my dear fellow," Sir Clifford protested with his refined Edwardian charm, "these artists draw with their brushes. For example, notice the lack of a line throughout the whole painting. Furthermore, demarcation of objects in space are produced by playing cold colour against warm colour. It's really quite astounding, don't you think?" Sir Clifford went on like this as we continued walking, with Holmes nodding his agreement from time to time. I was convinced that Holmes' taste in art, as I have said on other occasions, was simply ambiguous.

Sir Clifford turned to me and said, "Dr. Watson, your attitude is very normal. This distrust between contemporary artists and the public is generally mutual. To a successful businessman, an artist is little better than an imposter who demands ridiculous prices for something that could hardly be called honest work. On the other hand, among the artists it has become an acknowledged pastime to 'shock the burghers' out of their complacency. The consequence of all this is that the artists began to see themselves as a race apart, and generally stress their contempt for the conventions of the respectable.

"You must realize, Doctor, the impressionists have opened a new door of visual expression and are still in the process. The painting by Monet that Mr. Holmes and I were discussing was sold to an American collector for one thousand pounds. At the moment, it is on loan to the British government for the next three months."

"I had no idea!" I gasped. "One thousand pounds, you say?"

"That's correct."

"My word." In fact I had no words.

Sir Clifford went on, "Due to the efforts of a Mr. DuVeen, French impressionism has been selling in the United States to very rich American collectors such as the Vanderbilts and Mellons of New York and the Potter Palmers of Chicago."

Holmes turned to me with a somewhat bemused expression. "You must allow that my knowledge of this subject is greater than your own."

I did not reply.

We were at the far end of the building and leaving a hallway to enter a large gallery. Suddenly, there appeared before us a magnificent life-size portrait of a young woman.

"This is the painting you inquired about, Mr. Holmes: Lady Sybil Colefax, painted by Mr. Frank Sutcliffe," said Sir Clifford. We stood and admired the painting of a remarkably beautiful young woman in a lavish white satin gown. The skin glowed, the eyes were shining, the luxuriant hair was piled high on the proud head. Lady Colefax looked at us as if ready to speak. If ever there was a queen, this was she.

"It is quite remarkable," said Holmes. "A beautiful piece of technical skill which brings to mind the work of the American artist John Singer Sargent."

"True," said Sir Clifford, "but I believe Mr. Sutcliffe has, in this instance, surpassed the American. We are standing before great art, gentlemen."

There was no mistaking the pride and enthusiasm of Sir Clifford. I have to admit, I stood in awe. The artist's hand and eye were certainty itself, and could infallibly find in his model the wherewithal to convey all the force and completely realize his aim.

Holmes studied the portrait once more, then said, "What great art means, I cannot presume to know. It is in the end a cumulative decision of the literate public, not necessarily the individual decision of the critic. But tell me, Sir Clifford, do you know Mr. Sutcliffe personally?"

"Yes, of course, for several years in fact. I interceded with Lord Robert Colefax on his behalf to undertake this commission, and in the event of a successful completion, the painting was to be loaned to us and displayed for no less than three months. I felt that displaying this portrait would help foster and promote the young man's career."

"Without a doubt," said Holmes.

"He really is a charming young man, Mr. Holmes, with a naivete and freshness of feeling which is a pleasure to encounter in this matter-of-fact world of ours. The poor chap seems to be a good deal out of spirits at the moment."

"So I would imagine," replied Holmes.

"What was that, Mr. Holmes?"

"Nothing, Sir Clifford, nothing at all."

"Is your interest in Mr. Sutcliffe in any way connected with this terrible tragedy of Mr. Gaffney?"

"I am afraid it is, Sir Clifford. Frank Sutcliffe was the last person known to have been with Cecil Gaffney and, as I have learned this morning, he has left the country," replied Holmes.

"In regard to your first inference, I can assure you, Mr. Holmes, that Frank Sutcliffe and Mr. Gaffney were on close terms. Mr. Gaffney was planning a private showing this coming spring of Mr. Sutcliffe's work.

"In regard to your second point, that is easily explained: He goes to Paris many times a year and I am sure that he is there now, and will be back shortly."

"Why do you say shortly?" inquired Holmes.

"The only time he travels to Paris is at the end of the week, and he always returns by Sunday evening."

We had been walking toward the main gallery. Holmes turned to Sir Clifford. "I am sure what you have told us can be confirmed. You have been most helpful."

We said our good-byes and left through the main entrance. I was about to hail a cab, when Holmes said, "Let us walk. Simpson's is just around the corner in the Strand. A small repast would be welcome."

Later we were again walking toward Baker Street.

"You know, Holmes, that young man is a remarkable painter."

"I take it you are referring to Frank Sutcliffe."

"Yes, I am."

"It seems, my dear Watson, we have yet another impression of Mr. Sutcliffe through the eyes of Sir Clifford."

"Yes, I agree."

"He is remarkable, and something of an enigma."

"An enigma? How so?" said I.

"If you were along the Kennington Road this Sunday morning, you could have seen a smart pony and trap outside a house ready to take an artist for a ten mile drive, as far as Norwood or Merton, stopping on the way back at the various public houses—The White Horse, the Horns and the Tankard—on the Kennington Road. I stood outside the Tankard watching these illustrious gentlemen alight from their equestrian outfits to enter the alehouse, where the elite of the artists meet, as is their custom on a Sunday, to take a final quaff before going home to the midday meal. How glamourous they were, dressed in velvet or corduroy, with broad brimmed hats and loose ties. You know, Watson, sometimes a man can learn more in an hour's time in a public house than he could in several days of investigation."

"And just what did you learn?" I asked.

"Among other things, I learned Frank Sutcliffe, while being a prodigiously hard-working artist, also contrives to be a sporting country gentleman, hunting and shooting and the rest, as well as being a rather raffish man about town, enjoying parties, theater, and various gallantries."

"All that certainly does not coincide with what we heard from Geoffrey Banner and Sir Clifford," said I.

Holmes was about to reply as we turned into Baker Street. Instead, he said, "Can that be Inspector Hopkins getting out of that cab in front of 221 B?"

We were a good two streets away from our front door and I found it impossible to identify anyone at that distance.

"By Jove! It is he," said Holmes. "He is early for our appointment. It's only four fifteen. He must have some important news or nothing to report at all."

Hopkins was waiting in our rooms when we arrived.

"Well, you are early, Inspector. Help yourself to the brandy on the side table."

Dusk was beginning to fall and I poked up the fire and turned up the gas. We sat down together and it was immediately obvious the inspector had not fared too well. He looked rather crestfallen. Holmes had lit his briar pipe and was looking at him in a kindly way.

"Have you any news for us, Inspector?"

There was a pause, and Hopkins replied, "Unfortunately, nothing of great import. I am at my wit's end. Mr. Holmes, how many theories do I form, only to discard each in turn. First, Matthews' alibi was beyond reproach. There was no way we could hold him on suspicion. It was the same story with Geoffrey Banner. All my efforts to find Frank Sutcliffe have failed since I have learned he is not in the country."

"Yes, so we have learned also," remarked Holmes. "Have you uncovered any pertinent facts about the artist?" he inquired.

Hopkins opened his notebook. "He lives in Halfmoon Street just outside Green Park in Mayfair."

"Hmm. That's rather expensive," said Homes reflectively.

Hopkins turned several pages. "There's talk that he has a studio in the east end, borrows money continually from friends, and is something of a womanizer."

"Well, well," said Holmes. "You have done rather well. Pray, continue."

"That is all I have."

"That is all?"

"It's all so utterly unthinkable to have spent these past days and to net so little."

"Tut, tut, my dear Hopkins. It's not as bad as all that."

"The more I hear of Frank Sutcliffe, the more he sounds like several different people," said I.

"Now that is a strikingly original observation, my dear chap, and you are quite right. Here is a man of great talent, but little income. Nevertheless, he lives in Mayfair, has, I presume, a secluded studio in the east end, and is befriended by high society. From all accounts, his energy is indefatigable, he is genial and roguish, something of a Regency buck! And, he does considerable traveling out of the country. How does he do all this?"

"I haven't the slightest idea," said I.

"Nor I," said Hopkins, "but I must admit that you interest me very much. We have established the fact that he left the country on the night of the murder, and so far the police of France, Belgium and Holland have not notified us of his whereabouts."

"I should hazard an opinion he will be found in Paris, if he is found at all," said Holmes.

"But should he not be arrested?" said I.

Holmes looked at me sharply. "On what grounds? We know from Sir Clifford that he makes several trips a year. No, Watson, we must simply bide our time and continue our inquiries."

Holmes arose and went to his chemical table. "It will take about ten minutes to prepare a chemical test," said he. "If positive, it will determine one course of action. If negative, it will point to another direction."

He then quickly lit his Bunsen burner and measured out chemicals into a beaker. He then added water and began to heat the mixture. It appeared he was formulating a reagent of some kind.

I refilled Hopkins' glass and my own. It struck me, as the fire flared and threw fitful lights upon Holmes' face that he resembled a huge lank bird of prey sitting on his stool.

Finally he held a test tube filled with clear liquid in one hand and in the other, the envelope of white powder he had taken from Gaffney's medicine bottle. Slowly he poured a small amount into the test tube. The clear liquid took on a dull red colour.

"Without a doubt, that is conclusive," said he.

I do not know whether it was from the look upon Holmes' face, or from some subtle suggestion in his manner, but a feeling of horror came upon me as I looked at that dull red test tube in his hand.

Holmes was looking keenly at us, and said, "Cecil Gaffney was murdered, not once but twice, by two different individuals!"

It was one of those dramatic moments that Sherlock Holmes relished, especially as he saw our shocked and horrified faces.

"In God's name, why would anyone commit murder on a corpse?" I asked. "It seems so grotesque, so abnormal."

"Watson, the rarest thing in this world is what one would call normal. Take the case of Pearson in '82: All the outward signs of society's so-called normal individual, but deep in that twisted mind was a hatchet murderer."

"You appall me!" said I.

"I am not shocked by many things that shock other people. What fills you with horror only makes me shrug my shoulders."

Through all this, Stanley Hopkins looked visibly agitated, and no longer able to contain himself, cried, "Do you mean to tell me I have to apprehend two murderers?"

"Technically, no. The responsibility remains with the first person," replied Holmes.

"Are you positive about this chemical test, Mr. Holmes?"

"As I have said, it is conclusive. The medicine was laced with an extremely rare poison which you will find on page fourteen of this small monograph I have recently published."

Stanley Hopkins took the small book Holmes handed him, entitled "Diagnostic Toxicology of Common and Exotic Plants."

Holmes continued his dissertation, "On page fourteen there is a description of the lethal poison of the upas tree, which grows in the East Indies and Malaya, where it is native. Its technical name is Antiaris Toxicaria. It is especially common in Java, Borneo and the Philippines, where it sometimes grows to a height of seventy feet. When the bark of this tree is injured or cut, a sticky white fluid, with which the natives poison their arrowheads, flows out. According to some reports, those who stand under the Upas tree during a heavy rainstorm will be fatally poisoned.

"This poison is just as lethal in its powdered form, and when taken internally, death is but a few moments away. The powder of foxglove is also white, and it is odorless, but the Upas poison has a slightly acrid odor. I detected a slightly acrid odor on the dead man's lips and also in one of the bottles prescribed by Dr. Westcott."

Stanley Hopkins jumped to his feet. "Are you suggesting Dr. Westcott poisoned Cecil Gaffney?"

"Not at all, my dear Inspector. Essentially, what I am suggesting is that someone who knew Gaffney on very intimate terms laced his medicine with an extremely lethal poison."

Holmes had come back to his chair. On the side table he opened a box of cigars and handed Hopkins and myself each one.

Holmes stood lighting his cigar when Stanley Hopkins said, "The whole matter is becoming more and more extraordinary."

"Pray, let me elucidate."

"Please do," replied the Inspector.

With erudite authority Holmes launched into a discourse on his favorite subject. "It is one of the elementary principles of practical reasoning," he began, "that when the impossible has been eliminated, whatever remains, however improbable, must be the truth. Let us consider first, your initial report. It suggested to me the time of death. We know the housemaid leaves at five o'clock and no one came to the house all day. We also know that it was Gaffney's habit to arrive home somewhere between five and six o'clock. If he took the steam launch, which we can safely assume, he was home within fifteen or twenty minutes, the latest. Matthews came in at seven o'clock and heard nothing all evening. In fact, he thought it more quiet than usual. Therefore, the murder took place somewhere between five thirty and seven o'clock.

"Our impression of heart failure and a fatal wound from the letter opener, as described by Dr. Westcott, was unique, primarily because the stabbing took place some forty-five minutes to an hour after the heart attack. This deduction is based on a medical fact, namely a body that has been dead for an hour or so will not bleed with any great profusion from such a wound. And, as ou stated, Inspector, there was little blood from the wound. All this I knew before ever going to Greenwich."

"It's all simple and conceivable as you put it," commented Hopkins in undisguised awe.

Holmes continued, "When we arrived at the house, we determined no one had broken in from the outside. Evidence pointed to someone throwing out an object from the second floor window, which turned out to be the missing painting. On inspecting the death room, we find Gaffney was not alone when he died, as the Embassy cigar ash indicated. During that interview I believe there was a violent argument which brought on the heart failure, whereupon the murderer simply handed Gaffney the medicine laced with poison."

"One moment, Mr. Holmes. How could you possibly know there was an argument?" inquired Hopkins.

"Earlier I said the paintings were pivotal. Fundamentally, the first stolen painting was the one of paramount importance, primarily because it was found to be a forgery. I believe Gaffney became very curious as to who was responsible for it. The murderer did not want it known that the painting was not authentic; that is why it was stolen, but Gaffney would not let the matter rest. He enlisted my services to find it and when I discovered it in Paris, Gaffney disclaimed all interest in it. I believe he was threatened.

"The heart attack and poison combined gave the appearance of a massive attack, and that is exactly what the murderer wanted: That the death should appear as if from natural causes."

"That seems clear enough as you state it, but what of this second person?"

Holmes continued, "When the second person entered and discovered the body some forty-five minutes later, he immediately plunged the letter opener into Gaffney's chest and was about to leave with the second painting. Then he heard Matthews' bedroom door open, in all probability, to check all doors and windows, as was his habit.

"Waiting some time for Matthews to settle in for the night, our second murderer must have had some qualms as to whether to chance going through the house carrying a painting. Therefore, he slowly and carefully opened the window and threw it out. A short time later, he made his escape through the kitchen, picked up the painting in the garden and ran off."

"Why did he do that and how did he get into the house in the first place?" cried the Inspector.

"We may take it a working hypotheses that the second person wanted what appeared as a natural death at first to appear rather as a murder and theft."

"Mr. Holmes, you are completely beyond me."

"Not at all, Inspector. Our second murderer let himself into the kitchen with his own key and I would wager if you asked the house maid for her second key, she would not find it!"

I had been listening to Holmes' explanation almost transfixed. "Do you mean her young gentleman friend took the key?" I asked.

"Yes, and I fear that guileless young woman shall never see him again. I also believe this is the person who alerted the press and Mr. Geoffrey Banner."

"But surely he can be apprehended," said I. "We know his name...Peter Shaw! That was it!"

"Fictitious, of course," responded Holmes.

"For the life of me, I cannot fathom why this second murderer wanted the death to appear as a murder," said Hopkins wearily.

"That fact lies in the realm of conjecture," answered Holmes. "As I have said earlier, 'In the process of eliminating the impossible...' and believe me, Inspector, there are several impossibilities still to be eliminated. As I see it, this second intruder wanted Gaffney to appear as murdered and robbed for the sole purpose of igniting a scandal."

"A scandal, Mr. Holmes? For what purpose?"

"Ah, that is the question, Inspector. The only hypothesis that fits the facts is he wanted a public disclosure of forged paintings. Why that should be is yet to be ascertained.

"But, my dear Hopkins, you look positively exhausted. I insist you stay and have dinner with us. Watson, be a good fellow and ring for Mrs. Hudson." Holmes had gone to the sideboard and was already pouring three glasses of port.

CHAPTER FIVE

▼

SOMERSET GARDENS

We were halfway through our meal when Billy brought in a telegram for Holmes. He quickly read it and placed it in his pocket.

Holmes could converse on many divergent subjects, which ranged tonight from polyphonic music of the Middle Ages to the latest innovations of submarine warfare.

By the time we finished our meal and smoked a last cigar, Stanley Hopkins was in a more relaxed mood. Nevertheless, he brought the Greenwich affair back into conversation.

"Then you believe, Mr. Holmes, you see some light in this complex business?"

"I have noticed in this most curious world, my dear Hopkins, that anything is possible, and what seems highly improbable is merely beyond the current reach of one's imagination. You know my methods, I must have a free hand to bring this matter to a successful conclusion."

"I fully understand," replied the Inspector.

"You may rest assured I shall inform you at the first instance when we attempt to close the nets."

Stanley Hopkins left a little after eight thirty. I went to the window and saw his cab turning down Oxford Street. Rain that had been threatening all day began to fall gently against the window. The street was beginning to glisten. I felt tired and on such a night my old lounge chair and the novel beside it looked very appealing. I was just sitting down when Holmes handed me the telegram he had received earlier. It read:

63 CHETWYND STREET, SOMERSET GARDENS. WIGGINS

At my questioning glance, Holmes explained, "Wiggins is quite a young gentleman now, works in the Stock Exchange. Out of all the Irregulars, he alone has the natural instincts of a ferret. I employ him on a retainer basis."

"Is this Frank Sutcliffe's studio address?" I asked as I handed back the telegram.

Holmes was putting on a long traveling Ulster.

"You are going out?"

"Yes, I intend to burgle Sutcliffe's studio."

"Holmes!" I cried. "Dare you take such a risk? Think of your career."

"Any alternative would result in Sutcliffe being alerted to our interest. I fear he'll bolt under those circumstances, so it's best to do it this way. I see no other reasonable choice," said he.

"Then I shall accompany you."

"No, Watson. What is the point of compounding a felony?"

"Say what you will, but I insist!"

He saw my resolution and pondered a moment. "Very well then, but you must follow my instructions to the letter."

As we stepped out into the darkness, a sheet of rain was driven in upon our faces. Holmes hailed a cab, gave directions to the cabby and then sank back in his seat in silent meditation.

The rain pelted down upon the leather top of the cab, while the wheels splashed through large puddles, fanning the dirty water out behind us. I hugged my great coat around me and despite my weariness, watched the busy London night go past with quiet pleasure. After a while the road became dingy, the houses more crowded. Gaslights burned yellow and flat through the misty haze of the night. The road turned left into a line of dingy, eyeless houses. Above them rose a single block of flats: Somerset Gardens.

The cab slowed down and pulled over to the side of the street. In an instant Holmes was out. I followed.

"Here is a half crown, Cabby. Wait here until we return and there will be another for you.

"As your lordship commands," he said, smiling in his good fortune.

We turned a corner and walked half a block to Chetwynd Street, which was a narrow, sordid street in a wicked looking district. No. 63 was a large building, very ugly in its way.

Holmes, who knew London with the accuracy of a cartographer, cast a swift glance into the shadows. There was nothing but a line of flat-faced houses. The wet flagstones gleamed in the streetlight as we faced a discoloured door.

"The customary mode of entrance is quite impossible," said Holmes. "The door is formidable and there is too much light from the street lamp. We must go to the rear."

We turned into a mews where a rush of water in the gutters swirled forth toward the sewer gratings. To the rear of the house was an attached coach house.

"Watson, when I enter, wait a few minutes, then come to the front door and knock gently."

"How will you get in?" I queried.

Pointing up, he said, "Above, on the second floor. The left window."

We were both in middle life, but Holmes, with his catlike agility and strength, had clambered up to the roof of the coach house within seconds.

A drainpipe then brought him next to the window. He took a small jemmy from his coat and silently forced the window open. Swinging his leg over the sill, he entered quietly.

The door opened to my gentle knock. Holmes had his dark lantern lit, which cast a beam of light. Frank Sutcliffe's studio lay before us.

The room was very large and the ceiling ran up to the second floor with skylights in the roof. A set of stairs and a large balcony with rooms to the rear completed the studio.

In the center of the studio was a platform covered by Persian rugs and a large couch. Off the right side was a large easel. Dimly I could see paintings around the walls and art materials, bottles, pencils, bits of pastel chalk, nameless odds and ends that may come in handy to an artist.

Holmes had gone to a side table. "Hello, this is most interesting," said he. I watched as he picked up a small drawing and secreted it in his coat pocket. I followed him to the easel, where his lantern light played across a very large canvas. Before us, reclining on a couch, quite nude, was a beautiful young woman."Good Heavens!" I gasped. "It's Lady Sybil Colefax." I became thoroughly engrossed in the painting when suddenly Holmes drew his breath sharply in and seized my arm in a convulsive grip. At the same instant I heard the same sound that quickened him.

It was the front door latch being opened. In the next instant, Holmes sprang forward and motioned for me to follow. We quickly went up the stairs to the balcony, where we concealed ourselves behind a Chinese screen.

Through a partition in the screen we could dimly view the dark studio below. Suddenly, the door opened fully. A switch was thrown that bathed the studio in electric light and two figures entered. The balcony, thank God, remained in semi-darkness there was no mistaking Lady Colefax; her companion could only be Frank Sutcliffe. He was a handsome man, over six feet tall, slender, racily dressed with an especially dazzling cravat, very blond with a small golden moustache.

Darling, I promise you, this will be the last sitting," said he.

"It must be the last, I will not come again. It's much too dangerous."

"I know it's difficult enough with regard to your husband, but since this ghastly business with Cecil Gaffney, I understand through my friend Peter Daubeny that inquiries are being made as to my whereabouts."

"Who is making these inquiries?" asked Lady Colefax in an alarmed voice.

"Inspector Hopkins of Scotland Yard, and no less than Sherlock Holmes himself. All because I was the last person to see Gaffney alive. My God, I wish I had never gone that night!"

"What are you going to do?"

"I am going to finish what I have started, this painting. Then we shall have a late dinner and I shall take you to your train. As for myself, I shall return to France and stay until this affair blows over."

"But, darling, is that wise? They may think you are trying to escape."

"Perhaps, but with Mr. Sherlock Holmes on the case, I am sure he will find the one who is responsible for this atrocity in a very short time."

This conversation was taking place while the artist was laying out his colours and preparing his palette. Lady Colefax was undressing behind a screen at the left side of the platform. I held my breath as she emerged from the screen and reclined on the couch. Her beauty was intoxicating. I cast a glance at Holmes; his gaze was transfixed. His eyes were focused not on the scene below, but rather to the back of the balcony, where a narrow shelf ran under a window, which shed a ghost of light from the street outside. Under the window, against the wall were several paintings. I saw the familiar gleam in his eyes, that of triumph.

I returned my attention to the scene below. The model reclining on the couch was facing in such a way that she was obstructed from my view, but I could clearly see the artist mixing colours and very carefully applying a highlight here and an extended tone there. Outside we could hear the sound of carriages moving through the rain like the rustling of fall leaves in the wind. It was an awkward vigil and, I felt, incommodious, so I was greatly relieved to hear Frank Sutcliffe cry, "It is finished!"

He put down his brushes and brought out her clothing from behind the screen. Lady Colefax sat up on the couch and I could see the outline of a delicate shoulder just above it. Then a full view again for a tantalizing moment, as she put on her bodice and stertorously pulled up her stays. There followed the camouflage of her petty coat, the pulling on of knickers, more whale bone, more starch, the clamping down of an ample bosom, the fastening of sharp buckles, like the riveting of armour. The results of all this manipulation was a wasp waist, which I would venture was no more than twenty-two inches. All this, I learned much later, was derigueur for girls even as young as thirteen years of age.

Suddenly, the entire studio was thrown into darkness as the front door closed. Holmes sprang up to cross the balcony to where the canvas lay against the wall.

"What are we looking for?" I whispered.

Holmes was kneeling by the canvases and flashing his dark lantern over each one.

"We have found what we are looking for," said he. As he spoke he picked up one of the paintings and motioned for me to follow him downstairs.

CHAPTER SIX

▼

ENTER MYCROFT

It was shortly after two-thirty the following day when I entered our rooms. Holmes was seated at his chemical table where I had left him in the morning. He appeared to be deeply absorbed. Many years of experience have shown me I would be more of a distraction if I engaged him in conversation. I sat down by the fire and observed him handling his delicate chemical apparatus.

By this time in our association, Holmes' chemical equipment was highly sophisticated. Retorts had given way to Liebig condensers and fractional columns. The condenser was steaming its contents into an Erlenmeyer flask, which he then poured over a small piece of paper in a beaker. After adding several chemicals and stirring the beaker, the contents turned a dusty brown. Holmes' concentration was so great it seemed as if he did not know I was in the room. I was therefore surprised when he turned to me and said, "Tea."

"I think not," said I. "Mrs. Hudson will not be up until half past four."

"No, no, Watson, this tea, made with a small piece of Frank Sutcliffe's print." He held up the beaker with its liquid brown contents swirling. "This tea, as my tests have shown conclusively, has traces of tannic acid."

"Which proves what?" I asked.

"It proves that Frank Sutcliffe has faked a very early Manet drawing by coating its surface with ordinary tea to give the appearance of age. I seem to recall the Chinese doing something of the sort to age ivory."

I looked at Holmes in amazement. "A man of such superb talents! Why would he do such a thing?"

"One could surmise that this is the source of his large income, and I believe there is a connection to Cecil Gaffney's murder, but we can substantiate this by speaking with Geoffrey Banner. I have asked him to call upon us at four o'clock this afternoon. By the way, how is your old friend Colonel Hayter?"

"How do you know I met the Colonel? Surely I made no mention of the fact this morning."

"You told me yourself—that is, the clothing you chose to wear told me."

"I don't see the connection."

"Watson, it is so elementary that it hardly bears repeating."

"I should like to know all the same."

"You invariably forget that I know your habits well. This morning you took longer than usual to come down to breakfast. When you appeared, the room was positively redolent with your after shave and you were dressed in your finest. This fact ruled out any medical call you might have had. Stamford is on medical leave in Edinburgh, your billiard club does not meet until next week, your bank account would not allow your indulgence in the races until next month the earliest, when you receive your invalidity pension from the government. What is left? Colonel Hayter must be in London and you are meeting him for lunch."

"Perhaps I am meeting with a new woman friend about whom you know nothing," I challenged.

"Ah, but all the obvious signs are lacking. If that were the case you would be humming and positively aglow."

"Holmes, I think over the years you have made a profound study out of me," was my oblique reply. I was somewhat rankled at being so transparent to him.

He turned to me with a smile on his face. "The matter is of no practical importance, outside of keeping one's faculties finely tuned. So again, how is the Colonel these days?"

"He is leaving tomorrow for the south of France for an extended stay throughout the winter. He very much wants you to join us for dinner tonight."

"Dining is a capital pastime, but hardly conducive to the pursuit of…" He saw the disappointment on my face, then quickly added, "It's very kind of the Colonel."

I brightened, and he continued, "Perhaps a little break from the pursuit of crime is in order. I really can't think of anyone to burgle tonight, can you?"

I laughed and rang to send Billy round with a message for the Colonel.

I had returned to Baker St. feeling refreshed and lighthearted after lunch with the Colonel. We spent the time together reminiscing about days past and laughing anew at some of our experiences together. It was good to see him again, and I looked forward to our dinner that evening.

It was just after four o'clock when Billy announced Mr. Geoffrey Banner.

"Please come in, Mr. Banner. Thank you for coming. You remember Dr. Watson?" I shook hands with the art expert, and Holmes seated him by the fire.

"Well, Mr. Homes, I almost contacted you before you did me."

"Oh? Why was that?"

"Inspector Hopkins has been quite persistent in feeling I had some complicity in my partner's murder. As a consequence , I have had to

approach several of my friends and acquaintances to vouch for my partic-
ipation in Sir Reginald's Art Society gathering the night of the murder."

"And I am sure the Inspector is satisfied with your explanation," said
Holmes. "You must understand, Mr. Banner, our official police must
explore every possibility in order to narrow their investigation."

"I understand, Mr. Holmes, but when it borders on harassment, I
begin to wonder."

"More to the point, Mr. Banner, I have every reason to believe the real
murderer shall be apprehended soon. But first, I need your expertise."
Holmes arose and went to the bookcase. He picked up the painting he had
taken from Sutcliffe's studio and turned it toward Geoffrey Banner.

"What do you make of this painting?"

Banner looked across at the painting and said, "At a glance it appears to
be an early Renoir! But you must understand, Mr. Holmes, that only a
thorough examination would substantiate that premise."

"How do you go about that?" inquired Holmes.

Geoffrey Banner considered for a long moment. "It is difficult to
explain how you recognize a forgery. The first look at a work of art has to
give you the emotional response of truth or untruth. One could imagine
whole volumes being written on what this first look implies. It is a sum-
ming up of all the knowledge you have acquired, all things you have seen
of the artist, all you have read about him. From a technical standpoint,
colour is paramount. Colours on a newly painted canvas change as they
blend and mellow together in the process of drying. This process takes several years. That is why it is comparatively easy to discover a counterfeit five
years or more after it is done. It will have aged differently from the way the
original work of the artist aged."

"That is most interesting," said Holmes. "Please continue."

Banner contemplated the painting across the room. "Then, of course,
no one who produces a forgery can avoid putting his own personality into
it somehow, and that personality just is not the personality of the forged
artist. The better you know this personality, the easier it is to detect the

forgery." He continued to gaze at the painting, then paraphrased his last statement. "A work of art is a direct extension of the personality of the artist. This is something the forger cannot do."

Holmes had been listening intently. He arose from his chair, brought the painting across the room and placed it next to the art expert. Then he moved the lamp on the table closer and handed him his large magnifying lens.

"Would you kindly give us your opinion? And please, take your time."

Geoffrey Banner nodded in agreement. The room grew silent. I looked out the window; dusk was settling. I grew conscious of the wind blustering against the windowpanes and whistling down the chimney.

Some fifteen minutes later there was a knock at our door and Mrs. Hudson brought in tea on a large serving platter. Holmes thanked her and continued to keenly watch Banner's examination of the painting. At length, he put the lens down and took the cup of tea I offered him. Holmes brought out cigars and passed them to us. In this congenial atmosphere, the art expert leaned back in his chair.

"It is definitely a forgery."

"And executed by whom?" asked Holmes.

"It appears to be the work of Frank Sutcliffe."

"So I suspected," replied Holmes. "How is it that the forged Monet that Cecil Gaffney brought to you escaped that conclusion?"

"The fact did not escape me, Mr. Holmes, and I made Mr. Gaffney aware of the identity of the forger."

"You would have done well to have made mention of that fact on our first meeting."

"I am sorry, Mr. Holmes, but I really did not believe at the time that it had any bearing on the case."

"Do you now?"

"Well, it certainly puts Frank Sutcliffe in a bad light."

Holmes reflected a moment. "I should prefer you to keep this knowledge confidential for the time being."

"If that's what you wish, of course. But do you suspect Frank Sutcliffe of murder?"

"I shouldn't go so far as that, but we simply cannot dismiss the inconsistencies. In my limited knowledge of art procedures, I understand a definite certificate of authenticity is required in the sale of a painting."

"That is correct, Mr. Holmes."

"Are these certificates also forged?"

"Very seldom, to my knowledge. The French government recognizes certain individuals as experts, the aupres du tribunal, which means they have the legal right, gained by years of study and superior knowledge, to provide a certificate of authenticity for a specific work."

"I see," said Holmes.

"The weakness of this system, as well as the people in it, that is at the heart of this problem, for it is simple bribery plus the quality of the work itself that will merit certification, and they give their expertise usually without undue hesitation."

"In other words," said Holmes, "it is comparatively easy to obtain authenticity providing the price is right."

"That is correct."

"Have you encountered any other forged paintings beside Gaffney's Monet?"

"No, I have not, Mr. Holmes, but I understand there is a problem in the United States."

"Incidentally, would you happen to know where Frank Sutcliffe resides while in Paris?"

"Unfortunately, I do not." Looking at his pocket watch, the art expert rose to leave. "The hour is late. I would appreciate it, Mr. Holmes, if you would keep me informed of your progress. This has been a most dreadful business, and I shall not feel at ease until it is resolved."

"I quite understand, Mr. Banner. You have been most helpful and I appreciate your expert analysis."

It was just after six o'clock when Holmes and I stepped out into Baker St. and walked over to Oxford St. The night was cold and gusty. As I looked about, I felt there could never have been a period in history when city streets displayed so wide a variety of means of conveyance. The open-topped, horse-drawn omnibus was struggling for survival against the motorbus; the hansom cab against the taxicab; and the electric trams against both. Beneath the city the underground rail system had just been electrified, with escalators going down as far as a hundred feet.

Needless to say, Holmes hailed a hansom cab, and I directed the cabby to Stone's Chophouse on Panton St. Haymarket.

We met Colonel Hayter in the tavern room of Stone's, which was a few steps down from the adjoining dining room.

"My dear Holmes, I am delighted you have found time to come."

"It was kind of you to ask."

"Watson here tells me you're deeply involved in the murder of Cecil Gaffney."

"That is correct. Did you know him?"

Before answering, the Colonel indicated a table with three empty chairs and as we seated ourselves a waiter came to take our drink orders.

"Yes, I knew Gaffney on a business level," he answered when we were settled. "I bought some paintings over the years from him. It was shocking to read about this matter, poor chap."

"When did you first meet him?" inquired Holmes.

"About seven years ago at Sir Reginald's Art Society. I was inquiring about horse paintings and was introduced to Gaffney, who invited me to his art gallery. I bought a racetrack painting by the little known French artist, Edgar Degas. It certainly has appreciated in value and I consider it my best buy. However, at other times, I have lost considerable amounts of money, and as a consequence I have become difficult to please. Most other dealers no longer make an effort to talk me into buying a picture. Do you collect, Mr. Holmes?"

"No, I do not, but I have made it a point these last years to see as much as I can and I find a good deal of it self-serving, obscure, and almost deliberately poor. However, these impressionists are another matter. I sense a whole new direction, a total break from tradition. By the way, Colonel, do you know the artist Frank Sutcliffe?"

"I have not met him, but I have seen his stunning portrait of Lady Colefax."

Holmes reflected for a moment, then said, "Yes, Sutcliffe believes in intuitive perception, whereas the impressionists believe in direct observation."

I immediately understood Holmes affinity for the French impressionists by the revealing term "direct observation."

Our conversation was interrupted by the waiter, who indicated a table was waiting for us in the dining room. The room was large and each table had a sparkling white linen tablecloth laid with silverware and crystal goblets that lent a royal impression. As we sat down, I saw several wheeled carts at tables, piled with delicious smelling meals, which were being served by several hovering waiters.

"The service looks wonderful," said I. "What do you recommend?"

The Colonel turned to me and said, "The food is much better than the service, but they tell me the Dover sole brings tears to the eyes for grief that anything so innocent and tender should have to yield up its life."

We both laughed and ordered Dover sole.

After finishing a most excellent meal, we settled back over cigars and brandy.

"There is a distinct masculine atmosphere here, Colonel," said Holmes.

"Oh, yes, women are not included at Stone's. In fact, there are many bachelors of advanced years who think of Stone's as a club rather than a dining place. It has a long history going back to 1664, but in 1838 it was recognized as the only place in the west end where a clay pipe could be smoked after lunch."

Holmes looked about and said, "Without a doubt, a most excellent place." I concurred with their opinion.

The hour was growing late; a look at my pocket watch told me it was nearing half past eight when we bade Colonel Hayter good-bye, and he in turn bade us return to Reigate next spring for a visit.

"He's a splendid old chap," said I. "I had no idea he was so interested in art."

"He is an appreciator and collector," said Holmes, "whereas I simply appreciate. Who can deny that art through the ages is but a signpost for all humanity to behold and enjoy. On the other hand, when it becomes a vehicle for crime and murder, we must look anew."

We were thus conversing when we pulled up in front of 221B. Billy met us at the front door.

"Begging your pardon, Mr. Holmes, Mr. Mycroft is upstairs waiting for you."

"What on earth could bring him round at such an hour?" said I.

"So much for dinner engagements," said Holmes brusquely.

We ascended the stairs and entered our rooms. Mycroft Holmes was pacing back and forth in front of the fireplace.

"My dear Mycroft, I am delighted to see you, " said Holmes.

"Yes, yes, Sherlock, likewise, I am sure. But I have been waiting over an hour," said Mycroft in an agitated voice.

"Then, by all means, state your business," said Holmes as we all seated ourselves around the fire.

"You deduce business rather than a social call by the late hour?"

"Naturally."

"What else do you see?"

"Your business is of the utmost importance, since you just left the Prime Minister."

"Excellent!" cried Mycroft Holmes. "You caught sight of the envelope in my coat pocket with the P.M. emblem; the fact that I have waited an hour puts high priority on the affair."

"That is how I discern it,"

Mycroft leaned forward in his chair. The firelight danced over his somber features.

"You must drop it, Sherlock, you really must. This investigation of Cecil Gaffney's murder is of no consequence. Higher stakes, much higher stakes are involved."

Holmes stiffened momentarily, then, began filling his pipe with tobacco. It was one of the gambits he employed whenever it was necessary to play for time. He struck a match and held it over the bowl, saying, "I presume you are referring to the art forgeries."

"Yes, yes, what else! It is imperative they be stopped immediately. If the press gets hold of this affair and brings attention to the public the consequences are so appalling that the matter will simply not bear thinking about."

I had never seen Mycroft Holmes so agitated and animated. How did he know Holmes was on the Gaffney case? How did he know about the forgeries when we ourselves just learned about them the other night?

Mycroft composed himself and continued, "I shall start from the beginning."

"Please do," exclaimed Holmes.

"England currently favours the 'Entente Cordial.'"

"Which means," interjected Holmes, "the ambitions of the Kaiser must be contained."

"Precisely. The personality of the King has created a bond with France, which the agents of Germany have tried in many ways to undermine. As Prince of Wales he visited France frequently, and now coming back to his old friends as King of England, his popularity is at its highest. This popularity has aroused a feeling of gratification on the part of the French government and its people. As a consequence the two countries are allies. For the sake of the 'Entente Cordial' he must remain high in their esteem. But supposing it was learned an English art scandal involving French art was exposed in the process. What sort of effect would that have on French public opinion there? A disposition to distrust England's motives would be extremely damaging to our relations. The French people have an interest in art and music to a much larger degree than the British.

'It is a known fact to a few high government officials that this country is engaged in the manufacture of French art forgeries. A great fear has arisen over this knowledge. Any scandal at this moment could shatter years of work by the British government."

"Tell me, Mycroft, how came you to know of these forgeries?"

"We in government have our methods, but quite frankly, I don't mind telling you—and this is highly confidential!" as he looked directly at me, "Our American friends have put us on to it, and needless to say, that alone is highly embarrassing. It seems a Mr. Joseph DuVeen, an American art dealer who acts as a contact for the French painters, has experts who have encountered several forged paintings when they were sent to America. This fact was brought to our attention. Of course, the reaction of Germany, if she were able to break the 'Entente,' would be a new thrust for power, which we alone could not stop."

"You must understand, Mycroft, the Gaffney case is intrinsically woven into the art forgery business. The two are interlocked."

"Believe me, Sherlock, you cannot render greater service to your country. Concentrate all your powers on solving these forgeries."

"I shall require a list of all government workers in the foreign office."

"That's highly irregular, but you shall have it," replied Mycroft. "May I ask what you intend to do with the list?"

"I intend to cross check all the names for anyone associated with Sir Reginald's Art Society, then through the process of elimination, we should have a clear idea of who is supplying information to Germany. Since the press was alerted about Gaffney's murder, we can take it as a working hypothesis that the German agents had to know all about the forgeries. Their main problem was to make these facts public. They hoped that by making Gaffney's murder sensational, the forgery facts would come to light.

"So far, Scotland Yard has not put the two facts together, but I would strongly advise, Mycroft, that you inform Sir Charles and Chief Inspector Hopkins of the true nature of this investigation. I will need the complete cooperation of the Yard in order to resolve this problem."

"You shall have it," replied Mycroft Holmes. "You then see some light, Sherlock?"

Holmes had put his fingertips together in meditation, then answered, "As I see it, this entire situation hangs on one highly calculated gamble."

Mycroft looked up in alarm. "I have a horror of gambling and should always do my utmost to discourage others who have an inclination for it. Those who gamble will gamble on anything."

"That is a strikingly original observation, my dear Mycroft, but nonetheless, it is imperative that we go forth on that premise."

Mycroft Holmes rose from his chair to leave. No amount of persuasion could induce him to partake in the brandy that Holmes was pouring from the decanter. Citing the late hour and his missed presence at his club, he made his excuses to leave. Pausing at the door, he turned and said, "Spare no expenses, and remember, Sherlock, the entire resources of the government are at your disposal. Break up this art forgery business!"

After Mycroft departed, I turned to Holmes. "How in the world did your brother know you were working on the Gaffney case?"

"I have said it in the past," replied Holmes, "that sometimes Mycroft **is** the government. His remarkable storehouse of information makes him indispensable. However, he simply cannot understand an old hound cannot abandon the trail."

CHAPTER SEVEN

▼

COUNTRY SOJOURN

Very early on the following morning, I was aroused from my sleep by a tap on my bedroom door.

"Come in," I said sleepily. By the dim light of the gas lamp I could see Holmes standing at the doorway.

"Watson, there is no alternative. We must see Lady Colefax. Can you be ready in one half hour?"

Expelled from the snug comfort of my bed, I quickly washed and dressed. In minutes I sat down to a cup of tea and biscuits Holmes had set out.

"I have considered this problem through the night with the help of my shag tobacco. Since Mycroft has enlightened us, time is of the essence; therefore, we must seek the cooperation of Lady Colefax."

"Will she cooperate?" I asked.

"That remains to be seen, but I think she shall see reason enough."

Dawn was breaking when we entered King's Cross Station and within a short period of time the fogs of Baker St. were behind us. Holmes sat huddled in the corner of our compartment studying maps. He had brought along a rather large package, which rested on the rack above with our luggage. It was fully light now, and the day promised to be a pleasant one, at least in regard to the weather.

As I looked from the train window at the passing countryside, I could not help feeling a strange sadness. For miles along the way there were homes and estates newly built, that looked substantial, convincing and permanent. They were built high in the hills with commanding views of other homes. Such was the expansion of the suburban areas, which nullified the rural aspects of the countryside.

Holmes had put away his maps. "You seem keenly aware of the landscape, Watson."

"All this expansion—where will it all lead?" I reflected ruefully.

Holmes looked out the window. "More homes means more people, which means more than likely, more crime, especially in these isolated areas."

"It's not a very pleasant thing to contemplate," I said, more to myself than to him.

It seemed like a month had passed by since last Friday, and this being only Tuesday, the fourth of November. This Gaffney case had taken a bizarre turn. As it was, disquieting questions began crossing my mind. I turned to Holmes.

"Why do you consider a statement from Lady Colefax essential?"

"I have every reason to believe she can tell us where Frank Sutcliffe is."

"I find it insufferable," said I, "how can people of rank risk everything. Why, Lord Colefax is one of the wealthiest peers in all of England."

Holmes turned away from the window and tamped tobacco into his pipe. Short puffs of smoke escaped his lips as he stared at me over the bowl.

Finally, he said, "Watson, it happens every day. The most unlikely people commit the most unlikely crimes. Gentle old ladies poison whole households. Fine young gentlemen commit holdups. Bank managers with spotless records going back twenty years are found to be longtime embezzlers. Before we are finished, if I am not much mistaken, we shall add more impressive names to our list." While speaking, Holmes took down his large package from amongst our luggage on the overhead rack.

"But Holmes," I said, still bothered, "we are speaking of the highest ranks of society. What more could they possibly hope to gain?"

"Ah, there we come to the realm of conjecture. Who is to say what the motivating factor is? But one thing is for certain: The basic nature of some leans toward a fascination with evil." As he spoke, he suddenly, to my astonishment, took out sections of a fishing rod.

"But surely," I wondered, "you are not planning a fishing trip?"

"Why not?" he said with amusement in his eyes.

"Is it not a bit late in the season for fishing?"

"Nonsense, old chap, pike strike at the bait in all seasons. Our chances are admirable!"

My face must have betrayed my thoughts, that of total incredulity. Holmes quickly explained.

"Watson, since you took to publishing so many of my cases, we are unfortunately quite well-known. Since I do not want any scandalous implications cast upon Lord and Lady Colefax, we must appear as two tired professionals desiring relief from the fogs of London for the beneficial fresh air of the country. Furthermore, searching for the finny tribe is an excellent excuse to visit the village of West Tanfield, Yorkshire."

Sometime after boarding the local train at York, I began to notice a change in the landscape. We were well into Yorkshire now, and were quickly passing attractive villages in the Dales, a series of long valleys that pierce the eastern slopes of the Pennine Chain. Suddenly, we were running parallel to a river.

"According to my maps, that should be the River Ure," observed Holmes. "We should be coming into West Tanfield shortly."

Finally we pulled into a small wayside station and disembarked. Holmes sought the stationmaster.

"Can you direct us to the Rose and Crown?"

Pointing up the river, he said, "Follow the river to the bridge and cross over. You won't miss it."

There were few pedestrians at this time of day. A thin mist rose from the river and the opalescent light cast a pleasant somnolence over the scene.

"Have you been here before?" I asked Holmes as we walked along.

"No, but my guidebook tells me the Rose and Crown is the only accommodation."

The River Ure appeared to be a slow and placid body of water as we crossed the narrow bridge into the heart of the village. A slight bend in the road gave us a view of the village church reflected in the Ure's clear water. Without a doubt, West Tanfield's old buildings represented the essential parts of a medieval village from the time of the Saxon kings to Tudor days. There was a sublime charm to the winding streets and stone cottages.

The Rose and Crown proved to be a very old and rustic coaching inn. Being late in the season, the innkeeper was delighted to have guests, especially Mr. Sherlock Holmes. Holmes made a great show of his fishing equipment.

"Tell me, Innkeeper, where might the best pike fishing be had?"

"I would not know about that this time of year sir, but Lord Colefax's gamekeeper could tell you. I'll send round for him."

"Excellent!" exclaimed Holmes.

Our rooms were ancient but comfortable. We came down to the bar room and met Mr. Hawkins, Lord Colefax's gamekeeper. Holmes ordered pints all around.

"Well, Mr. Holmes, it's a bit late in the season for pike fishing," said Hawkins. I cast a glance at Holmes.

"Nevertheless, we should like to try," replied Holmes.

The gamekeeper scratched his head. "Through the season the river at any point is usually good, but now I should imagine about a quarter of a mile north of the village where the river widens into a large pool would be the only spot to try. I have a boat along the shore that you may use."

"Capital!" cried Holmes. "Another round of drinks, Innkeeper."

"Best you watch out for the shooting parties, Mr. Holmes. Lord Colefax and his party are out every day from morning till late afternoon."

"Oh," said Holmes, "what is hunted in this area?"

"Mostly pheasants and partridges, occasionally deer."

"Are the shooting parties very large?"

"Oh Lord, yes. The woods are fairly bursting with birds, but Lord Colefax employs no fewer than ten beaters to put up the birds. Mind you, I wouldn't want it repeated, but it strikes me as a bloody massacre at times."

"Indeed," reflected Holmes. And you say he spends almost all day at this?"

"Yes, sir."

"I understand an acquaintance of mine, Mr. Frank Sutcliffe has hunted with Lord Colefax?"

By now Mr. Hawkins was in a talking mood, which was encouraged by the ample libations Holmes provided for him.

"Oh yes, I remember the gentleman quite well. I heard he painted a picture of her Ladyship while he was a guest at the hall."

"I have heard Mr. Sutcliffe is an excellent shot." said Holmes.

"That he is, but Lord Colefax is rarely seen to miss a shot and is ranked among the six best shots in England. Young Mr. Sutcliffe kept right up with him, until they had an altercation one day."

"An altercation," said Holmes. "Why, I have never heard of Mr. Sutcliffe disagreeing with anyone."

The gamekeeper lowered his voice. "My boy Jimmy was with them that day. The altercation, which turned into a violent argument, was about her Ladyship."

"Well, well," said Holmes. "That is extremely interesting, but if we are to fish today, we must get started. I have enjoyed chatting with you, Mr. Hawkins. Innkeeper, make sure Mr. Hawkins has another pint."

"Thank you, Mr. Holmes. It's been a pleasure to speak with you." Mr. Hawkins was beginning to slur his words.

Holmes gathered his equipment and we left the inn to follow the river northward. The cool air was filled with the chimes of the nearby church.

"We are getting a rather late start," said I.

"Yes," replied Holmes, "but we now know we can interview Lady Colefax tomorrow with no interruption from his Lordship."

The river ran by fields that were bounded by low woods, and at the foot of a high down was the pool we were seeking. The boat was moored on the near shore, as the gamekeeper had promised. The air had grown cold.

"Holmes, are you serious about this fishing? It seems like self-inflicted torture to pursue this any further."

"The light won't last too long, Watson. We will give it a try until it falls."

"Very well, but if I catch my death of a cold…" I took the oars and guided him along the shoreline while he cast his bait to and fro.

"With some luck we could have baked pike for dinner tonight. What do you say to that, Watson?"

"I think it highly improbable," I said with some asperity.

In the far distance we could hear the booming of the huntsmen's guns.

"It's well they are no closer!" exclaimed Holmes. "By Jove, I believe I have one on. Yes, yes I have one, Watson! Hold that net carefully. Now, Watson—now scoop him up!"

We boated a good ten-pound pike that thrashed madly about. Holmes looked exultant.

"The gods have smiled upon us. We certainly have magnified our piscatorial impression."

"Can we leave now?" I implored, laughing with him in his good fortune.

"By all means, dear boy."

We moored Hawkins' boat in the same place we first found it and walked back the way we came. As we approached the village, everything grew muted and somber.

Wednesday, November the fifth dawned damp and gloomy. Apparently it had rained during the night. Thank God our fishing expedition was behind us, I reflected as I looked out of my bedroom window.

I found Holmes bent over his maps in the sitting room. He looked up as I entered.

"Watson, when we finish breakfast, we had best make our way to Colefax Hall." Looking out the window, he continued, "This weather may terminate Lord Robert's hunt earlier than usual."

At breakfast, Holmes talked with the innkeeper about the mighty pike caught the day before.

"Without a doubt, Mr. Holmes, this is the latest seasonal catch I can recall."

"It certainly made a delicious meal," replied Holmes. "We shall not fish today, but Dr. Watson and I should like to drive through your picturesque countryside for a few hours before we return to London."

"I will have a dog cart waiting for you after breakfast," said the innkeeper.

"Excellent," cried Holmes. "Well, Watson, are you ready for a sojourn into the country?"

"The weather does not look too promising," I replied, more to myself than to him.

Later, as we stepped out into the courtyard, heavy clouds moving over the rooftops made the damp day even more depressing.

Holmes took the reins of the dogcart and set off in a northern direction. Colefax Hall lay a good five miles from West Tanfield, and we drove that distance slowly, as the night's rain had made the road nearly inaccessible.

Sheep grazed near hedgerows and there was a strange bleakness from the road to the horizon line in the distance. Holmes drove in deep thought during the time. We climbed a hill. Patches of fog lay in low ground here and there.

At a crossroad Holmes stopped to consult his map. He turned to the left and made west over empty moorland. The sun peered briefly from the clouds before it disappeared completely. To our left, in the far distance, we again heard the reports of guns.

"I wonder if there is a massacre on today," said I, looking toward the direction of the sound.

"In this weather, with such difficult, wet terrain, I hardly think so," replied Holmes.

Quite suddenly we came to two high pillars crowned with heraldic carvings, which flanked the opening of a winding avenue. After a short drive we could see a long, many-gabled mansion covered with ivy: Colefax Hall. Upon closer inspection the Hall appeared to be a crenulated mass of grey stone. One could hazard a guess that it was built at least two centuries ago.

After alighting from the cart we crossed a large stone terrace to the massive entry. Holmes clapped the doorknocker, which thundered in reverberation on the other side. After a moment or so, a butler swung the heavy door slowly open.

"We should like to speak with Lady Colefax," said Holmes.

"And whom shall I say is calling?" inquired the butler.

"Mr. Sherlock Holmes and Dr. Watson."

"Please step in gentlemen." The butler turned and walked across the large entrance hall and ascended a very old, ornately carved staircase. Mullioned windows cast feeble streams of colour onto the tiled floor before us. A few minutes later he returned.

"Madam is indisposed and cannot see you."

"In that case," said Holmes, "please take this message to her." Holmes scribbled a short message on the back of his card and handed it to the butler.

"What did you write?" I asked when the butler left.

"I wrote, 'Frank Sutcliffe will spend the rest of his days in prison unless you assist me.'"

Several minutes elapsed before the butler returned.

"Madam will receive you in the study in ten minutes. Please follow me."

We entered a very large room lined with bookcases from floor to ceiling, which resembled a library more than a study. From the bay window, I could see the yew hedges in the adjoining gardens, a lake and then a park stretching on out to the horizon line. As I looked about the room, it appeared that Lord Robert Colefax was surrounded by possessions that had been in the family since the reign of Charles II. Soon after, Lady Sybil Colefax appeared at the door and entered the study. Her angelic appearance was marred by confusion and defiance written across her features. With instant embarrassment, I recalled her posing in Frank Sutcliffe's studio. She stepped forward, looking from one to the other of us.

"To what do I owe this impertinent intrusion?" she demanded, holding up Holmes' card.

Holmes opened the interview with a directness that jolted Lady Colefax.

"We are aware of your involvement with Frank Sutcliffe."

"I have no idea what you are talking about."

Holmes stood by the bay window, tapping his heel on the highly polished floor. "We also are aware of the improprieties you have exhibited, such as posing unclothed for his painting."

The first stage of this disclosure was to bring Lady Colefax to a near faint. With great effort, she mastered herself, but her countenance took on an ashen pallor.

"My God, is there no such thing as a gentleman?"

"You do him an injustice, Madam. I have never met Mr. Sutcliffe."

"Then how could you have known?"

"It is my business to know."

"Are you here to blackmail me?"

"We are here to find Frank Sutcliffe."

"I do not know where he is!"

"Well, we have come a long way, but I see we must go." Holmes moved toward the door.

"Stop!" she cried. "What is the meaning of this message?" She held Holmes' card forward. Quiet fell over the room. A small bird perched on the window ledge, chirping and fluttering. Holmes half-turned to look at it, then turned quickly back to Lady Colefax.

"The fact is no longer secret, Frank Sutcliffe is an art forger."

She looked from Holmes to me in a dazed state.

"Do you realize what you are saying? Do you realize what this means?" She stepped forward a few paces, then slowly began to collapse. I sprang forward and caught her before she touched the floor. We brought her over to the chair by the window.

After a moment, with supreme effort, she recovered and composed herself.

"Madam, we are not the official police. I have no intention of exposing your indiscretions. If you ever had any feelings for Frank Sutcliffe, you had best tell me where I can communicate with him.

"If I had any feelings for him…" she repeated. "I love him." Her hands were clutching the side of the chair.

She looked up at us with the set, rigid face of a desperate woman.

"My husband is many years older than myself. My family convinced me the union would benefit their dwindling fortune. I tried my utmost, but I could not love him then, or now. I quickly found he thinks more of hunting and his hunting hounds than anything else in this world. He is at this pastime continually. Our marriage is a disaster, and I resolved to leave.

"Lord Colefax is proud of his heritage and his possessions. I am one of his possessions that he likes to display. When he commissioned Frank Sutcliffe to paint my portrait, I was not especially interested, but a short time later, I fell under his influence. At first, we talked of every day occur-rences, then he opened the world of art to me. His enthusiasm is bound-less. He spoke of the great artists of the Dutch school, the masters of the French and Spanish schools. He spoke at length about Goya, his life and his painting of the Duchess of Alba, both clothed in formal wear and in the nude. In time, my qualms about posing unclothed were dispelled.

"As the sittings grew from weeks to months, his passion for my portrait became an obsession. His powers of rendering were reaching their zenith. I knew he had fallen in love with me, and as a married woman, I am ashamed to admit, I was ardently attracted to him. This attraction turned into a deep love and respect. In a moment of weakness I allowed myself to be overcome by his desire. I thought this horridly improper, but rather grand and daring.

"My husband sensed a liaison was developing and terminated the commission after a heated dispute with Frank in the hunting fields. Thereafter, I posed when I could get away to London so the portrait could be finished. Finally, I suspected that I was being followed by my husband's agents and had to give up meeting Frank. I resolved to give up everything and go to Frank. Then all this happened—the murder of Frank's benefactor, Cecil Gaffney, and now this accusation of art forgery."

We listened intently to this extraordinary statement. By and large, Holmes was immune from sentiment, but he looked down at the distraught young woman and said, "If I had a daughter, she would be close to your age. Have a care, madam, have a care. One cannot play with fire for too long without getting burned."

"Mr. Holmes, what am I to do?"

"You must wire Frank Sutcliffe. I will dictate the message to you."

Before we left Colefax Hall, Holmes assured Lady Sybil he would do everything in his power to assist Frank Sutcliffe, providing he would cooperate in the investigation.

As we came outside and down the terrace steps, much to our misgivings a heavyset gentleman carrying a large cudgel in his hand came toward us.

"I am afraid," said Holmes, "this is Lord Colefax approaching."

He appeared to be a quiet, wary type of man, this Lord, with thin lips and heavy eyelids. There was suspicion written over his features as he faced us. His rather large jowls twitched with a nervous disorder as he spoke.

"And what might you be doing on my property, since I do not recall inviting you here?"

"We have merely stopped to pay our respects to her Ladyship," answered Holmes. "My name is…"

"I know who you are, you're that infernal busybody who sticks his nose into everybody's business, Mr. Sherlock Holmes. I demand to know what your business is with my wife."

"That is not for me to repeat to you. I am sure if her Ladyship so desires, she will communicate what has transpired."

Lord Colefax's wrath was enduring as well as fiery. He half raised his cudgel when he spoke.

"If I ever see you on my property again, I shall have you horse-whipped."

Holmes did not shrink from this verbal attack. "And you, sir, would find yourself prosecuted for such actions, and you may be assured that your private affairs will be exposed in every newspaper across the country."

With that we turned, mounted our dogcart and drove down the avenue.

On the road back to West Tanfield, Holmes reflected, "That woman is blessed with beauty and a high degree of intelligence. Unfortunately, it could prove to be a lethal combination. If my inferences do not deceive me, I believe Lady Colefax is heading for trouble."

"Are you referring to her husband's outburst just now?"

"I am afraid our visit will put undue hardship on her, but I dare say, she should have thought about these consequences beforehand. The perfidy of women never ceases to amaze me."

I considered what Holmes had said and concluded there was no way I could condone Lady Colefax's indiscretion. But after experiencing Lord Colefax's wrath, I felt some pangs of sympathy for her.

I turned to Holmes and said, "On the whole, it was a very unpleasant episode in high society."

Later that afternoon we left our lodgings at the Rose and Crown, and made our way back to the small rail station. Holmes dispatched three brief telegrams before we boarded the last train to York.

We were well into our journey when Holmes, who had been silent for a time, turned to me and said, "The more I turn this matter over in my mind, the more certain I am of a hidden force."

"A hidden force? What do you mean?"

"All the strands of this web lead to one man, the mastermind of the forgeries. I intuitively feel his presence and influence."

"Let us hope," said I, "Frank Sutcliffe can throw some light upon his identity."

"I rather doubt the artist has any idea who it is." He saw the question forming on my face and quickly added, "But I will go over my findings and conclusions in detail when we meet Inspector Hopkins at Baker Street."

CHAPTER EIGHT

▼

AN ARTIST'S LIFE

We arrived at King's Cross Station near seven o'clock. Holmes dispatched two more telegrams, which were longer in content. One message was the dictated message from Lady Colefax and the other was his own to Frank Sutcliffe.

"I am quite sure we shall see Mr. Sutcliffe tomorrow evening."

On our way to Baker St. we stopped at the Diogenes Club. I waited in the cab while Holmes went in. He returned shortly with a large envelope in his hand.

"I wired Mycroft to have this waiting for us," he said as he entered the cab.

"The list of government names?" I asked.

"Precisely, and it will prove interesting when it is cross checked against Sir Reginald's Art Society members."

Arriving at Baker St., we found Inspector Hopkins waiting for us.

"I received your wire, Mr. Holmes. Are there any new developments?"

"Ah, my dear Hopkins, very good of you to be so punctual. There are many developments, but we must plan our strategy. I trust Sir Charles had made the true nature of this investigation clear to you?"

"Yes, who would have imagined this turn of events?"

We all sat down around the fire. "Well, Inspector, we have come a long way from what appeared to be a commonplace murder and theft in Greenwich."

"Have you come to any conclusions?" inquired Hopkins.

"I shall give you a concise, cursory summary of the steps through which I have reasoned thus far. If you recall, when last we met, I brought your attention to the significance of the paintings. All my findings signified they were the motivation for the murder. We learned later, through Geoffrey Banner, that the first painting was a forgery. That fact brought the murderer onto the scene. Next, we found that a second party visited the murder room. His purpose was to make what looked like a natural death into a scandalous murder and theft. I have every reason to believe this individual discovered that the painting was forged quite by chance."

Inspector Hopkins interjected, "Did the second party assume the painting he took was a forgery?"

"Not at all. What could not be substantiated was by and large pure conjecture on his part. His primary goal was to use the murder to focus on the paintings, which, under Scotland Yard's dogmatic investigation, would eventually prove to be forgeries. Hence, a scandal would commence, which could topple governments."

"As you put it, Mr. Holmes, that is clear enough, but who is this second party?"

"We should have that answer shortly," exclaimed Holmes. "In the meantime, we have to consider the identity of the murderer himself. I have stated to Dr. Watson that each new development brings his presence closer. He is a man alone with perhaps one accomplice. I feel this hidden force, this leader, this mastermind of forgeries."

"Are you referring to the artist, Frank Sutcliffe?"

"Not at all, Inspector. The artist is of no real importance to this case, outside of supplying certain bits of information."

I was surprised at Holmes' lack of concern toward the artist who was responsible for the forgeries, and casually asked the Inspector if he had been located.

"We have had no word from the continent, which suggests to me he is lying low, and I might add, that is extremely suspicious under the circumstances," replied Hopkins.

Holmes made no comment, but resumed his original line of thought.

"Our chief concentration must be centered on the one man who is the leader of the forgery gang, and, as I have told my brother Mycroft, our only hope is a calculated gamble."

"I am afraid this significance escapes me," admitted Hopkins.

Put in another way, we must take a long chance at identifying him."

"If you do, will you have enough proof?"

"We will, up to a point."

"But will it hold up in a court of law?"

"Ah, that is the question, my dear Inspector. Offhand, I would say no. Therefore, we must force his hand."

"You have a plan?"

Just then there was a knock at the door and Billy came in with an envelope addressed to Holmes.

"This should be from Sir Reginald. Watson, take this list of the government names and kindly read them off." Holmes held Sir Reginald's list and regarded it with great interest. I read off all the names. When I finished, Holmes looked up with an exultant expression.

"We have him! Mr. Charles Holroyd."

Holmes had undergone a transformation, from his somewhat staid attitude to a man of action. He leaned forward in his chair and addressed Hopkins.

"Now then, Inspector, you must present yourself to Sir Reginald's Art Society at one o'clock this coming Friday. Have a sergeant accompany you. You will wait in the library until we bring in Charles Holroyd. It is essential that he is put under arrest immediately. Allow him no visitors. In the meantime, have Gaffney's housemaid, Emily, on hand and ready to confirm his identity. As I am sure you will remember, she shall know him as Peter Shaw. Best you check his lodgings for the stolen painting."

"Would he not have destroyed this evidence, Mr. Holmes?"

"That my be," replied Holmes placidly, "but nonetheless, I suggest you look into it."

"In light of these developments, I will do as you suggest."

"Excellent. I shall inform Sir Reginald of our course of action when we meet tomorrow. If there are no other questions, Inspector, I should not detain you further." Hopkins rose to leave.

"I shall be at sir Reginald's on Friday."

"Very good," said Holmes.

When the Inspector left, I turned to Holmes and asked, "Whom do you suspect is the ringleader?"

"To a great extent, that depends on how well Frank Sutcliffe cooperates with us."

"But you said in all probability he did not know."

"So I did, but you must understand, Watson, his knowledge may point the way." With that he would say no more.

The sky was grey and soiled with heavy mist the next morning. I had just finished my eggs and toast when Holmes came in.

"You have had breakfast already?" I asked.

"No, I spent the last hour with Mycroft and he concurs that if my course of action is successful, we shall have to meet with the Prime Minister. I am expecting Sir Reginald at two o'clock this afternoon. Your presence would be most helpful if you are free."

"I have no plans," I answered.

"Capital. I believe some breakfast is in order now." He rang for Billy.

Later, when he had finished, he pushed his plate aside and began to fill his pipe with yesterday's dottles.

"I can't understand how you can smoke those filthy dregs," I commented.

He looked up, rather surprised. "Absolutely no worse than one drinking yesterday's warmed over tea," he answered.

"That also does not sound too appetizing," I remonstrated.

Billy announced Sir Reginald precisely at two o'clock. Holmes rose and greeted him warmly, "Thank you for coming, Sir Reginald. This is my friend and associate, Dr. Watson."

I shook hands with our visitor, who was middle-aged, well fed and clothed in the Edwardian fashion: Cuffs turned up to his dark blue, four button coat, a sapphire pin in a heavy cravat, spotless wing collar, and antique cuff links completed the picture. An observer could sum him up as a wealthy bachelor, literate and, above all, an aesthete, perhaps even a dilettante.

"My dear Mr. Holmes, I am delighted to see you again. I received your wire yesterday, and sent your highly unusual request for our membership names as soon as they could be copied.

"I received the list and it proved most helpful." Holmes pulled up a chair for Sir Reginald and we all sat down.

According to the society columns of the daily press, Sir Reginald's gay exuberance had earned him friends in all walks of life. It was easy to see why, as this effusive gentleman spoke.

"I shall never forget your help, Mr. Holmes."

I turned and looked with surprise to Holmes. In answer to my look he said, "It so happens, my dear Watson, I was of some slight assistance to Sir Reginald several years ago."

"It was not slight to me, Mr. Holmes. My world was about to collapse. Without your advice and discretion—well, I hate to think of the consequences."

"Tut, tut, surely you exaggerate, Sir Reginald. Your problem was simplicity itself, but I did not ask you here to review the past. We have more immediate problems to discuss at the moment."

"What problems are you referring to, Mr. Holmes?"

"The case I am working on, the murder of Mr. Cecil Gaffney."

Our visitor's brows deepened. "This is a most inexplicable business," he said. "There has been precious little news in the press."

"There is a reason for that," answered Holmes, "but I understood you dined occasionally with Gaffney?"

"That is correct. I dined on the average of once a month with Cecil, and, of course, he dined at the Art Society with my other guests. He was a constant, brilliant, unbearable guest, spreading wit, terror and gaiety. A piercing mimic, incisive and merciless in his attacks, infallible in his taste, narrow-minded, yet lucidly passionate. He was always throwing mud at artists, at the schools, at the aloof poseurs, and especially at the artists who were bent on success. I can still hear him."

"You have characterized Cecil Gaffney in a most enlightening way, Sir Reginald, but I have been led to believe he was the benefactor of the artist, Frank Sutcliffe, and that does not correspond with your description of 'throwing mud at artists.'"

Sir Reginald reflected for a moment. "Frank Sutcliffe was the only exception, perhaps because he is far from being haughty or stiffly withdrawn, as so many artists are. Frank Sutcliffe is always approachable and affable. Moreover, he is much admired by his fellow artists, especially for his technical skills. But unlike most other artists, he is not afraid of responsibility, but welcomes it, up to the highest degree, enjoying, as he does, a superb self-confidence."

Holmes and I looked at each other. Here again was a completely different impression of the artist.

"Be that as it may, Sir Reginald, we have heard much to the contrary. For example, his bluntness has caused offense to some; others have accused him of using friendships to further his ambitions and fortune."

"If you are referring to Lord Colefax's commission of the Lady Colefax portrait, you may be right, Mr. Holmes. But consider the result: Her Ladyship's portrait is the most important art event in several years. It is a masterpiece of technical skill and sensitivity."

Holmes took a few moments to light his pipe before responding, "Sir Reginald, I am afraid her Ladyship's portrait was much more a work of love than the techniques you attribute it to; however, that is neither here nor there. We know, for example, that one of your members is a German agent, and more than likely, another is a murderer."

"My dear Mr. Holmes!" he expostulated. "Do you mean to imply that I play host to thieves and murderers?"

"Forgive me, Sir Reginald. I expressed myself clumsily. I realize your Art Society provides a setting where like minds can meet on neutral ground in an atmosphere of easy hospitality, but nevertheless, what I have stated is true. Of course, we cannot prove it in regard to the murderer of Cecil Gaffney, but it is an assumption which the evidence permits. As far as the German agent is concerned, there is no doubt whatsoever."

Sir Reginald was visibly agitated, but he contained himself before he spoke. "It is dreadful to contemplate the consequences if you are correct, Mr. Holmes."

"Not necessarily so. If you would be so kind as to follow my instructions, I believe we can expedite this highly unusual situation."

"What do you suggest then?"

"First, it is necessary that Dr. Watson and myself attend your Art Society tomorrow."

"Mr. Holmes, that is impossible."

Holmes had been speaking in a relaxed manner, but, in fact, was now concerned. "Impossible? Why?"

"You must understand, we have a board of directors. The very least would be a week's time for them to review a guest. As far as a candidate for membership, at least two months. Aside from that, the Society meeting rooms are being redecorated, and the members are meeting temporarily at my home in Mayfair until the work is done."

"Sir Reginald, these are deep waters, very deep waters. If necessary, I could have the Prime Minister request our presence. Of course, I should not like to go that far."

"The Prime Minister!" said an awestruck Sir Reginald. "What in the world has he got to do with this?"

"I can't reply to that now," replied Holmes.

"I can see you have not told me the whole story, Mr. Holmes."

"It is a question of national security, but I am prepared to say that your government would be highly appreciative if you would comply with our request."

"In light of what you are saying, Mr. Holmes, I see I have no recourse, but to comply."

"Capital. I am glad we are in accord on this matter. Now, then, Sir Reginald, at one o'clock tomorrow, Chief Inspector Hopkins from Scotland Yard will present himself to you. He will be accompanied by a sergeant. Please have them await our arrival in the library. I will want to discuss some of your membership in detail when I arrive, if that could be arranged. Privacy would be most helpful. I need hardly mention that all this is of the most confidential nature and will in no way be brought to the attention of the press."

"But what about the police? A scandal could be ruinous," lamented Sir Reginald.

"Sir Charles Spencer, the head of Scotland Yard is personally responsible that no information of this situation reach the press. Rest assured, there will be no blemish laid upon your Art Society."

"Well, Mr. Holmes, you seem to have this affair under control, but I must warn you, we are subject to high criticism from the membership with you and Dr. Watson being admitted without invitation."

"We must risk that. And now, Sir Reginald, I do not wish to detain you any longer." We bid a much cooler Sir Reginald good-bye.

"His life revolves around that Art Society. I suppose we represent some kind of threat," reflected Holmes after Sir Reginald left.

"It strikes me that if he knew the true nature of this business he would have been highly cooperative."

"That is true, Watson, but under the circumstances, that is out of the question."

I spent the rest of the afternoon putting my notes in order, while Holmes was occupied with a large volume entitled *"The Nobility of England from 1800 to 1900."* After an early dinner he sent several telegrams.

A little after seven o'clock, Holmes began to pace the floor. By eight fifteen he was extremely agitated.

"Where can he be? He must come." As if in answer, there was a rush upon the hall stairs, and abruptly our door burst open. The handsome face of Frank Sutcliffe was hardened with anger and wariness. He hesitated momentarily as if uncertain whom to address.

"I am Sherlock Holmes and this is Dr. Watson. Please sit down, my dear sir, and try to calm yourself."

"Calm myself!" What is the meaning of these telegrams from you and Lady Colefax? I am told I shall go to prison unless I speak with you!"

Holmes wasted no time in preliminaries or equivocation, but came to the point at once. "If you wish to avoid prison and save yourself, I would suggest you sit down and listen to what I have to say." Holmes directed him to a chair by the fire.

"I know everything about your part in the art forgeries," he began, "and unless you tell us what we want to know, it could be very difficult for you."

The anger drained from the artist's face and was replaced by trepidation. He took the proffered seat in a subdued manner.

"How is it possible that you know I have been involved with the art forgeries?"

"How I know is elementary, but perhaps I'd best summarize the events."

Holmes sat opposite Frank Sutcliffe. All he needed was a wig to duplicate the effect of a High Court Justice about to address his condemned prisoner.

"Now then. First you had been exposed to Cecil Gaffney as an art forger by Geoffrey Banner. Your benefactor, Cecil Gaffney, confronted you with the evidence last week Thursday in Greenwich. You denied the accusation, and a heated argument followed. The next morning, you went to Paris to confer with an accomplice to break from the forgery gang. Your accomplice, in turn, threatened to expose you and Lady Colefax as lovers by evidence of a photograph taken of her nude painting. You had no recourse, but to return to England and seek out Cecil Gaffney to confess everything and hope for forgiveness and mercy. You returned on Sunday and were shocked to learn your benefactor had been murdered, and inquiries were being made about you. You understood immediately that you could fall under suspicion by virtue of the argument you had with him the night of the murder. You met Lady Colefax the same day and later departed for Paris. You hoped that by lying low in Paris, the murder would be solved and you could return cleared of any implication."

Looking down at the floor, Frank Sutcliffe agonized a moment. "Everything you have said is true, Mr. Holmes, but since you agree I am innocent of Mr. Gaffney's murder, why should I go to prison? I could leave the country forever."

"This forgery business is by no means something that can be easily dismissed. Indeed, it cuts very deep. The Entente Cordial is at stake. A scandal of this magnitude could destroy years of work by the British government, and ruin the reputations of many of the leading men in France. Yes, I concur, you are in no way implicated in murder, but you are deeply involved in an illegal activity, which could put you behind bars for many years to come."

"My God, Mr. Holmes, I had no idea whatsoever. What you say shocks me beyond belief."

"Then I suggest you tell us everything from the beginning. We must have the names of your accomplices," answered Holmes.

A now thoroughly subdued and dejected young man looked from Holmes to me sitting on the side chair.

"I can assure you, Dr. Watson is the soul of discretion. Any statement you make will be held in the strictest confidence." Frank Sutcliffe nodded his head in gloomy acquiescence.

Hesitantly, as if not knowing where to begin, he finally began talking in a low voice of concentrated passion.

"It is hard luck on a fellow to have expensive tastes, great expectations, aristocratic connections, but no actual money in his pocket. Worse still is having a profession which is not known or appreciated.

"I met Cecil Gaffney through Sir Clifford Dawes at the National Gallery. Sir Clifford convinced Mr. Gaffney that I had great promise, and a small allowance was arranged for me. Mr. Gaffney brought me into Sir Reginald's Art Society. I worked hard to get ahead, but temptations were great and my debts began to be pressing. It was now a matter of survival, like a fox that is being run to death by the hounds.

"One evening I met Peter Daubeny at the Art Society. He, too, was looking to find ways of meeting his debts. Suddenly, he suggested I try making a copy of a painting he had in his family. He suggested it could be sold for a thousand pounds if it were good enough. I jumped at the chance. This led to periodic trips to Paris, where a Mr. Jacques Raindre supplied me with paintings and photographs that were completed here in London. I had enough money to set up a studio on the East end to complete these pictures. When Sir Clifford interceded on my behalf to obtain a commission from Lord Colefax, I made a decision to stop doing the forgeries. But it was too late. Raindre threatened to expose me and ruin my reputation. I saw no way out. In this beastly life of ours, which is wholly a struggle, one is never too well-armed. I know I have not been honest with myself or others in pursuing my ambitions, and I have no recourse but to accept my fate."

The room grew silent. Holmes had listened attentively while the young artist spoke. He reached for his pipe and began filling it with tobacco.

"How were you paid for your services?" he asked.

Frank Sutcliffe, somewhat dazed from telling his own dishonorable story, hesitated. "I was paid by Raindre in Paris, about once a month."

"What was the sum of these payments?"

"A thousand pounds."

"Do you realize that some of these paintings sold for as much as ten thousand pounds?"

"I had no idea."

"Were there any other individuals involved in this activity?"

"None that I know of," said the despondent young man.

"You realize we are not the official police, Mr. Sutcliffe. Your statement rings true as far as I can discern. You have a great talent that should be allowed to mature. I am sure you realize, after this extraordinary lesson in life, that there are no short cuts to fame and fortune. Therefore, I propose I shall be the judge and Dr. Watson the jury. How does the jury find the defendant, guilty or not guilty?"

"Not guilty," said I.

"Nor I, but I must suggest, and I might add, strongly suggest, that you leave the country for at least five years. The United States would be a good choice. Also, you will not, under any circumstances, communicate with Lady Colefax. The old adage 'Out of sight, out of mind' should work very appropriately in this instance. Last, but not least, destroy the painting of her Ladyship. I, in turn, shall destroy the photographs. Is all that clear?"

It seemed as if Frank Sutcliffe could not believe his ears. He lifted his head up slowly. "I am sure I am very grateful, if you are quite sure, Mr. Holmes?"

"Quite sure," responded Holmes. "But I must remind you, should you fail to follow my injunctions, I assure you the full weight of the law shall be brought to bear upon you."

Frank Sutcliffe was acceding to Holmes' conditions, when suddenly there was a knock on our door. I rose to open it. To my amazement, standing in the doorway was Lady Colefax.

Frank Sutcliffe cried out, "My God, Sybil, what are you doing here now?"

"Frank, Frank, I'm so glad I found you." She leaned against the doorway as if to faint. I gripped her arm, as Sutcliffe sprang from his chair to her side and held her.

"Darling, what has happened?"

"I have left Lord Colefax. I will never go back." she was in a state of shock, and we brought her over to the chair by the fire. I poured a small glass of brandy and handed it to her.

She removed the lace veil from her face, and we were horrified to see a long red welt across the left side of her beautiful cheek, which looked like the mark of a riding whip.

"My God, Sybil! Did he do this to you?"

With quivering lip and downcast eyes, she nodded.

I interjected, "Please drink this. I am a medical man, and you need this stimulant."

She slowly sipped the brandy while tears rolled down her cheeks.

"I have a good mind to horsewhip that blackguard myself," said Sutcliffe.

Holmes looked sharply at the artist. "You will do no such thing. You have just agreed to keep my injunctions. You must understand this is a complex business that becomes even more complex with the arrival of Lady Colefax."

At the mention of her name, she looked up at Frank Sutcliffe. "Darling, I will go wherever you go."

"Will you go with me to the United States?"

"Yes, yes, anywhere."

Holmes became concerned. "Your Ladyship must understand that Mr. Sutcliffe must leave immediately. Are you prepared to do so?"

"Yes, I am, Mr. Holmes. The sooner, the better."

Holmes reflected a moment. "I have already compounded several felonies on this case. I suppose one more should not matter. Then it is settled. You will both leave together. First of all, be sure to destroy her Ladyship's painting. Second, I would advise a steamship to Sweden, where you can book passage to America. This will put time on your side. More than likely, Scotland Yard will be watching for you, so take every precaution."

"We will do as you say, Mr. Holmes, and God bless you for giving me this chance to make amends, and, as God is my witness, I shall."

Lady Sybil was recovered enough to give Holmes a warm smile of appreciation.

"Then it is settled. I suggest you leave through the back door. Dr. Watson and I wish you 'Bon chance.'"

After the young lovers departed, I turned to Holmes and said, "How in the world did you know about Sutcliffe being blackmailed by a photograph of her Ladyship's painting?"

"I have more than once received important information through my agents on the continent," said Holmes. "We now also have the necessary information to make tomorrow's visit to the Art Society rather interesting."

CHAPTER NINE

▼

SIR REGINALD'S ART SOCIETY

The November afternoon was clear and bright as we hailed a cab in front of 221 Baker St. Holmes was in a state of high nervous energy. I sensed the prospects of Sir Reginald's Art Society presented more of a problem than he anticipated.

We drove a short distance to Wilton St. in the heart of Mayfair. Our cab pulled up in front of an elegant Georgian facade, where a footman in livery and knee breeches immediately opened the cab door and led us up the steps to the main entrance. As we stepped inside the entrance hall, an impression of great wealth encompassed me.

Sir Reginald's butler inquired after our names, then led us into the adjacent study. We moved silently across luxurious carpeting, past a profusion of priceless paintings and attractive pieces of period furniture. In a few minutes, Sir Reginald stepped into the room.

"My dear Mr. Holmes, I beg you accept my apology for my confusion and temperament yesterday."

"There is absolutely no need for an apology, Sir Reginald."

"But there is, Mr. Holmes. It was a great shock to me to learn that my Art Society harbours spies and murderers. You must understand, it put a great strain on me in regard to what a scandal might do. That was most selfish of me and I feel I owe you an apology."

"Not at all, my dear Sir Reginald. If I were at liberty to relate the true nature of these inquiries, you would not have had the slightest hesitation. But we must get to the business at hand."

"How can I be of assistance?"

Holmes took a slip of paper from his coat pocket. "These two names are most significant. I would ask you to supply us with whatever knowledge or information you may have about each name on this paper."

Sir Reginald took the paper from Holmes and considered for several moments.

"The first name, Peter Daubeny, has been a member for the last few years. He is an English subject, but of Norman ancestry. Daubeny has spent several years in Paris art schools, but has never succeeded in an original concept. His great interest is the French impressionist school of art."

"Who introduced him to the Art Society?" inquired Holmes.

"Why, Lord Pomeroy sponsored him."

"Does he pursue his art as a means of livelihood?"

"Heavens, no. In all probability, his family grants him a substantial allowance. He appears to be in funds at all times."

"Do you consider his art of any worth?"

"He is mediocre in his work, and in all probability, there are many reasons why Daubeny may not have been a great artist, but he is a great character, which is what the English relish and admire."

"I see," reflected Holmes.

"With regard to the name Jacques Raindre," continued Sir Reginald, "we see him but a few times a year. He is a French citizen and has, I have been told, a small art gallery in Paris. He speaks fluent English and continues to keep up to date on new art movements."

"Did Lord Pomeroy sponsor Mr. Raindre?"

"No, I believe Sir Clifford Dawes sponsored him. Sir Clifford acquires art pieces from him from time to time."

"When he does make an appearance, with whom does he associate?"

"Well, that is rather hard to answer, Mr. Holmes. He seems to know everyone, but if memory serves me, Peter Daubeny is the one he usually inquires about and spends more time in conversations with him."

"Singular, most singular," commented Holmes. "It is best you return to your guests now, Sir Reginald, and when Mr. Charles Holroyd arrives, please come back and inform us."

Sir Reginald had a questioning look on his face, but did not make any inquiries as he left the study.

"Well, Watson, what do you make of it?"

"I can't make anything of it. There seems to be nothing here to incriminate Daubeny or Raindre."

"Nothing but their association," reflected Holmes.

Sir Reginald returned a short time later.

"Mr. Holroyd just arrived."

"Very good," said Holmes. "You must, on any pretext, bring him to the library. We shall await you in the entrance hall where you shall introduce us and invite us to the library also. Oh, incidentally, has Peter Daubeny arrived?"

"Yes, he has, Mr. Holmes."

"Thank you, Sir Reginald." We left the study and awaited Charles Holroyd.

The gentleman with Sir Reginald was a handsome man with a pale, trailing moustache and large blue eyes that stared straight at the observer with a gaze so cool, direct and penetrating as to be somewhat unnerving.

"Why, Mr. Holmes and Dr. Watson. How nice of you to stop by. I was just telling Mr. Holroyd of my newest acquisition. Please come along and share my enthusiasm."

"With pleasure, Sir Reginald," answered Holmes.

We entered the library and Holmes quickly turned the key in the lock. Holroyd caught sight of Inspector Hopkins and the sergeant.

"What is the meaning of this, Sir Reginald?"

Holmes stepped forward. "It means time has run out for you, Mr. Holroyd."

"What are you talking about?"

"I am talking about your activities for the German government."

"This is preposterous! I really must protest, Sir Reginald."

Holmes turned to Inspector Hopkins. "Make sure Emily sees him as soon as you return to the Yard."

Hopkins came forward. "I must warn you, I am arresting you for suspicion of spying for the German government, and anything you say may be held against you in a court of law."

Frustration spread over Holroyd's features as Hopkins put handcuffs on him.

"You were right, Mr. Holmes. The painting was found in his quarters."

As Inspector Hopkins led him to the side door, Holroyd suddenly turned and addressed Holmes, "We shall meet again, Mr. Holmes."

"I have heard all that many times in the past, even the late Professor Moriarty suggested that if I dispatched him, he would indubitably dispatch me. But alas, here I still am. And now, Sir Reginald, we must partake of your Art Society."

"I must say, I am in a state of disbelief, Mr. Holmes. This man is a foreign agent in my Art Society?! It is almost impossible to believe."

"Not at all, my dear sir. As I have recently remarked to Dr. Watson, the most unlikely people commit the most unlikely crimes."

A somewhat stunned Sir Reginald led us into the main Art Society. As we entered the main hall, the immensity of wealth overwhelmed me. Cigars and cigarette smoke laced the air, small groups of people, some in formal attire, stood sipping refreshments and conversing about artistic matters. From the sideline, Sir Reginald began to identify his guests for Holmes.

"And that is Peter Daubeny, in that group at the far side of the room." We moved forward in that direction when Holmes held Sir Reginald back from joining the group. Rather, we listened by the sidewall next to a potted palm. Peter Daubeny was speaking. He had a rather didactic manner about him.

"You begin to paint, and within a half hour, you have completely forgotten all the petty vexations that were previously occupying your thoughts and weighing you down—you are a free man again, and whatever the ultimate fate of your work, no one else in the world could have made a precisely equivalent pattern of design and colour upon the canvas. It is yours and yours alone."

Holmes stepped forward, and we followed.

"Your enthusiasm is quite infectious," remarked Holmes.

Sir Reginald made introductions. Daubeny was immediately on his guard.

"Mr. Holmes, what brings you to the Art Society?"

"We are investigating the death of Mr. Cecil Gaffney. Were you acquainted with him?"

"I knew him only casually, but the dapper Cecil Gaffney, with his cryptic humour, was the sort who could tell a droll story at a crowded table and have everyone laughing at the expense of his subject. Needless to say, his untimely death was a shock to all of us."

Through all this, Holmes was regarding the various small groups in the room. His attention was drawn away by the arrival of two gentlemen. Holmes drew Sir Reginald aside.

"Who is that tall, bristling man?"

"Why, that is Lord Pomeroy," answered Sir Reginald.

As we spoke, Peter Daubeny crossed the room to greet Lord Pomeroy. Holmes watched keenly as the two had a brief discussion while Pomeroy puffed on a cigar. Suddenly, Daubeny left the room. In the next instant, the impeccable Lord Pomeroy was at our side addressing Sir Reginald in a distressingly loud voice.

"Really, sir Reginald, I was led to believe this is a private Art Society for members and guests alone. These persons," he said dyspeptically, while gesturing toward us with his monocle held between thumb and forefinger, "are neither members or guests, and have no right to be allowed to participate." There was a moment of embarrassed silence as several heads turned to look in our direction. The insult was so outrageous, so insufferable, that I fiercely turned on Lord Pomeroy.

"Do you realize this is Mr. Sherlock Holmes, who received from Queen…"

Holmes gripped my arm and quickly said, "Please forgive our intrusion, Lord Pomeroy. We are investigating the death of Mr. Cecil Gaffney, and were about to leave." Still gripping my arm, Holmes led me out of the room.

"Don't say another word, dear boy, until we are outside."

As we left, we could still hear Pomeroy's loud voice. "The rules are very clear on this point, and I should strongly suggest, Sir Reginald…"

Once outside, I could no longer contain myself. "Really, Holmes, how could you tolerate that pompous ass? The effrontery of that man! Damnable upper class!"

Holmes responded jovially, "My dear Watson, impetuous as usual, I see."

"That's still no excuse for such incorrigible manners," said I in indignation.

"There, there old fellow. This is nothing new. Disraeli put it very aptly when he spoke of the rich as compared to the common, 'They are like two nations between whom there is no intercourse and no sympathy, as if they were dwellers on different planets.' I suspect one of these days the aristocracy of England will enter into the twentieth century. However, I am sure you will agree that 'old ideas die hard.'"

As if in complete disregard of his own words, Holmes hailed a motorized hansom cab. It clanged and wheezed it's way back to Baker St.

"You certainly did not have much time for observation at the Art Society," said I, still smarting from Lord Pomeroy's brashness.

"On the contrary, I saw all that was necessary."

"But Holmes, there was a vast array of participants. It looked like half the House of Lords were present."

"Watson, you have correctly characterized the situation, however you have seen what I have seen and you have heard what I heard, but you have not observed and analyzed. If you would but apply my methods, you would know that all we need is proof to terminate the activities of the forgers and the murderer of Cecil Gaffney. I have no doubt we shall have that by next week Friday."

Holmes would say no more. I made an attempt to review and analyze the day's events, but could see no indication which Holmes alluded to. Over the years, he almost bordered on obsession when it came to not disclosing his findings until the very last moment, and then only if he could realize a dramatic effect. I retired with a head full of theories, but no tangible clue.

The following morning, Saturday, the eighth of November, was eight days since we viewed the scene of the crime in Greenwich. Holmes spent the morning in Whitehall with Mycroft and Sir Charles Spencer. They were closeted with the Prime Minister for more than an hour. When he returned to our rooms at a quarter past twelve, he made it clear that nothing could be done with regard to the forgery case until the following Friday.

"The Prime Minister concurs with me, that in order to apprehend the leader of the forgers, we must bide our time and continue our inquiries."

"What if he becomes suspicious and leaves the country?" said I.

"We must risk that possibility, although I doubt we will have to contend with that eventuality."

I contemplated that bit of intuition, and he went on, "I have asked Stanley Hopkins to step around to our rooms at one-thirty this afternoon."

We finished a light lunch and soon after, Billy announced the Inspector.

"Ah, Inspector, just in time for coffee." Holmes motioned him into an armchair.

Stanley Hopkins looked somewhat puzzled. "Mr. Holmes, we can't get a word out of this Holroyd individual."

"I suggest, and I am sure Sir Charles will concur, that this man must be kept in solitary confinement until he decides to confess. The Prime Minister feels strongly that information he has is vital to this government, and in addition, wants this man to be used to send false information back to Germany. I should imagine in a week or two Holroyd will be more than ready to cooperate. In the interim, never let up the interrogation."

"You can rest assured, Mr. Holmes, he will talk."

"Incidentally, Inspector, when you were going through Holroyd's rooms, did you find any printing supplies?"

"Yes, we did, and according to his landlady, this is something of a hobby with him."

"Hmm, so I thought," reflected Holmes. "It was a clever way of informing the press and also Geoffrey Banner of Gaffney's murder by the simple fact that these printed messages would be almost impossible to trace—unless, of course, the press itself were found. We can safely assume the press is nearby. When it is found, it will prove to be as good as one of his own fingerprints to further incriminate him. All this should have its proper effect on him."

"Well, to be truthful, Mr. Holmes, I somewhat lost sight with regard to those printed messages, in view of all the other events which have occurred."

"A capital mistake, my dear Inspector. One must keep under scrutiny the infinite as well as the infinitesimal. I have remarked to Dr. Watson many times, it is invariably these small incidents which will make or break a case."

"On consideration I am sure you are quite right, Mr. Holmes, but I am sorry to report we briefly caught sight of Frank Sutcliffe last Thursday night, but lost him completely. Strangely, in this area of Baker St."

Holmes looked momentarily uncomfortable. "I must confess to you, my dear Inspector, that I did have an interview with Frank Sutcliffe." Hopkins looked at Holmes in amazement.

"And you let him go?"

Holmes picked up his oldest briar pipe and began to fill it. "In the past I spoke of a gamble that must be taken in this investigation. That gamble was Frank Sutcliffe, and it has paid well with pertinent information. Now it follows logically from this information we may draw new inferences which in all probability will call for us to gamble again."

"How is that?" inquired Hopkins.

"Sutcliffe supplied the missing links to the chain of events; without those links, our progress could have been seriously hampered."

"Again, you are beyond me. What did he supply?"

"Names of associates"

Light began to dawn on Hopkins countenance. "But surely, he should have been put under custody."

"On the contrary, he should be allowed to fade away. This case cannot tolerate any notoriety whatsoever. This is also applicable to Peter Daubeny and Jacques Raindre."

A questioning glance crossed Hopkins' face. Holmes continued, "Daubeny is the English connection for the forgers and Raindre is the French source. What steps the French government takes with Raindre is not our concern. However, Daubeny is ours. Therefore, it is of predominant importance that he be put under observation directly, and then on next Friday morning, be arrested without fail. He must be treated in the same manner as Holroyd. Following that, I would suggest at least six Scotland Yard detectives be spread around Sir Reginald's home no later than one o'clock."

Comprehension was emerging in Hopkins' eyes. "You are planning a trap!"

Holmes looked at me with a twinkle in his eyes. "You might say I was planning a fishing trip. Therefore, we must provide the proper bait."

CHAPTER TEN

▼

UNDERGROUND SEPULCHER

Sunday was a deceptively tranquil day for Holmes and myself, preparing me not at all for the turbulent events I was to witness by the end of the week.

I recognized his remote, restless mood as eagerness for action, and by midday Monday he had already received an unusual amount of telegrams and messages. On Tuesday and Wednesday he was a flurry of activity, rushing in and out of our rooms throughout both days.

No longer able to contain my curiosity, I inquired about the case late Wednesday night.

"Holmes, you've been running about like one possessed. Is there any way in which I can assist you?"

"I am afraid not, old fellow. I am doing what Mycroft explains as my running here and there, to cross-question chambermaids and lie on my face with a lens to my eye, which, if you remember, is not his metier."

I smiled at this. "Yes, I remember."

"Tomorrow I shall be gone all day. Our net is getting full, and if I am not much mistaken, we will have our catch on Friday afternoon."

I spent most of Thursday putting my notes in order. Holmes arrived back in Baker St. in time for a cold dinner. When he had finished, he sat down by the fire. A glass of rich port, which I had poured, was upon the marble-topped table at his elbow. The strain of the week's efforts showed upon his face as I sat down opposite him.

"I have just left Sir Charles at Scotland Yard. It appears our friend, Charles Holroyd, has confessed all. Making the most of a sharp mind, diffident manner, and a wonderfully ingenuous open face, he had collected what is probably the most complete file in existence. He knows all the inner workings of the government. In this fashion, he quickly and methodically passed on to the German government all the information he gathered. I tell you, Watson, we have much to concern ourselves with regard to our German antagonists."

"You make it sound as if we are at war," I said, somewhat alarmed.

"You have touched upon the essential; in a way, it is a war—a war of nerves. This Holroyd is but an infinitesimal part of the whole, a mere microorganism in the stagnant pond of government. Unless the pond is disinfected, it will prove contagious and possibly fatal."

"Do you mean to imply there are more foreign agents?"

"What I suspect, my dear Watson, is that our government is honeycombed with agents which will stop at nothing to harass England's progress in all fields of endeavor. The future does not bode well."

"You horrify me! Is there nothing we can do?"

"The government plans to use Holroyd to dispatch false information back to Germany."

"But is there not great danger using this man as a counter-agent?"

"Exceedingly so, but the heads of state concur: We must use any means at our disposal to counter this insidious situation. In the meantime, they go about with impunity, living their double lives."

Over breakfast the next morning, Holmes looked up from his newspaper.

"I trust your old service revolver is cleaned and oiled?"

"At all times," I answered.

"Then I suggest you bring it with you this afternoon."

"Do you anticipate trouble?"

"When one is forewarned, it is wise to be forearmed."

"Holmes, can you give me any indication as to what we may encounter?"

"Only that we have arrived at our second calculated gamble."

Early that afternoon a light fog began to drift down the street. By two o'clock it was a dense blanket that obliterated everything. Holmes became impatient with it as we were about to leave for Sir Reginald's.

"Watson, I did not anticipate this abominable weather. It could wreak havoc on our plans. We will have to consult with Stanley Hopkins the minute we arrive."

Shortly after three o'clock we gathered in the somber library of Sir Reginald's. Holmes immediately instructed Stanley Hopkins to bring his men closer in. Hopkins left and returned shortly after.

"I have passed the word on to my men. I have one man at the front door. The rest are spread around the house."

Holmes was peering out the library window. "This fog is getting worse; it could be ruinous to all our plans."

At that moment Sir Reginald entered the library.

"My dear Sir Reginald, I am extremely sorry that we have to infringe on your hospitality once again in this manner, but I can assure you it will be the last time."

"Well, Mr. Holmes, I was rather surprised when I received your telegram yesterday. What can I do for you this time?"

"I am afraid it is very much like the last time. You must bring one of your guests into this library again."

Sir Reginald took out a handkerchief and passed it over his forehead. "My God, Mr. Holmes! Do you mean to imply we have more spies or murderers in our midst?"

"Essentially that is correct. Now I shall accompany you to the Art Society and indicate who you shall bring in. I shall follow right after you. Is that clear?"

Sir Reginald acquiesced in an agitated manner.

"Inspector, you and Watson station yourselves at the left of the door." As the Inspector and I arose to comply with Holmes' instructions, Sir Reginald and Holmes left the room.

Several minutes later Sir Reginald entered the library with Lord Pomeroy. Hopkins and I were astonished that this was the man Holmes had directed Sir Reginald to bring forth.

Supple and lean, his bearing stodgily expressionless, a practiced eye roving constantly around the room, he looked every inch the kind of aristocrat he had been all his life. When he caught sight of Hopkins and me he turned to Sir Reginald.

"What is the meaning of this?"

Holmes came in just behind them and closed the door but left it unlocked.

"It means we wish to have a few words with you in regard to forged paintings," answered Holmes.

A moment of uneasy silence passed while Lord Pomeroy tried to absorb this intolerably dangerous implication.

"I suggest we sit down by the table," said Holmes. Instinctively we crowded closer in a semicircle around Pomeroy. He was watching Holmes with a faintly puzzled air. Curiosity seemed to take the upper hand and he complied by sitting down. Doubtless, he found the situation odd.

"I should be careful making statements I could not prove, Mr. Holmes."

"Lord Pomeroy, we know that you run a network of forgers, Frank Sutcliffe being one of many. We also know of your trips to Paris." Pomeroy listened in silence, fingering his watch fob, which appeared to be engraved with his family's heraldic symbol.

"That proves nothing."

"Does it? Peter Daubeny would not agree."

Pomeroy's face underwent a change, that of alarm and chagrin. "You seem to be asking for a libel suit, Mr. Holmes. I can assure you, if you persist in these baseless accusations, I will be forced to…"

"Come, come, Lord Pomeroy, it won't do, it simply won't do. Daubeny has been arrested and has confessed."

Pomeroy underwent another change of composure. He arose from his chair. "Since we are talking at cross purposes, I suggest that you contact my solicitors." It appeared he was about to leave.

Holmes looked hard at the aristocrat across the table. "We are not talking at cross purposes, Lord Pomeroy, we are talking about murder. You are the one who murdered Cecil Gaffney. The Upas tree poison is interesting in its lethal effect, don't you agree?"

Pomeroy turned slowly and faced Holmes, a hard glint coming into his eyes.

Holmes continued. "I suggest you go along quietly with Chief Inspector Hopkins."

Hopkins stepped forward and was about to warn Lord Pomeroy of his rights, when suddenly he cried out, "You meddling fool! I will not go anywhere with anyone!" In an instant, he bolted for the door, brandishing a small revolver. "If anyone tries to follow me, I shall use this!" The door opened and closed, and he was gone.

"Quick!" cried Holmes. "We must not lose him."

None of the foregoing had prepared me for the shock of Lord Pomeroy's action. Holmes was up and out the door. Hopkins followed with me closely behind. Sir Reginald was too unnerved by all he heard and saw to follow.

The front door of the entrance hall was wide open. Two men were getting back on their feet: Sir Reginald's footman and Hopkins' detective.

"Quick, which way did he go?" cried Holmes.

The detective pointed down the street into the dense milky fog.

"Watson, follow me. Hopkins, alert your men."

We ran down the street. There was no sign of Pomeroy.

"Could he have taken a cab?" I said breathlessly.

"This is a residential area. He is heading toward Knightsbridge Road."

We came to the corner of Knightsbridge and Wilton Place.

"There he is Watson! He is getting in that cab—no, it's occupied. He sees us! He's running—run, Watson, run!" Holmes quickly outdistanced me. I could barely see him in the fog. Hopkins came up with three men, all breathing hard.

"Where is Mr. Holmes?" cried the Inspector. I pointed up Knightsbridge Road as we all ran up the street. We approached the Hyde Park underground station. There was no sign of Holmes or Pomeroy. Hopkins directed two of his men to continue up the street. We dashed into the underground entrance and began running down the stairs. About a hundred feet down, Holmes was just turning a corner.

"There is Holmes!" I shouted.

At fever pitch we went down. Crowds of pedestrians were concluding their day's work and the platform was filled to capacity when we reached it. We made our way to Holmes, who was about to enter the center of the crowded platform. Pomeroy entered the crowd at this point.

"Fan out and keep a sharp outlook," cried Holmes.

We were moving through the crowds when suddenly there was a cry from the front of the platform. There was someone on the tracks. We pushed our way to the front of the platform. I could see Pomeroy nimbly leaping over the rails.

Holmes shouted, "Come back! The rails are electrified. Come back—watch out! He's going to shoot!"

Two shots rang out and reverberated throughout the tunnel. Pandemonium broke out on the crowded platform. Pedestrians were running and shouting in all directions. In the midst of this chaos, Pomeroy turned momentarily with diabolic triumph on his face. I struggled in the jostling crowd to aim my revolver, but in the next instant the aristocrat lost his footing and fell forward. I was about to go down when an ominous sound reached my ears above the cries of the crowd: The faint roar of an approaching train. I shouted at Holmes to come back. It was maddening that he could not hear me over the cacophony all around me. Holmes stopped and held Hopkins back; he had heard the approaching train. They quickly regained the platform.

"Holmes, what can we do?"

"We are too late to do anything."

The train roared into the station. By now, constables had arrived and were directing people into the train and leading others out.

"My God, he must not have known the rails have just been electrified," said I.

"I think not, Watson. Desperate situations always call for desperate measures."

Hopkins gathered several constables for assistance and when the train departed, we all went down onto the tracks.

"We have only ten minutes before the next train approaches," said Holmes. "Have your men quickly remove the remains after I have inspected the area."

We trod our way carefully over the rails to the spot where Pomeroy had fallen.

The body was mutilated beyond all recognition. Along the side of the track lay Pomeroy's watch fob with its heraldic symbol crushed. It was as if fate had ordained such an inglorious end.

Holmes stood silent, looking down at the body. Finally he spoke, "A higher power has judged this man, greed and murder has brought him to this end, and in a way, justice has been served."

We left the underground, which to my mind took on aspects of a sepulchre. Hopkins stayed on to finish supervision of removal of the body.

It was late that foggy afternoon when we returned to Baker St. When we arrived, the full shock of the events that had just transpired seemed to have caught up with me. I sat down heavily in my armchair. I turned to look out our window. The fog of the afternoon had thickened into a driving rain.

"Watson, you look positively done in. I would suggest a glass of brandy." Holmes went over to the cupboard and poured two glasses. I concurred and accepted the glass he handed me.

"I am sure you will agree we have had enough excitement and exercise for one day," remarked Holmes.

I was about to answer when there was a knock on our door. Billy announced Inspector Hopkins.

"Oh, Inspector, just in time for a glass of brandy," said Holmes as he helped him out of his wet coat. "Come, sit down by the fire and warm yourself."

"That would be most welcome after all this excitement, Mr. Holmes. After you left the underground, we discovered that one bystander was wounded by Lord Pomeroy's discharge of his revolver."

"Was it serious?" I asked.

"No, thank Heavens, it was only a superficial wound, more than likely a ricochet off the wall. You know, Mr. Holmes, the whole affair was a close thing. We were fortunate in finding you in the underground under the circumstances of that heavy fog."

"Yes, the fog almost gave Pomeroy a providential chance to escape us." Holmes passed cigars around before sitting down. "This case has been of considerable interest."

"Yes, but I must admit I am still in the dark with regard to how you knew Lord Pomeroy was the guilty party."

Holmes lit his cigar and sat back in his chair and considered for a moment. "Perhaps, Inspector, when you have taken the time to consider the smallest detail and then apply it to your special knowledge, you really would have no trouble. The cumulative effect is certainly considerable if one does this."

"But what was this small detail, Mr. Holmes?"

"Well, as I have remarked to Dr. Watson, early in this case I felt all the strands of this web led to one man, one man in charge of the entire operation of forged paintings, who in all probability worked alone or perhaps with one confederate. I felt his presence from the very beginning."

This hypothesis seemed to me altogether tenable. Holmes abhorred the proclivity to explain his methods during a case, but now he expressed a relish in relating its details.

"In the course of this investigation you both, no doubt, remember the Art Society as a large smoke-filled room. Of all the members smoking, only a handful were cigar smokers. The only Embassy cigar was smoked by Lord Pomeroy, the same kind of cigar found in Gaffney's ashtray. That fact, when equated to the liaison between Pomeroy and Daubeny, justified further investigation. When the first ray of light indicated Pomeroy's complicity, I myself became guilty of excessive reluctance in reaching such a seemingly fantastic deduction. That was erroneous. There was no alternative but to continue, which confirmed one fatal fact after another. By Thursday this week, my case was complete. However, proving Pomeroy's complicity was another matter."

"It is fantastic," said I, "considering Pomeroy's outburst and arrogance toward us at the Art Society."

"Bluff, all bluff, dear boy. Pomeroy sensed the danger of our presence immediately. Of course, Daubeny informed him who we were. I might add, he terminated our inquiries most effectively."

"I must admit, it certainly was a small detail, and I completely overlooked the fact," said Hopkins with undisguised admiration. "But you also spoke of two calculated gambles?"

"Simply put, the first was whether we could intimidate Frank Sutcliffe sufficiently to expedite his return to England and divulge his associates. The second was to goad Pomeroy into a situation where escape was his only alternative. At the mention of the special poison he administered, he realized the game was up and he bolted."

"According to your monograph on toxic plants," said I, "you stated the rarity of the upas poison. How did Pomeroy obtain such a poison in England?"

"My inquiries led me to the Pomeroy family physician—a Dr. Westlake, who has a reputation beyond reproach. Dr. Westlake was a personal friend of Pomeroy's, and it was interesting to note that the good doctor had recently returned from an extended trip to the East Indies. I think we can safely postulate Pomeroy stole the poison.

"Upon reflection, I must say, Lord Pomeroy certainly had flair. He was known to gamble away one thousand pounds in a single night. He lived in a five-story mansion on lower Belgrave Street, which, as you know, is the heart of London's fashionable Mayfair district. His clothes were tailored by the distinguished firm of Barton and Hogwell."

"Sir Reginald's home is at Wilton Place," interjected Hopkins. "Why didn't Pomeroy make his escape the short distance back to his home on Belgrave Street?"

"Because he determined to go to the family estate in Kent, more than likely to pick up his fortune and leave the country. I learned of the family estate through Barton and Hogwell, as all his country squire clothing was sent there. On Thursday I visited the estate, which was considerable. When I found that only three years ago the estate was on the brink of bankruptcy and was now in the process of restoration, when I found that popular rumour had it that Lord Pomeroy had acquired great wealth from a deceased uncle who made his fortune in South African gold, and when I found through his bankers that the South African gold did not exist, the conclusion was inescapable.

"On the whole we can safely infer that Pomeroy, through his agent, Daubeny, learned that Gaffney was infuriated by the forged painting and was going to take the matter to the police. This, of course, is what Frank Sutcliffe told Daubeny. When Gaffney learned from Geoffrey Banner that the painting was the work of Frank Sutcliffe, he called me to locate the painting. In the meantime, Pomeroy acted quickly by sending a threatening letter to Gaffney. Whatever the letter stated, Gaffney, as a result, elected to drop the matter. Safe for the moment, but not for the long run, Pomeroy then and there planned to eliminate Gaffney, and, I might add, his method was unique in the annuls of crime. These inferences are based on many facts I uncovered, which I hardly need go into now. As far as Daubeny is concerned, you must release him, Inspector."

Holmes' incisive statement startled the Inspector. "But Mr. Holmes, his complicity in forged paintings...?"

"I appreciate your point of view, but you are forgetting we can have no publicity in regard to this affair. Daubeny has served our purpose by being indisposed when we set our trap for Pomeroy. We had him arrested but he confessed nothing since we asked him nothing. I have always felt that perversion of the creative instinct, men such as Daubeny, failed artists, are capable of anything and are usually responsible for social upheavals. He must be watched in the future, for if I am not much mistaken, he shall fall to temptation again, which in all probability will be his complete downfall."

"The same fate has befallen Holroyd," replied Hopkins. "He is under the strict custody of Sir Charles."

"My dear Inspector, these are conditions beyond our control, but, except for Holroyd's all-consuming drive to embarrass this government, he, in all probability, could have gone undetected for years."

"It is still frustrating to have no case against anyone," retorted Hopkins.

"Nevertheless, you have gained a great deal of experience in this affair, even though you cannot share credit for its successful conclusion."

"Without a doubt, Mr. Holmes, my own career has been forwarded by your kind assistance over the years. I have never failed to learn something when I have been fortunate enough to be associated with you in an investigation. Would it not be a grand thing if you were to write a treatise on the detection of crime!"

Holmes, as I have stated on other occasions, was not adverse to flattery. Inspector Hopkins' sincerity was so genuine that I detected a note of approval for such an undertaking.

"On the face of it, your idea has merit. Several years ago I stated to Dr. Watson, which I believe was at the time of the case of the Abbey Grange, the possibility of doing just such a thing in my declining years. Perhaps an earlier start on such a project would not be out of order. There has been universal reluctance on the part of your colleagues to accept the fundamental premise of deductive reasoning. I might even go so far as to say my methods are the principal reason why I have incurred the odium of Scotland Yard from time to time. I have been told these methods are not practical, but I can assure you without hesitation that virtuosity in solving crime is either a natural gift or a combination of enthusiasm and assiduous practice. In the collection of observable facts, one cannot be overly cautious. But in the invention of theories, especially in a field so unique as ours, where analogies are drawn from past experience and knowledge, a canny and sober circumspection would be the greatest mistake. As I have said before, the really fundamental thing is sound observation."

"To think," said I, "all this has transpired because a man became curious about a painting and was murdered for it."

"Yes, Watson, it was a commonplace murder until it took on serious undertones of complexity. You have summarized it well as far as you have gone. However, the other factor one has to take into account is man's inherent weakness to life's temptations."

Later that night when I retired, I recalled many of the cases Holmes and I shared over the years. It appeared that the affairs of men were some kind of gigantic hoax. This inexorable drive—this ceaseless rhythm of getting and spending—this unquenchable thirst for power—all of it invariably seemed to destroy those who partook in its quest. One way or the other, I felt the hopelessness of it all.

Epilogue

▼

Several weeks later, a wet sticky snow was falling, which quickly melted when it touched our windowsill. I had just finished breakfast and was working on the second draft of this narrative. Among the plethora of titles that crossed my mind, I was struck by the simple title "The Curious Connoisseur." Tracing the course of events afterwards, primarily at the beginning of this narrative, I commented somewhat critically on Holmes' character. Now, however, upon reflection, I felt I gained yet another insight, which, as I turned it over in my mind, certainly personified my friend. It was clear that Holmes saw life and work as complementary, somehow elevating each other, the quality of his work connecting to the quality of his life. The nature of this connection in a man like Holmes resists explanation. For him, a separation between life and work seemed artificial, for they mix and overlap. Indeed, Holmes felt in a sense his hours and days spent on a case were privileged. He was then in complete control of his material, in which there was a beginning, a middle and an end; he was freed from the contingencies and boredom of everyday life. Everything, then, was relevant.

Holmes had been out all morning. When he arrive back at our rooms at noon, there was a look of quiet desperation about him. The London criminal had indeed become a dull fellow. Very few cases of interest came to my friend's attention. Small petty thefts and lost persons comprised the majority of his work that winter. As a consequence, Holmes, in complete desperation to fulfill his craving for work, had plunged into the production of a two-volume compendium entitled *"The Whole Art of Detecting Crime."* Foremost with this massive tome was the use of deductive and inductive reasoning based on observed facts. As it were, this opus took him well into his retirement years.

Later that evening, after dinner, I sat with the London Times spread out before me. My friend began prosaically enough by asking, "Anything new?"

"I see nothing of interest in your line," I answered. "But there is a small notice that the police are still investigating the death of the unidentified man killed in the underground last November." In reality, the police in charge of this affair, by the winter of 1902, had worked with infinite patience and care to solve what appeared to be an impenetrable mystery. The true nature of Lord Pomeroy's death was never made public. a normal amount of reticence was only to be expected in a crime such as Pomeroy committed, which entailed such international intricacy and portent.

"The news," I continued, "seems to be nothing more than one topic of scandal after another—divorce, government, high society." I closed the paper in disgust "It's as if the devil himself were let loose upon the earth. What has our society come to?"

Homes put his manuscript down. "Watson, you positively emanate light today. I rather believe you are correct. It's as if the powers of darkness have encompassed all of society. However, as you well know, I am certainly not a Biblical scholar, but if memory serves me correctly, your answers lie in the book of Job, chapter one, verse seven. I am sure you realize we are in a dawning new century with a promise of being vastly different and possibly worse than what you and I have come to maturity in. As for me, as I grow older, I take pleasure in the simpler things of this world, such as this." Holmes had picked up his oldest briar pipe and was contemplating it. "What the botanists call Erica Arborea."

"Is that the Latin name for your old pipe?" I asked.

"No, it is the Latin name for briar. One should consider this tough little shrub, which is a member of the heather family."

"Consider it in what way?"

"Well, think of the strong mountain winds that tear at this hardy little plant. The soil resists its efforts to grow. But the briar drives its roots into the tiniest crevices and forces them wider little by little. Fighting tenaciously, first for a foothold, then for growth, the little shrub develops a tightness of grain, a hard solidity where it is in contact with the earth that makes it unique among the plants of the world. A parallel could be drawn by many persons we have met over the years. I gather that you agree?"

"It would hardly be an exaggeration," said I, "to suggest that the majority of people seem to be distracted by simply trying to survive such as the Erica Arborea."

Several days later an extraordinary occurrence took place. Holmes was working on his manuscript one afternoon, when Billy brought in a large embossed envelope. It was from Windsor Castle, addressed to my friend. He read the contents with relish, and when finished, looked up at me with a mischievous smile.

"It may distress you to learn I have refused His Majesty's offer of Knighthood last week."

"But Holmes! How could you? Such an honor to be bestowed—how could you ignore it?"

"I have no prejudices against letters after one's name or before it. I have never been a public figure and I do not wish to become one. No, no Watson, your protests will not do. I simply cannot see myself as Sir Sherlock, who would be called upon to open things, lay foundation stones, make after dinner speeches... You must understand, Watson, I treasure one thing above all, and that is my privacy, my anonymity. However, this is another matter." He handed me the embossed letter with the Royal Coat of Arms at the top.

It was a summons from King Edward, who wished to bestow in person the Royal Victorian Order upon my friend.

"Holmes, this is wonderful! I give you my heartfelt congratulations."

My enthusiasm must have been infectious, for Holmes smiled and simply said, "Thank you, Watson. It is an honour I can readily accept, since it does not infringe upon my privacy. As I understand it, the King awards Five grades of the R.V.O., the highest being 'Knight Grand Cross,' which he feels fit to bestow upon me."

We were both in a state of some elation. "This calls for a toast," I cried. I poured two glasses of brandy from the sideboard. As I handed Holmes his glass, I said, "This most certainly is the crowning achievement of your career, and I congratulate you again."

In this instance Holmes did not reply in a deprecating manner upon receiving a compliment. Rather, he responded in a way that touched my heart.

"Thank you, Watson, but none of this would have been possible," he indicated His Majesty's letter, "had it not been for all your help over these many years. Therefore, I propose a dinner celebration at the Cheshire Cheese." It was one of those rare moments when Holmes expressed his gratitude and regard for me.

"That sounds excellent," said I, "but why the Cheshire Cheese?"

"Elementary, my dear Watson, it so happens that was Dr. Samuel Johnson's favourite restaurant, and what more fitting place is there for me to honour my Boswell?"

BOOK THREE

THE ILLUSION OF GLORY

AUTHOR'S NOTE

▼

"Stand with me here, upon the terrace, for it may be the last quiet talk that we shall ever have."

From *His Last Bow*

I could never quite accept the fact that the "last bow" was the last adventure of Sherlock Holmes. Quite the contrary, this was more than likely the tip of the iceberg.

Under the circumstances of *The Von Bork Affair*, it would be hard to believe Whitehall could or would let Holmes simply return to the South Downs to tend his bees. Surely he was asked to use all his powers to infiltrate German Intelligence, and Holmes being Holmes, simply could not reject this immense challenge or ignore his country's war time needs. No wonder he could fatalistically say to Watson, "It may be the last quiet talk that we shall ever have." The dangerous mission facing him could very well mean his demise in front of a firing squad as a British spy.

CHAPTER ONE

▼

THE SOUTH DOWNS

Toward the end of December, 1902, I left Baker Street for what proved to be the last time as a resident. The occasion was my second marriage and consequent move to an apartment on Queen Anne Street. My new domestic duties and renewed medical practice left very little time to see my friend Sherlock Holmes.

It was therefore sad and, I must confess, quite disconcerting, when I read the published account of "The Case of the Blanched Soldier," written by Holmes early in 1903, especially when he spoke thus of me: "The good Watson had, at that time, deserted me for a wife, the only selfish action which I can recall in our association. I was alone." Those words echoed and reechoed in my mind and I therefore resolved to make every effort to see Holmes when I was free from my busy practice.

During 1903 my notes show I was able to participate in "The Adventures of the Three Gables," "The Mazarin Stone" and "The Creeping Man." In regard to the latter adventure, it became apparent Holmes no longer could carry on. His incessant smoking of shag tobacco played a very large part in his obvious poor health which I observed that September. Of course he remonstrated that the state of his health was not a matter in which he himself took the faintest interest. However, I prevailed upon him to visit a Harley Street specialist and as I suspected, it was found he was in the advanced stages of "tobacco amblyopia." This, coupled with irregular hours and poor eating habits forced him into an early retirement.

By the spring of 1904, somewhat to the consternation of my wife, I spent a fortnight in assisting and establishing Holmes in a small farm cottage five miles outside Eastbourne on the Sussex Downs.

His condition called for a complete change of scenery with regular hours, small amounts of work with more than normal rest, and of course, no smoking. As I have said in the past, Holmes had a feline attitude with regard to his personal appearance and attire. On the other hand, his possessions were always in a state of disorganization. He had a horror of destroying any of his articles that he acquired over the years, and loathed parting with any document that pertained to a criminal activity.

As a consequence, papers were lying about in the most inconvenient places and the general disorder was a nightmare to anyone who places emphasis on good management. I suggested the attic for his vast hoard of books that he had accumulated and was surprised when he agreed to my proposal. However nothing I could say or do would prevent him from affixing his bills with a penknife on the mantle over the fireplace. I found this particularly annoying since he had a small desk that sat in the corner, fundamentally unused.

The violin, the smoking pipes, Persian slipper sans tobacco, the chemical corner, all were in place after a few days, and in a way it was our Baker St. sitting room in a modified version.

Far from being an invalid, Holmes readily adapted to his new environment and a relaxed pace of life. His time was taken up in completing his massive tome "The Whole Art of Detecting Crime," plus a new pursuit, the study of bees.

Over the next few years, Holmes developed a hermit-like existence on the South Downs. I managed to come down and visit once or twice a year. He, in turn, came up on occasion to London, where we would meet at the Northumberland Hotel. I noticed during these visits that he spent considerable time at Whitehall, which I surmised was with his brother, Mycroft.

In the latter part of August, 1909, I received a letter from Holmes stating briefly the events of "The Lion's Mane," which he proposed to author himself. To the best of my knowledge, this was the last case he participated in until the Great War.

The fall of 1911 found me a widower once again. London no longer held any interest for me and I readily accepted my young niece Catherine's kind invitation to reside with her in Edinburgh. When Holmes learned of my bereavement, he suggested an extended stay on the South Downs. My visit took place in the spring of 1912.

Over a year had gone by since I last saw Holmes. When he greeted me upon my arrival at Eastbourne Station, I was astounded by his renewed vigor. His health was improved by such a large degree, he appeared to have taken a new lease on life. That he was able to do so with such apparent ease was due largely to a single extraordinary fact.

"Holmes, you look a picture of health. How did you manage such a transformation?"

"Bees, my dear fellow. I owe it to my bees and all this fresh Sussex air."

"I can understand fresh air," I replied, "but how on earth can bees affect one's health so salubriously?"

"Ah, there lies the beauty of it. It is their honey and one's consumption of it. The benefits from it are astounding. I am writing a small monograph on the subject. Meanwhile, from a purely practical point of view it is clear that what we eat is what we are; that is to say, from a standpoint of our general health. Have you ever heard of Mohandas K. Ghandi?"

"No, I don't recall the name. Who is he?"

"Ghandi is an Indian who studied English law several years ago here in England. At the time, he promoted the vegetarian way of life, which did not take hold of the public's imagination until several years later. Ghandi's methods of food consumption clearly have great merit over English eating habits. Through his teaching of moderation, I am even able to smoke once or twice a day."

I was greatly impressed with the change that had occurred in Holmes' health. During that April and May, when the weather permitted, we took long walks high on the precipitous chalk cliffs overlooking the channel. At other times when wind and rain kept us indoors, I spent many hours in the attic browsing through Holmes' extensive book collection.

From time to time Holmes would suggest I put certain adventures before the public. Accordingly I reviewed cases from my notes for future publication. Holmes took a keen renewed interest in certain cases as he recalled the past.

"No, I'm afraid not," he replied to a suggestion of my own. "'The Giant Rat of Sumatra' is a story that the world is still not prepared for. However, I see no reason for holding back 'The Adventures of the Abernetty Family.' It has been many years since that affair and the family is dispersed in various parts of the world now."

And so the time passed, Holmes working at intervals on his book and tending his bees. I, in turn, alternately worked on my own writing and absorbed the fresh beauty of spring.

By the first of June, I found my self once again back in Edinburgh. One afternoon several months later, my niece, while serving tea, commented, "What a long time it has been since you heard from your friend Mr. Sherlock Holmes." Upon reflection, she was quite right. Between completing adventures that Holmes had sanctioned and traveling down to London to handle all the complications involved with publication, I quite lost sight of time.

"I'd best send him a letter in the morning," I answered.

Several days later I received a cryptic communication from Holmes' old housekeeper, Martha, stating that Holmes was in the United States and would be gone for an indefinite period of time. I was surprised that I was not informed of any impending trip, but then Holmes was always unorthodox with his comings and goings. Nonetheless, I felt a little piqued.

At the close of a sultry summer day in August, 1914, when the sunlight was fading from the sky, I found a telegram addressed to me on the hall table. As I opened it, I felt a sense of thrill. It was from Holmes and read thus:

> *Your assistance vital in a matter of national*
> *security. Take last train to Harwich August*
> *2nd. Do not fail.*
>
> *Holmes*

The manner in which Holmes apprehended the foremost German agent just prior to the World War and all that transpired that fateful August night is recorded in what I call "The Adventure of His Last Bow." His prophetic statement on Von Bork's terrace will be forever engraved in my memory: "Stand with me here upon the terrace, for it may be the last quiet talk that we shall ever have. There's an east wind coming, Watson."

"I think not, Holmes. It is very warm."

"Good old Watson! You are the one fixed point in a changing age. There's an east wind coming all the same, such a wind as never blew on England yet. It will be cold and bitter, Watson, and a good many of us may wither before its blast. But it's God's own wind nonetheless, and a cleaner, better, stronger land will lie in the sunshine when the storm has cleared."

It was clear that Holmes was working for British Intelligence in the capacity of a secret agent. Apparently he felt the gravity of his future work would separate us. Indeed, there was the possibility of never meeting again.

The east wind blew down upon England at twelve o'clock on August 4th, 1914. Britain was at war, though the first armed German had not invaded Belgium. Britain's entry in no way dismayed the German General staff. They had already allowed for it and discounted it, confident that they could smash through Belgium to a decisive victory in France within four months before Britain could get major forces on the continent.

CHAPTER TWO

▼

THE CLARION CALL

I returned to London that August and rejoined my old service. However by virtue of age and experience I was enlisted into medical administration. My niece closed the Edinburgh apartment and joined me in London. Our residence was on Charles II Street off St. James Square, not far from Charing Cross Hospital.

The rest of 1914 was taken up with a myriad of duties, which left no time for reflection or inquiries into the whereabouts of Holmes. 1915 came and went. All that year I also heard nothing of my friend, which gave me some concern. The war raged on, our work increased.

By the spring of 1916 the Verdun offensive was underway. The philosophy of attrition became a household word with all its connotation of horror and carnage.

During the following spring of 1917, I had one of my infrequent leaves of absence for a fortnight. The first few days were spent in recuperating from the consequences of working longer than twelve hours a day. One afternoon after experiencing the invigorating effects of a Turkish bath at

Neville's on Northumberland Avenue, I strolled down the Strand to the Criterion Bar. I sat there and reminisced how many years had gone by since young Stanford suggested I take lodgings with Sherlock Holmes. Memories flooded through me. What momentous changes had taken place. Where was Holmes? Why had I not heard from him? All my past inquiries were to no avail. I looked around at the unfamiliar faces, pushed my unfinished drink aside and rose to leave.

During my walk I unconsciously gravitated toward Baker Street. Somehow I seemed to see reflected headlamps of hansom cabs intermingled in opalescent sunlight and fog. Down the corridors of time I heard the clatter of horses' hooves—the most evocative of all the sounds of London. I shook my head sadly; it was all another day, a vanished age. In retrospect, I always considered it a privilege to have known and assisted Holmes, but it was all in the past. I pondered as to where he could be.

I took a long last look down the street at 221B, the starting point of so many adventures. Perhaps it is not wise to return to old landmarks where nostalgia can grip one's emotions. The changes that take place over a period of time can only fill one with sadness. Baker Street was now a paved and widened thoroughfare, the old gas lamps replaced with modern electricity, motorcars moving to and fro. In terms of logic, nothing in life is more certain than change; still, we resist change. The Baker Street of yesteryear was gone, but the fog still swirled. I turned slowly and walked away.

Upon returning home that evening I was surprised to find a message addressed to me from the War Department. It briefly stated I was to meet a Major Saunders at nine o'clock the following morning at Hyde Park corner. This was a strange communication. What on earth was it about, I wondered. I resented any interruption while on leave; however, there was no alternative but to comply.

Duly at nine o'clock I arrived at the entrance of Hyde Park. Immediately a man approached me from the other side of the street.

"Dr. Watson!"

I looked keenly at the man addressing me. "Yes, I am he," I answered.

"I take it you do not remember me, Doctor?"

I looked even more carefully at this man with salt and pepper, greying hair and smiling, intelligent eyes. "I am sorry, but you have the advantage. I am afraid my memory is not what it used to be."

My companion looked bemused as we began to walk down the gravel path into the park. "I am sure you remember the Stonehenge mystery back in '84."

"Yes, of course," I acquiesced. Suddenly a flash of recollection came before my eyes. "You're not the same Constable Saunders of the Salisbury Constabulary?" I asked in amazement.

"The one and the same," replied he, smiling broadly. "I was but a lad at the time, but I have never forgotten the experience. Mr. Holmes was a tremendous influence upon me, and thanks to you and your stories, I have kept abreast over the years. Mr. Holmes' methods have been my guiding light throughout my career."

"I recall now," said I. "Holmes said he felt you would go far in your profession."

"Well, it has brought me to the rank of major in Military Intelligence."

"Well then, Major Saunders, what is all this about? Why has Military Intelligence sent you to me?"

"Basically it is in regard to your friend, Mr. Holmes."

"What! You have heard from Holmes? You know where he is?"

"Easy, Dr. Watson, I can say yes to both your questions. However, you will find Colonel Carrington more knowledgeable on the subject. He would like to meet you tomorrow at two o'clock. I am to accompany you. Can you meet me at a quarter past one at St. Pancras Station?"

"Yes, yes, but can you tell me no more?"

"I am afraid not." My companion was looking to and fro when suddenly he stopped walking. "I must leave you now. Until tomorrow then, good-bye." Major Saunders abruptly left my side and walked off at a brisk pace down a side path that led out of the park to Stanhope Gate and Park Lane. I stood there alone watching his figure disappear into the hedges and trees. At the far end another pedestrian was quickly walking in the same direction.

   Precisely at a quarter past one the following afternoon I stood at the St. Pancras Station platform. Major Saunders appeared as if out of nowhere.
   "Quickly, Dr. Watson, we must board this northbound train."
   We had no sooner sat down in our compartment when the train lurched forward and began to move out of the station.
   "Well, Major, that was a near thing."
   "Quite."
   "It seemed to me you encountered some kind of problem in the park yesterday."
   "Well, it is easy to see you have been influenced by Mr. Holmes over the years. You also are a keen observer."
   "You flatter me Major, but in all truthfulness, I could never come anywhere near to Holmes' astute observation. However, I did see the other individual taking the same path as you out of the park."
   "Yes, I thought I had lost him earlier yesterday morning, but today I made doubly sure."
   "What is all this about, Major?"
   "I am sorry, Doctor, but we must leave all that to Colonel Carrington's discretion, should he decide to broach the subject."
   A short time later we were sitting in the parlour of a large Edwardian house in the north London suburb of Enfield. The room was dimly lit and the walls were crowded with military pictures, most often of officers sitting upon horses. There was a pretty garden outside. The house itself, I was told, belonged to two kindly ladies who had offered it to the government for the duration. Major Saunders indicated it was now the headquarters of Military Intelligence.
   So there we were, the two of us, waiting some fifteen minutes for this Colonel Carrington. Suddenly the door opened and a very tall, distinguished man with a manuscript entered the room. Major Saunders

introduced us. We all sat down, the colonel at a very large desk. He began to address me.

"Mr. Holmes has requested your assistance for a very important mission. We have cleared the way at Staff Hospital for you to participate, if you so desire.

If I so desire, I reflected. My God, what a reprieve from the monotony of detail and duty, the never-ending problems. To be able to see and work with Holmes again. Indeed, to restore a sense of adventure after all these years.

I responded enthusiastically, "It would be a singular honor to serve my country in this capacity."

"Excellent," said the Colonel looking very keenly at me. "You must understand, Dr. Watson, the necessity for spies has been an age-old concept. During a war there will always be secrets that one side shall guard and which the other will use every means to unearth. Some men out of malice or greed will betray their country. There are also some rare men who from sheer boredom or a high sense of duty will risk death to secure information valuable to their country. Mr. Holmes fits the latter description. It was a sense of high duty that brought him out of retirement.

"You must also understand, Doctor, that in the event of an unforeseeable problem, you may be faced with it alone. We will make every attempt to help if it is at all possible. If you should fall into enemy hands, you are essentially on your own. Do I make myself clear?"

"I understand, and you can have every confidence in me."

CHAPTER THREE

▼

THE ROAD TO WAR

Back in London the following day, Major Saunders outlined a condensed course of training that included anonymous country houses, anonymous instructors, some travel and, looming ever larger, the prospect of seeing Holmes again.

Several months later my traveling orders came down from Colonel Carrington. My instructions were to proceed by a circumspect route to Switzerland. Evidently the German Secret Service was posted at all major seaports in western France. I bid my niece good-bye and left her with the impression of taking a holiday in Cornwall.

Debarkation was from Plymouth on a troop ship bound for Marseille. Apparently the North Sea routes were not considered safe enough from the escalated German submarine attacks. Landing at Marseille we immediately departed by troop train, northward to Belfort, which was only some twelve miles from the southernmost part of the Hindenburg line.

A light rain was falling when I stepped into the Belfort station. A young French lieutenant approached me and inquired in perfect King's English if I were Dr. Watson. Somewhat surprised that a total stranger found me so quickly, I realized how thoroughly organized my mission had been planned.

The lieutenant had a motorcar waiting to take me across the French-Swiss border to Basel. As I looked through the rain splashed car window just outside of Belfort, I witnessed my first scenes of war. All around me were bombarded, crumbling houses haunted by sad faces that appeared like wraiths in the broken windows. To think that conditions such as this extended as far north as Flanders was appalling. My young driver must have observed my dismayed expression. He turned slightly and addressed me.

"Humanity must be mad to do what it is doing—hell cannot be so terrible. What you see here is nothing compared to the horrors and carnage at the front. Up there one must smoke as much as possible to beat the stench of the wind."

To be honest, I had taken very little notice of this young officer, but as I did so now, I clearly saw a strangeness in his eyes. They were deep set and had a hollow, timeworn look far beyond his years.

"I have every reason to believe this conflict will be terminated in our favor in the very near future," said I in a feeble attempt to cheer him. He shook his head.

"I return to the front after this assignment—I feel my luck is running out."

There was a tone of fatalism in his voice to which I had no idea how to respond. I knew in my heart this immense bloodletting was upon a scale at once more frightful than anything witnessed before. This war had raged on for three years and in reality the end was nowhere in sight. We drove on through the rain in silence.

Arriving at Basel I wished the young lieutenant good luck and good-bye, and caught the midnight train to Zurich. This was the last leg of my journey as per Colonel Carrington's instructions. At Zurich I was to take rooms at the Glarnischof Hotel and await Holmes.

It was a beautiful, cool night and through the window I watched the silhouetted landscape bathed in a soft argent glow against a starlit sky. Far in the distance I could just make out the Bernese Alps—"The Final Problem;" Meiringen; The Reichenbach Falls, and the infamous Professor Moriarty whose bones are still submerged in that immense black cauldron. How long ago it all seemed.

At five-thirty in the morning the train halted at the Hauptbahnhof station. I took breakfast in the station restaurant, but I did not venture to draw attention to myself by extravagance. A half hour later I hailed a cab for the Glarnischof Hotel. A quarter of an hour after crossing the Bahnhof Bridge we pulled onto Seegarten Strasse. It appeared now in wartime Zurich was as deserted as it must have been before the world at large discovered that Switzerland was the playground of Europe.

The Glarnischof was a small German hotel of the second class, spotlessly clean and the sitting room had a nice view of the lake. It was furnished with brightly varnished wood. I half expected to find Holmes waiting for me in the lobby, but it was empty except for the desk clerk. I inquired at the desk but there were no messages for me.

That first day I feared leaving the hotel in case I would miss Holmes. By the second day I was having misgivings: Had something gone wrong? Where was Holmes? Pacing my room on the third day, I knew I must leave the hotel for some fresh air and exercise. My mind was in a turmoil. I was quite sure Colonel Carrington's plans had somehow misfired. What was I to do, stay on or go back to England?

I walked for the better part of an hour along Belerive Strasse adjacent to Lake Zurich. Feeling somewhat refreshed, I looked forward to the dinner hour. As I entered the hotel, a tall but bent old man with white hair and drooping mustache brushed against me. I turned to excuse myself, but in an instant he was gone.

After inquiring at the front desk, I found there was still no message. For some reason the dining room struck me as somber that evening. As per usual, I sought a far corner table as I did not want to be drawn into conversation. I soon found it was unnecessary, as the dozen or so guests were more intent on eating than conversing. In all probability, wartime conditions made people wary of speaking in public.

Halfway through an excellent dinner, a man and woman entered and crossed the dining room and sat down at a table near me. He was discoursing in animated German while she listened intently, interjecting a comment here and there. She was an extremely beautiful woman, possibly in her late thirties. I could not help but think how incongruous her presence was in this second-class hotel.

They seemed to bring a breath of fresh air into the heavy atmosphere of the dining room and everyone in it seemed suddenly more alert. The man appeared to be somewhere in his early fifties and of exuberant vitality. He exuded health and well being, and his round face was bathed in the light of his childlike smiles. Only his eyes gave any indication that he was not as innocent as his appearance and manner seemed to imply.

I was startled when he addressed me in English. "My wife and I felt you must be an Englishman," said he.

I stammered something to the effect that I was. He introduced himself and his wife as Mr. and Mrs. George Manning. His wife was German, but he was English like myself. He felt fortunate to find someone recently from England who could relate the latest news.

"And how did you guess I was English and just arrived here?"

"I never guess." His penetrating gaze did not waver from my eyes. A moment later he seemed to catch himself and beamed forth gestures of friendliness.

"I work in customs and your luggage and copies of your papers passed through our department," he justified himself smoothly.

"I see," I answered. This man was very astute to have searched me out like this. Was there anything more to it than merely wanting to talk with a countryman, I ruminated.

"Won't you join us for coffee and schnapps, Mr. Waterford?" For a moment I forgot I was traveling under that name. Not wanting to look unsociable or draw more attention to myself, I agreed, and left my table to join them.

"What part of England are you from?" inquired Mr. Manning.

"London for many years, but recently Edinburgh. And you?" I ventured.

"London, of course. Hammersmith to be exact," he shot back. "What brings you to Switzerland, Mr. Waterford?"

"Primarily for health reasons. I plan to visit the Bernese Alps."

Mr. Manning looked at me as if he were weighing the possibility of my health being impaired in any way. "You seem to be the picture of health."

With what assurance I could muster, I lied that I recently became affected with tuberculosis. Again he eyed me sharply.

"One would never guess," said he, smiling.

Our coffee and schnapps arrived and Mrs. Manning proposed a toast to the end of the hostilities. She spoke English with a heavy German accent. Her husband explained she was born and raised in Germany but would never return until the war was over.

"How is it you have not returned to England?" said I.

"My wife would find it difficult to live there, and furthermore, I have good employment here." Mrs. Manning turned and addressed her husband in German. He laughed.

"She said the real reason I stay is my passion for archaeology." Manning's face lit up as he warmed to the subject of his ardor. "Perhaps you are familiar with New Stone Age man, commonly called the Swiss Lake Dwellers of this area."

I confessed my lack of knowledge on the subject.

Manning became more animated. "Think of it, Mr. Waterford, we are dealing with the seventh millennium B.C." His face had a look of sheer awe. "We shall be taking a walking trip tomorrow to an area I have been assured has many relics. We would be delighted if you were to accompany us. My wife puts up a wonderful pack lunch."

This was a dilemma. I did not want to be away all day in case Holmes came or sent a message. On the other hand, these people were taking an extraordinary interest in me. If I refused to go it would look most ungracious to their friendly overtures.

I rose to leave and said, "I appreciate the invitation, but I shall have to see how I feel in the morning with regard to an all day outing."

Manning appeared again to weigh my remark. "Excellent. We shall await your decision when we meet at breakfast."

With that I bade the Mannings good evening and returned to my room. I had grave qualms. The last thing I wished was to be entangled socially with anyone while awaiting Holmes. These were exceptional people, but I wondered how authentic their purpose was in making my acquaintance. I sensed a great deal of shrewdness in both of them, but then again perhaps I was being over cautious.

I retired at an early hour but lay tossing for what seemed several hours. Suddenly I thought I perceived a shadow fall on the opposite wall. My senses were brought to an immediate alert. I continued to gaze at the wall, which was thinly glazed by moonlight through the open window. Nothing stirred, nothing moved. It must be my imagination, I told myself. I turned over and resolved to get some sleep.

Suddenly I heard a voice, "Watson, are you awake?"

"Holmes! Is that you?" I asked, startled. I moved to turn on the lamp next to the bed.

"Don't light that lamp until I close this window and draw the drape."

"Is it really you Holmes?" I repeated.

"Yes, my dear Watson, it is I."

"How on earth did you get in? I heard no one."

"That is to be expected when I enter and do not wish anyone to know that fact."

I had the light on now and standing next to the bed looking down at me was Holmes. "Time has been kind with you, Watson."

Was this Holmes? In appearance he looked like some retired Prussian aristocrat with his close cropped hair. His down-turned mustache gave him a menacing expression.

"My God," I commented. "In 1914 you looked like a replica of Uncle Sam with that horrible goatee." I arose from bed, put on a dressing gown and pushed a chair over to Holmes. "Now you look like a German nobleman. I can barely recognize you."

"I was aware of that fact when we met earlier this evening."

"Don't tell me that was you, that bent old man with long white hair, who brushed up against me?"

"Naturally it was me."

"But why, Holmes?"

Holmes ignored the question. "I see you have met Frederica Von Strada and George Granville this evening."

I looked hard at Holmes. "You don't mean Mr. and Mrs. Manning," I said incredulously.

"Precisely, Germany's top secret agents."

"Great Scott!" I cried. "Is this hotel a nest of spies?"

"Not exactly," smiled Holmes, "but your waitress, Fraulein Erna Benke, reported some of your conversation to me. I might add it was in this fashion that I have been able to observe your movements for the past three days."

"Holmes, I am overwhelmed by all this, but why, if you knew I was here, did you not contact me sooner?" I remonstrated somewhat testily.

"Simplicity itself, old fellow. I knew these people would approach you. When, however, I did not know. Until their suspicions are allayed we cannot move forward with our plans. Furthermore, I am awaiting vital information in connection with your mission."

"Which is?"

"All in good time," replied Holmes.

"Why then are you going about in disguises, such as earlier this evening?"

"Oh, you mean Herr Brandt, the book seller! You must understand, of course, I know these people. If my presence here were known it would cast great suspicion on you and, in all probability, terminate your assistance." Holmes lit a cigarette and continued, "On our very first case together, which you so dramatically entitled 'A Study in Scarlet,' I told you, 'What you do in this world is a matter of no consequence. The problem is convincing people what you have done.' Believe me, Watson, when I tell you that statement is more applicable today than when I first said it so many years ago. But aside from all that, tell me what transpired over coffee and schnapps this evening."

I briefly sketched to Holmes my meeting with these people whom I shall continue to refer to as Mr. and Mrs. Manning.

"What were your impressions of them?" inquired Holmes.

"They struck me as fascinating and stimulating people who appear extremely intelligent but also very shrewd, motivated by reasons I still fail to understand." I mentioned Manning's interest in archaeology and his proposed trip for tomorrow.

"I am glad you are here. I shall refuse to go with them."

"On the contrary, you must accompany them."

"I must?"

"You will arouse their utmost suspicion if you do not. At this very moment a dossier is being prepared, entitled 'Mr. Waterford.'"

"Good Lord, it's hard to believe."

"Not at all; German intelligence checks and re-checks everyone coming into Switzerland, especially the English. I went through the same process, but much more intensified.

"For all intents and purposes, you handled your encounter with Manning reasonably well, but you definitely should have been more outgoing in your attitude and given the appearance of someone with time on his hands who would welcome the acquaintance of new companions."

"Should I conduct myself in that manner tomorrow?"

"By all means, and since you have tuberculosis, I should do some coughing and complain of fatigue. Insist on stopping from time to time to rest. Tell them nothing more than your hospital work in England, your despair over your health and your planned trip to the Bernese Alps for rest and recuperation on the following day."

"If they ask where in the Bernese Alps, what shall I tell them?"

"Tell them Lauterbrunnen. In the meantime, I shall cross the Bodensee by steam launch to Fredrichshafen, Germany. By the time you return tomorrow, I should have my information and will meet you in these rooms at nine in the evening."

I was fully awake after all this, but I could see on closer inspection that Holmes appeared tired. I was extremely curious as to what had transpired in the last two years, but refrained from making inquiries at this time.

Holmes, after a short reflection, lit another cigarette and continued, "Granville has had a nasty record; extortion, petty larceny, held many times on suspicion of murder, but somehow has always managed to slip out of the clutch of the law. That is, until the Lord Norton affair. I am sure you remember the details."

"Lord Norton," I repeated. "Was that not a blackmail murder case?"

"Quite right. It was in the fall of 1912. I followed the case with great interest while on the South Downs. At any rate, Granville found England too hot for comfort and fled the country undetected. So much for the police work at the time. He made his way to Germany and has been working for the German government ever since. At the outbreak of hostilities he offered his services to the war department and has risen high in the profession of spying. He is intelligent, ruthless and extremely dangerous. Under no circumstances underestimate him. His companion, Frederica Von Strada, is in every respect a reincarnation of Irene Adler with regard to intelligence. The combination of great beauty and intellect are virtues in a woman I have always found invariably dangerous. In her case it is doubly so because she has nerves of steel and will stop at nothing to see Germany gain predominance throughout Europe."

Holmes took out his pocket watch. "The hour grows late. I must leave you now."

"Can you tell me nothing with regard to my mission?"

"I am afraid not, old fellow. If for any reason I do not receive the information I am awaiting, there may not even be a need for your assistance. One last word: Under no circumstances underestimate these people." With that he rose, turned off the light and was out the door as quietly as he had entered

CHAPTER FOUR

▼

THE MANNINGS

I awoke to a glorious spring morning with a deep blue sky. I arose and went to the window. As I looked out new buds of greenery were radiating a pastoral symphony. It was sheer joy to breathe the fresh air.

An hour later when I entered the hotel dining room I caught sight of the Mannings waiting for me.

"Oh, there you are," cried Manning, gesturing to join them. "What a glorious day. I do hope you have decided to accompany us. It would be such a pity to stay indoors today."

I concurred that indeed, it was a beautiful day and yes, I would join them.

"Splendid! We have all the provisions necessary—knapsacks, walking sticks and so on."

Mrs. Manning was attired in alpine dress, consisting of knickers and heavy walking boots. Even in this outrageous apparel she appeared fresh and beautiful. Manning himself wore lederhosen and also had heavy walking boots.

"I am afraid I do not have the appropriate clothes."

Mrs. Manning was gracious and charming. "We felt sure you did not, so we brought a pair of boots for you."

"That was very kind, but you do not know my size."

"Oh that is no problem. If necessary, we shall stop at the boot shop."

After breakfast I put on the boots she gave me. To my amazement, they fit perfectly. I could not fathom how they knew my size.

We left the hotel at eight and walked in a southerly direction along the eastern shore of the lake. Later as we approached the Riesbach area, the terrain began to rise and fall with rocky outcrops extending into the crystal clear water. The few dwellings we had encountered were rapidly receding into the northern horizon. Manning was an absolute fanatic, clambering over rocks with such agility I felt weary just watching him. I complained of fatigue throughout the morning with intervals of coughing.

"Mr. Waterford, you must look at this. It is a colossal find."

I laboriously made my way over the rocks and found him holding some decrepit broken piece of pot. He was ecstatic in his delight.

"Just think, Mr. Waterford, what I am holding may be some seven thousand years old." He carefully put the crusty pieces into his knapsack.

Mrs. Manning was strangely silent throughout the morning. I had the feeling she was watching me carefully. We continued walking. Manning was exuberant, continually expounding on the life and times of New Stone Age man.

"You must understand, Mr. Waterford, early in the epoch the inhabitants of this region sought protection by making their homes over the waters of the lake."

"How did they do that?" I asked, trying to show some interest.

"They drove posts into the mud as far as they could with the tools they had. Then they piled stones around the bottoms to make them more secure. When a sufficient number had been erected in this fashion, they placed a platform on the top. A square or rectangular house was then built upon the platform."

"Indeed, they sound like a most ingenious people," I replied, "but now I must insist on stopping to rest."

We were on high ground overlooking the lake. Mrs. Manning suggested a small repast of cheese, sausage and bread with a bottle of wine, which she began to remove from her knapsack. We sat down on rocks, which gave a good view of the lake.

"There, Mr. Waterford, there. You can see for yourself." Manning was pointing down at the water's edge. "Do you see those posts under the water?

I acknowledged I saw the posts.

"We certainly must explore this area after lunch," said he excitedly. His manner was overdone. I had the distinct impression he had been over this ground before.

Mrs. Manning handed me a cup of wine, then addressed me slowly and deliberately. "Perhaps Mr. Waterford is not interested in New Stone Age man."

I confessed my newness to the subject, but asked that they excuse my lack of enthusiasm due to my fatigue.

"But of course," she replied. "But tell me, Mr. Waterford, do you not have some relatives in the War? I have a young brother at the front."

Here it was at last, the subject of the war. I replied that I did not and informed them I was a widower. Since the impairment of my health, I was forced to retire from my administrative hospital work, which I described at length. The Mannings seemed to consider my statements for some moments.

She continued, "My husband receives so little news from England, really nothing more than what is stated in the newspapers. Do you feel this war will come to an end soon?"

A leading question, that was, and I cast about in my mind for an answer. "I have no way of knowing that, but the casualties are mounting."

The Mannings became immediately alert. Manning put his cup down and took up the questioning.

"Have the English sustained heavy losses?"

"Before I retired, my work had increased immensely. The whole war strikes me as inhuman savagery."

"Here in Switzerland there have been rumors the Americans may join in the conflict on the side of the 'entente.' Have you heard anything about it back in England?"

I reflected a moment. "Yes, there have been rumours, but I seriously doubt it."

"Why do you say so?" They were both vigilantly attentive to the conversation.

"Oh, I don't know," I said offhandedly. "The Atlantic Ocean would be a formidable supply route, for one thing. For another they are not prepared for war."

"You are quite right," answered Manning, somewhat relieved. "How long will you be staying in Zurich?"

"I am leaving for the Bernese Alps tomorrow."

"Where will you be staying?"

"Lauterbrunnen." Will there never be an end to these questions? "Perhaps we should finish lunch in order to get on with our walk," I ventured in the hope they would refrain from further questions.

"By all means. You will find Lauterbrunnen very beautiful, Mr. Waterford," said Mrs. Manning.

Several minutes later we moved down to where Manning had observed the sunken posts. Manning picked up a small stone on the shore.

"Mr. Waterford, I command your attention to this small piece of flint. Possibly of the earliest epoch." His voice took on tones of pure rapture. There was no doubt the man was quite expert on the subject of New Stone Age man. And so it went until four o'clock when we arrived at the small lakeside village of Kusnach.

I can seriously say I was thoroughly done in and made no secret of my discomfort and weariness to the Mannings.

"Really, I must say this has been an exhaustive trip for me. I had no idea you would come so far. I think you have shown a dismal lack of consideration for my well-being. After dinner I shall hire a carriage and return to Zurich. You may accompany me if you so desire." In reality if I walked back I should be extremely late for my appointment with Holmes. The Mannings were beside themselves with remorse and apologies for my fatigue and inconvenience. They insisted on paying for dinner and the carriage.

On our way back to Zurich the subject of the war was brought up again. Manning looked keenly at me. "Mr. Waterford, we understand shipping between England and the continent is severely restricted due to German submarine attacks. How did you manage your trip here?"

Blast the man! I felt sure he was trying to trip me up. As nonchalantly as I could, I replied, "On the whole I had no trouble. I booked passage on a Greek ship bound for Athens. I felt an ocean journey would be more beneficial to my health rather than an overland journey in France. Our first port of call was Marseille, which met my needs admirably since it was the shortest route to Switzerland."

Manning mulled this over and apparently was satisfied. But suddenly he shot back, "I simply do not recall any passenger ships leaving England over the past year."

"It was a cargo ship, shipping coffee and produce to Athens," I answered somewhat testily. "If you don't mind, I would like to rest for the remainder of the trip. Today's outing has completely exhausted me." I coughed a few times, then settled back in the carriage and closed my eyes.

The road we traversed was far from the lakeside and consequently not a direct route such as we had taken earlier on the walk. We arrived in Zurich a little before nine o'clock.

I bid the Mannings good night and good-bye. Manning studied me closely. "Perhaps we shall meet again. At least my wife and I hope so, and I guarantee not to tire you out next time." I did not answer as I wearily climbed the stairs to my rooms.

As I entered, Holmes was sitting in the chair near the window with the shades drawn. He held his finger to his lips indicating silence until I closed the door. Next to him on the side table was a decanter of wine. He poured a glass and handed it to me.

"Since Von Bork acquainted me with Hungarian Tokay, I have developed a definite taste for it. You appear exhausted."

"I am. That man climbed over rocks like a Swiss mountain goat."

Holmes smiled, "Sit down, Watson, and tell me about it."

I sat down with a sigh, tasted my wine, then related my misadventure in detail.

Holmes' countenance took on a judicial air. "All in all, I believe you have satisfied their curiosity, but on the other hand, one can never be too sure with people like these. However, your trip to Lauterbrunnen will disclose how well they accepted your story. If you have no more encounters with strangers, we can safely assume you are in the clear. Any move made from here to Lauterbrunnen would take place either on the train or in the town itself. It is interesting the Mannings have heard rumours about the Americans."

"They seemed very keen for information," said I.

"You did well to negate the possibilities of the Americans entering the war. That information will be received in Berlin even as we sit here and talk."

"It is hard to believe," said I, "that a personal opinion could be so regarded."

"With the Germans, everything is regarded in minute detail. As far as the Americans are concerned, the best information available to me is that we should more than likely see their presence in Europe no later than the fall of this year."

As I sipped my wine and listened to Holmes, I felt my vigor returning. I ventured to inquire about the last two years.

"You know, Holmes, you gave every indication on Von Bork's terrace in 1914 that there was the possibility of never meeting again. Can you tell me nothing of your activities since then?"

Holmes looked at me with a drawn expression. With a gesture of resignation, he took on his old familiar professorial attitude.

"I was not prepared to relate my work at this present time, but recent situations have developed that may terminate my activities in Germany. It was primarily for this reason that I called for your assistance.

"By and large the general public has a romantic concept of a secret agent. Believe me when I tell you it is a difficult and hazardous profession. If the average person knew what was involved, he would avoid it at all costs.

"The Von Bork affair was a mere child's game compared to the vastness of this complex war situation. It is not unlike a gigantic game of chess being played for very high stakes, stakes so high that on any given afternoon, sixty or seventy thousand young men are slaughtered on the western front. I tell you in all sincerity, Watson, I have used every vestige of my powers, every resource at my disposal to quell the dogs of war. This conflict is of epic proportions and must be stopped."

I wholeheartedly agreed with this premise as I filled and lit my pipe and settled back in my chair.

Holmes continued, "In the quest for vital information—information which could bring the hostilities to an end, new situations, new problems continually crop up necessitating reevaluation and redirection of energies. It is a never ending duel of thrust and parry."

▼

CHAPTER FIVE

SHERLOCK HOLMES, BRITISH AGENT

"I will tell of my activities for the first time, filling in certain lacunae to make it as concise as possible. You may recall, my dear Watson, on our yearly visits in London I spent considerable time at Whitehall."

"Yes, I remarked to my niece about it."

"I was already engaged by the British government to review all foreign agents and their associates within the confines of England. Close cooperation with the foreign office and Scotland Yard netted all the subordinates in the Von Bork affair. You may also recall that in order to bring that operation to a successful conclusion I had to spend time in the U.S.A.—Chicago, to be exact—in order to acquire background for my Irish-American pseudonym of Altamont."

"I remember it clearly."

"This time it was necessary to return to the United States to the city of Milwaukee where I pursued several chemical tests and brushed up on my German."

"I fail to see the connection. Why Milwaukee?"

"It was necessary to affiliate myself with all the pro- Kaiser elements that flourished in that city. If you could have been in the Stadler Hotel on any given Sunday afternoon during the winter of 1914, you would have seen a gentleman participating in the vigorous exercise of pounding nails into a gigantic German cross."

"Pounding nails into a cross!" I repeated in disbelief.

"Yes, Watson, each nail cost five dollars. There was hardly room to hammer in the five I had purchased. All the money collected in this manner was but one of many contributions to German War Relief. Through this dubious pastime I met many German sympathizers, some of whom were directly involved in the assassination attempt on President Theodore Roosevelt in 1912."

"It's incredible, I had no idea the Americans were so pro-German."

"That was also my impression at first, but in reality these pro-Germans are found only in a few larger cities throughout the States. All in all, it would be safe to say the majority of Americans do not share in their feelings. At this time I was using the name of Mueller—Dr. Erich Mueller. I made it strongly known at these nail and cross functions and other meetings that I was personally prepared to go to Germany to offer my services to the war effort in whatever capacity. All this gave me sufficient background to return to Europe. I returned by way of Lisbon, Portugal, then made my way to Switzerland, making Zurich my base of operations.

"Britain at this time had secret agents in various locations throughout Germany, but too many were being caught and executed. What was desperately needed was a central control to systematically gather information to transmit to London, then, in turn to spread false information back to Germany. Upon the direct request of the British government this was the task I was asked to create and oversee. To this end I set about creating a network of both British and German agents. Both types of agents have produced staggering amounts of data. The important factor was to see that their efforts and results did not overlap, or to expend their energies attempting to gather the same information.

"I then made my way to Berlin and established myself as a sympathizer to the German cause. I found that I was something of a novelty. I often heard remarks expressing amazement that an American would come so far to assist them.

"I made calls on the German chemical manufacturers with the express wish to be of some assistance. I relied on my knowledge of chemistry to suggest alternative methods of manufacturing explosives, primarily with the use of ether-alcohol nitro- cellulose with a higher concentration of nitrogen than previously used.

"Of course I realized very few if any would change production methods in the middle of a war. On the other hand, if some manufacturer felt a need for improvement, I would certainly oblige, while making sure every explosive produced would be unstable to the same extent as nitro glycerin. I thought this was a rather ingenious method of sabotage, don't you agree?"

"Most ingenious," I commented. "Did anyone require your services?"

"Unfortunately not, but it accomplished my primary goal."

"Which was?"

"To maneuver myself into German high society. I did this through the auspices of Hr. Wilhelm Schmidt of Gewerkschaft Werks G.M.B.H., who very conveniently introduced me to Karl Hauffe.

"Herr Hauffe was quite taken with my coming from America to assist Germany. He suggested I accompany him to the Baroness Von Gildenstuble social gathering on the following Saturday. This was the very opportunity I was seeking, as such social functions usually have government and military people of considerable influence on the guest lists.

"The Baroness had a perpetual look of disdain written on her features, but like Herr Hauffe she was quickly taken with my enthusiasm for the Reich. Early in the evening she introduced me to Professor Otto Steiner of the University of Berlin. He was quite famous for being able to reconstruct an entire prehistoric animal from a single bone. He took the straightforward view that Germany must be the master of Europe. His immense degree of learning lent authority to his view. Such a man as this burns with a kind of heroic frenzy, or *eroici furori*, who truly believes he can bring salvation to the human race. Professor Steiner was avant-garde in all his political views and that is always perilous. I have always felt that a man who is one step ahead of the crowd is a leader; if two steps he is a radical; if three, he is either mad or a charlatan. Our Herr Professor appeared to be just between steps two and three.

"As the evening wore on, still in the company of the professor who seemed to cling to me like glue, we found ourselves in conversation with several government people. A distinguished looking gentleman approached our group. Steiner's enthusiasm erupted. 'Ah, Von Kleingardt, you have arrived rather late! Here is someone you should meet.' The professor indicated in my direction. 'Let me introduce Dr. Mueller from the United States.' Heads turned as Von Kleingardt shook my hand. The professor turned and addressed me. 'I must leave you now, but you must discuss your ideas with Hr. Von Kleingardt. Perhaps he can suggest a course of action to pursue since he is attached to our Embassy.'

"As peculiar as Steiner was, I was tempted to dismiss him as an eccentric, but later I had to admit a debt of gratitude to him. This was precisely the kind of individual I was hoping to meet. It was not until several months later that I learned indirectly that Steiner had sent a message to bring Von Kleingardt to the gathering with the express purpose of meeting me. After a few minutes of general conversation it was easy to ascertain Von Kleingardt was a genuine aristocrat, a man of considerable culture and refinement. I also received the distinct impression that the probability of his being a German spy was very high.

He seemed to take a keen interest in my views and listened attentively as I expounded on my theories of chemistry with regard to high explosives. His real interest was my desire to be of service to the German Reich. I quickly found he had a disarming way about him. Within the hour he was speaking to me like an old friend.

"Several days later it did not surprise me when I received a note from Von Kleingardt asking me to meet him at his office the following day. It was a bitterly cold January day and it had just begun to snow when I arrived at his office.

"He was in appearance a perfect example of his class. He was exactly what one would expect a German diplomat to be. His rise in the diplomatic service had been rapid and, though doubtless it had helped him to be connected by marriage with powerful families, his assent had been chiefly due to his own merit. He knew how to be determined when determination was necessary, and conciliatory when conciliation was appropriate. He was also one of Germany's top recruiters for the secret service, as well as an agent himself.

"Von Kleingardt greeted me warmly. He made some passing remarks about the Baroness, then quite suddenly asked what my plans were. Again I alluded to whatever service I could render to the Reich. He looked at me very carefully, then began talking about various political problems as related to the war. He was astute in every aspect of the geopolitical aspirations of Germany. I listened attentively and when he finished I casually remarked I had hoped he would furnish me with a letter of introduction to one of the larger chemical manufacturers.

"'No,' Von Kleingardt said, 'what I will do is get a bottle of cognac I keep in this cabinet and we will talk in complete confidentiality. You must understand, Doctor, Germany is in need of intelligent men like yourself. Especially men with enthusiasm and dedication to the Fatherland. Your knowledge of America and your command of the English language could be invaluable to certain members of our secret service. I am in close association with the War Department and if you are interested, I would be happy to intercede on your behalf.'

"Here it was, at last. The months of preparation finally bore fruition. I told him I would be honored to perform in this capacity if he felt I could be of service. Von Kleingardt went to his desk and quickly wrote a letter.

"'Then it is settled. Here is a letter of introduction to Colonel Von Reichter at the War Department. I would not let too much time elapse before making an appearance.'

"'I shall go tomorrow,' I replied.

"'Excellent, then we can presume our little talk has born fruit. Here, let me fill your glass before you leave. It is bitterly cold today and we must take every precaution to maintain your good health.' Von Kleingardt stood up and held his glass outstretched. '*Deutschland ueber Alles. Prosit.*' I, in turn, stood and repeated the toast.

"The following day at precisely two o'clock I presented myself at Koeniggratzer Strasse 80, which is a typical Prussian building of adminis-tration. Solid, but unpretentious, it is the very embodiment of Prussian efficiency, and like all official buildings in Germany, it is well guarded. The door attendant and commissar, a noncommissioned officer, takes down one's name and the party one wishes to see. He enters these later in a book, then telephones to the person required and one is either ushered in or denied admittance. When sent up, one is invariably accompanied by an orderly who does not leave until the door has closed behind one. This happens no matter how well one is known. When one leaves, there is the same procedure and the very duration of the visit is entered and checked in the attendant's book. As you can well imagine, I took great interest in that book.

"I was admitted immediately. After passing through three anterooms occupied by private secretaries in civilian dress, I was shown into Colonel Von Reichter's private office. He wore the undress ranking uniform of the Imperial Army. The secretaries and men of general office work, however were all civilians; this for a reason. The heads of all departments are

German officers, recruited from the old feudal aristocracy, loyal, to a degree, to the throne. They find it incompatible, not withstanding their loyalty, to soil their hands with some of the work connected with certain government duties, especially those of the secret service.

"Von Reichter was seated behind a large mahogany desk covered with a large green blotter. I noticed the room seemed like a private library; books, memoranda, letters and dispatch cases littered not only the desk, but the tables and chairs. He was seated with legs crossed in a huge leather armchair.

"When I came in he was reading some document and without a sign of recognition, he continued to read. Now and then he glanced at me from above the top of his document. Abruptly he told me to have a seat. As I sat down he pulled open a drawer and removed a folder that I surmised was a dossier regarding myself. There was another period during which he seemed to be unaware of my presence.

"Fortunately I had gained a great deal of data concerning men in high government position, and here sitting directly across from me was unquestionably one of the most highly esteemed militarists of the day. A diversified, creative man among whose achievements was the establishment of the military officers' school at Kreuznack.

"After twirling his fingers several times he finally said, 'I see you have come from America and also have been to England.'

"'That is correct.'

"'I presume you are familiar with their military strengths.'

"'Up to a certain point.'

"'What point?' he asked quickly.

"'I am afraid I am only familiar with what I have read in the newspapers.'

"He arched his enormous eyebrows and stared hard at me. 'Is America preparing for war?'

"'There are such plans.'

"'How do you know that? On what grounds do you make that ascertainment?' His agitation was ill concealed.

"'I have no specific proof,' I replied, but it is common knowledge. The Americans are mobilizing since Germany has sunk much of its shipping.' He pressed me for further details but I answered only in vague terms.

"During this interrogation Von Reichter impressed me as being one of those typically intolerable Prussians. Presumably, through centuries long contact with races of the east, the Prussian type presents the bland, imperturbable, incommunicative, almost inane expression of the oriental that hardly gives one any criteria of the tremendous power of perception and concentration beneath the mask.

"My unsatisfactory answers seemed to displease Von Reichter. Suddenly he took a different approach.

"'Von Kleingardt speaks highly of you. Have you any idea what this line of work entails?'

"'What would be required of me?'

"'Before my entering upon that, are you averse to applying methods that may appear against all ethics?'

"I could see it intrigued him to evaluate, from a detached position, what he would later describe as 'the agent potential': To devise minute tests of character and behaviour which could inform him of the qualities of a candidate. This part of him appeared bloodless, almost inhuman. I had to guard myself warily from spontaneous reaction.

"'Ethical considerations are of no consequence if the cause is just,' I answered.

"I noticed a peculiar smile cross his features momentarily. Then, looking me straight in the eyes and using the sharp, incisive language of a German officer, he declared, 'We make use of the same weapons that are used against us. There is no way we can afford to be squeamish. The interests at stake are too high to let personal ethics stand in the way.' It was obvious he regarded introspection as unhealthy, un-German and unpatriotic.

"Von Reichter continued, 'You would be required to gain information for us such as we seek. The means by which you acquire this information will be left entirely to your own discretion. We expect results. We place our previous knowledge on the subject required at your disposal. You will have our organization to assist you, but you must understand very clearly that we cannot and will not be able to extricate you from any trouble in which you may become involved. This service is dangerous and no official assistance or help could be given under any circumstances. Do I make myself perfectly clear, Herr Doktor?'

"I reflected a moment, then said, 'Perfectly clear, Colonel.'

"'Do you accept these terms?'

"'Yes, I do,' I replied.

"An uneasy silence settled on Von Reichter's face that also registered an unspoken question. Finally he said, 'You have not inquired about payment, Herr Doktor.'

"'Remuneration is not necessary—I have private funds at my disposal.' I judged this answer would display my loyalty. To the contrary, my remark brought on a longer and more awkward silence. Von Reichter eyed me suspiciously.

"Then, as if making up his mind, he finally said, 'That will not do, Herr Doktor. Our policy dictates that all agents shall receive payment. We have this policy for two reasons: In the first place, it gives us a definite hold on our men. Secondly, your expenses could become very high in the course of your duties.' He raised his eyebrows inquiringly.

"'Very well. In that case, I accept.'

"'You made up your mind quickly.'

"'It is my way Colonel, if I see no alternative. I take a thing or leave it.'

"'That's what I like Doktor: A quick decisive mind.' That seemed to please him and I felt I had passed the last hurdle.

"'Very well then, to be of use to us you will need a great deal of technical coaching. Are you ready to start tomorrow?'

"'I am ready to start today.'

"'Very good,' he said, 'but tomorrow morning at ten o'clock will do. Then you will give us daily as much of your time as we require.' He called in one of his secretaries, gave him a brief command and in a few minutes the man returned with an order for three hundred marks.

"'This, Doktor, is your first month's living expenses. Retaining fees are paid quarterly. This scale of pay is only the beginning. As your use to us and the importance of your missions increases, so will your remuneration. That, of course, depends entirely on you.'

"As I pocketed the cheque I remarked, 'Will I be working in your department or elsewhere?'

"No sooner had I put the question to him than I regretted it. All traces of geniality vanished from Von Reichter's face. It was stern and serious. 'Doktor,' he said very slowly, 'Learn this from the start and learn it well. Do not ask questions. Do not talk. Think. You will soon learn that there are many unwritten laws attached to this service.' With that he began working at something on his desk, which signified I was summarily dismissed.

"On the way out I casually asked the door attendant if Ambassador Von Kleingardt had arrived. I glanced over his shoulder as he checked off the names in his book.

"'No, he has not come in today,' was the reply.

"'Well, then I shall go directly to his office,' I answered. Among the many names in attendance was the singular name of Frederica Von Strada.

"For the next two weeks I took intensive instructions daily at Koeniggratzer Strasse 80. I cannot emphasize strongly enough how extremely thorough the German spy system is—nothing, absolutely nothing is left to chance.

"It was within that same month, while attending a social gathering at Baroness Von Gildenstuble's, that I met Frederica Von Strada. This introduction was no accident; it was arranged. It was obvious she worked in Intelligence. I later found out through my own channels of inquiry, her explicit orders were to substantiate whether or not I really was what I claimed to be—a German-American with sympathy to the Fatherland—and above all, whether I could be trusted with truly vital information. I studied her closely. She was a fanatic. Her patriotism was aggressive, but disinterested. She was obsessed with the notion of the superiority of all things German. She loathed England with a virulent hatred because in that country she saw the chief obstruction to the diffusion of German interests throughout Europe. Her ideal was a German world with the rest of the nations under its influence enjoying the benefits of German science, art and culture.

"Later we were thrown together on small missions. On occasion after occasion I have nearly been exposed by her clever intelligence. She soon learned her womanly charms and feminine wiles were of no avail in dealing with me. As a consequence, I felt strongly she did not completely trust me. All this resulted in her testing me at every turn. I had always to be on guard while in her company.

"She is at the forefront of virtually every allied disaster that has occurred, like some voracious carnivorous flower that consumes its victims. Without a doubt, Frederica Von Strada is the most dangerous woman in Europe.

"The following month, which was February of 1915, both she and I were summoned to Von Reichter's office. Von Reichter wasted no words. He looked unusually grim as he informed us there was valuable German naval intelligence seeping back to allied lines (all of which was my doing).

"Von Reichter continued, 'These incidents do not offer any conclusive proof of such information coming from this department, but they do suggest provocative questions that demand investigation.'

"I quickly agreed. Von Strada was watching me closely. Then as if making up her mind, suggested three names to be reviewed and further indicated I should take charge of the investigation. All her doubts about me were going to be put to the test. I am quite sure she had a definite idea who the informer was. Werner Blucher was a valuable agent to England's cause, who was attached to the naval offices and supplies. I warned him of his danger through a complex numerical code, which I used only in extreme emergencies. Doing this was a serious risk to my own safety and situation, which had taken close to two years to establish.

"Two days later I had no recourse but to inform Von Reichter who the informer was, hoping Werner Blucher was long out of the country. But he hesitated in his departure, apparently trying to make arrangements for his family. He was arrested, accused of being a traitor, tortured, confessed nothing and was executed by firing squad. Losing this valuable agent was a serious blow. Not only the loss of life, but the problem of replacement was extremely difficult. By and large, most potential agents desire the end, but hesitate at the means. On the other hand, this situation made possible the passing of a critical test and henceforth I was above suspicion.

"My assignments now became more frequent and later I was able to replace another man back in the naval department. Although my practical work fortuitously threw light upon certain German agents, these have never been my exclusive or even main concern. The broader issues of significance were where war production was located and major troop movements. Believe me, my dear Watson, when I tell you volumes could be written on some of these exploits."

"Let us hope some day they shall be written," I said in earnest.

"By the latter part of 1915 the Supreme Army Command concurred that 'unrestricted U boat warfare could bring England to her knees within six months.' All in all, the war during 1915 was something akin to a stalemate. The allies realized they needed vast numbers of men and machines to penetrate the German line in order to pour armies through to victory.

"On the German side they felt they could contain the allies indefinitely, but this was an untenable position. What was needed and wanted was victory, so the proposal of unrestricted U boat warfare was declared the only remaining measure capable of saving the situation.

"I threw all my energies and efforts into the disclosure of U boat activities and manufacture. In the very beginning the *unter sea booten* were extremely limited in far ranging activities. They were often spotted by British seaplanes even when they were disguised as sailing vessels. They were sunk, sails and all by the Royal Navy. Information concerning U boats was forwarded to the Admiralty through normal channels from our headquarters in Zurich. Later, Germany perfected these U boats with greater range and firepower, with deadly consequences for us. They look upon their U boat warfare as the *ultima ratio regis.*

"There is mounting evidence as should be clear by now, our fantastic losses of troops and warships are due chiefly to the Reich's dramatic increase in U boat production. Alone during the first ten days of April, over two hundred and fifty thousand tons of allied shipping was lost. Building goes on feverishly by day and by night.

"This activity continues not withstanding the fact that numerous agents have lost their lives while trespassing the verboten North Sea coastal areas. I myself have gone out to the general areas and have found them so extensively guarded along the entire coast that it is impossible to say with any exactitude just where these sites are. Through these efforts and an unfortunate event, my activities have been seriously hampered."

"What event hampered you?" I asked curiously.

"Earlier I mentioned the doorman's book at Koeniggratzer Strasse 80. Recently I viewed a name on that list which in all probability could terminate my service on the continent. It was for that reason, my dear fellow, I have sent for you."

CHAPTER SIX

▼

WATSON'S MISSION

I had listened in rapt admiration to Holmes' discourse on his penetration into the German Secret Service. To think he was privy to the inner workings of the German war machine was nothing less than the most immense accomplishment of his entire career.

I was about to ask Holmes what service I could render when suddenly he posed a question. "Perhaps you remember one of my monographs I wrote during my hiatus from crime detecting using the pseudonym of Sigerson?"

"Offhand I am afraid I cannot."

"Well, if you had, I am quite sure you would have found my impressions of Tibet rather interesting."

"Tibet!" I remonstrated. "What has…"

"Yes, for example, that country offers peculiarly favorable conditions for psychic phenomenon. My own theory is that the very high level of the land and the great silence in which the landscape is bathed is helpful."

I looked at Holmes, totally perplexed. Had I come all this distance during a war to hear a dissertation on the esoteric merits of eastern mysticism? "But Holmes, what has this to do with the war? Or my mission?"

"Everything."

"Everything?" I repeated in amazement."Watson, Watson, still pragmatic as ever. But I assure you, as Shakespeare so aptly wrote, 'There are more things in heaven and earth, Horatio, than are dreamed of in your philosophy.'

"I still do not understand."

Holmes continued, "I made the long, tedious journey into the mountain cities of Tibet to embrace the curious knowledge of that land. As a result of my experiences I have had many vivid impressions of various psychic phenomenon that cannot be satisfactorily explained within the limited framework of our accepted knowledge. One thing is for certain: These powers do exist. Therefore your mission is to go to France in the capacity of a courier. You will deliver a map and a letter to Professor D'Eslon, a clairvoyant."

For a moment I sat in stunned silence. I was critical of this aberration on the part of my friend. Logic had been the foundation of Holmes' career—now, as if out of nowhere, he was going to rely on psychic forces.

I am sure he caught the extreme doubt on my face when he sharply added, "The application of active imagination in conjunction with incisive reasoning is what is called for."

"But Holmes! To rely on a clairvoyant..!"

"Over more years than I care to remember I have stated repeatedly to you, when you have eliminated all the impossibilities, whatever remains, however improbable, must be the truth. Believe me Watson, too much is at stake not to use every conceivable recourse open to us. Furthermore, as I have stated earlier, all other efforts have failed. The most logical approach to this problem is to make an inquiry of this nature."

Sherlock Holmes' proposition appeared to me as incredible as if I could single-handedly terminate the war within the hour. How could I tell him

I felt such an excursion was nothing more than a wild goose chase? What could I say? He seemed determined I should go to France.

"All right, if that is what you want me to do, I shall go," I said with some asperity, mingled with disappointment.

"Capital. I knew I could count on you."

"But I must tell you in all sincerity that it strikes me as mere balderdash."

"On the contrary. It is of paramount importance you get through and back to Zurich. Regardless of how you feel now, I assure you this mission is imperative. All allied agents are known. You are unknown. Therefore, your chances for success are greater. I should go myself, but as I stated, my activities have been severely hampered and I must be available here for further developments."

Holmes took a large envelope from his valise on the floor and handed it to me. "Earlier I spoke of your trip to Lauterbrunnen. If you have no suspicious encounters on the train we can assume the way is clear. On the other hand, if you have any doubts, you must desist and return forthwith. Is that perfectly clear?"

"Yes."

"If all is well you will spend the day sight-seeing. You will take the cable car to Murren and register as a patient at the sanitarium. Again, if you have any doubts, desist. Early the following morning you shall leave Lauterbrunnen by train. Proceed to Chamonix, France. In all probability, you will have no encounters after Lauterbrunnen and can feel the greater threat is over. You will give the envelope to Professor D'Eslon and bring back his answer. Guard this envelope well, Watson! Its contents may well be pivotal with regard to the war. By the way, do you have your old service revolver with you?"

"Yes, I do."

Holmes drew from his coat pocket a slim automatic. "You will find this an interesting and ingenious piece of ordnance. Much more efficient than your bulky old service revolver."

"What is it?" I inquired.

"A nine-millimeter German Luger, known as the pistole 08." Holmes handed me the slim automatic that lay and conformed to my hand like a glove. Its weight was centered over the back of the hand and gave a feeling of exceptional balance. It was a wonderful example of a mechanical contrivance that almost approached a thing of beauty.

It was well after midnight when Holmes left my rooms. Sleep was almost impossible now as I pondered the magnitude of Holmes' overwhelming mission. After a few hours of fitful tossing, I arose early in the morning and made my way to Hauptbahnhof Station.

The trip to Lauterbrunnen was uneventful. I arrived in the valley town and made my way to Murren by cable car, which had to be nearly three thousand feet high. I registered at the desk of the Murren Sanitarium. No one took especial notice of me and I decided to make the most of my sight-seeing for the day.

I was surrounded by the Bernese Alps. There must be few vistas in the world more wonderful. Names like the Grosshorn, Jungfrau, mountains well over the thirteen thousand foot elevation were awe-inspiring. What apocalyptic forces brought all this into being? It must have been aeons since the titanic conflagration occurred. Indeed, one felt thoroughly inconsequential in this vast landscape. It was incongruous to think a war of epic proportions was raging less than a hundred miles away, and here before me was all this peace and beauty.

Again the day passed with no suspicious encounters. I had no feeling of being watched. However, since my experience with the Mannings I was doubly on guard. I retired early and slept well for the first time in days.

Arising just as the first rays of light were creeping through the valley, I caught the early cable car to Lauterbrunnen, and then the train to Chamonix.

As I went down the aisle to the breakfast car, a man came toward me. He was smartly attired. His ivy green redingote was beautifully cut and flared out a little at the knees. He was slight of figure and not very tall. He was smoking a small cigar. In the crook of his arm he carried a curious case. On closer inspection as we passed, I observed the case was covered with snakeskin.

I thought nothing of this incident until I returned to my compartment after breakfast. This same man was going through my bag.

"I say there, what do you think you are doing? That is my bag."

"Oh, dreadfully sorry. This bag looks ever so much like my own. Ah, there is my bag piled in the corner on top of the rack." He produced a bag quite like my own. He apologized again and introduced himself as Helmute Stekel of Steinheil Manufacturing Company out of Basel, Switzerland. I mumbled something and sat down. The man was not attractive. He had a wolfish grin showing a row of small teeth and a dark moustache that ended in points that were waxed.

I picked up the book I had brought along and opened it to discourage further conversation. This was a dilemma. This man had been definitely searching my bag. Should I return to Zurich? I clearly recalled Holmes' injunction to desist if in doubt. On the other hand, my journey was nearly over, and Holmes' anxiety about my getting through to Professor D'Eslon prodded me to make every effort to finish the trip successfully.

I alighted at the small station at Chamonix and was considerably relieved in my mind when Helmute Stekel was not among the passengers who left the train. Nevertheless, the incident that occurred on the train was ominous. It was a wise decision to carry Holmes' envelope on my person.

I was immediately struck by the pristine beauty of the town in its mountainous setting. It was still early in the afternoon when I took lodgings at the Albert Hotel on Rue DuPaccard. Here in the secluded northeast corner of France the war seemed an eternity away.

I took lunch on the hotel patio and observed all the grandeur around me. Europe's highest mountain, Mont Blanc was on my right, reaching up to the incredible height of 15,781 feet. I reflected a moment on the most determined attempt to reach its summit in 1900, which ended in tragedy. McDonald and Fraser, two of Britain's finest climbers, were seen at a height of 12,000 feet on the north ridge, reached after many hours of exceptionally difficult climbing. They disappeared into the clouds and were never seen again.

Directly before me the town and surrounding valley stretched out to infinity, which brought me back to the reality of my purpose here. I still could not fathom Holmes' emphasis on this occult inquiry. From my point of view this was a most astonishing development. After all these years of association with Holmes, I was now relegated to a messenger in search of a French fortuneteller. And the like had always struck me as so much blather and nonsense.

Lunch finished, I made inquiries as to the whereabouts of Rue Des Moetieux and then set off walking through the town. Flowers were everywhere. The houses sat decently in their own gardens. Most of the curtains were drawn, first the lace and then the brocade. Everything had a delightful quaintness. My walk took me to the outskirts of the town into the surrounding foothills. A short time later I found the address I was seeking. The house stood on a high hill. The ground fell steeply away beneath the side windows. Heavy trees stretched into the distance. I knocked at the front door, which opened shortly. The man who stood before me had an inquiring look spread over his features.

In my broken French I asked to see Professor Armand D'Eslon. *"Etes vous Professor D'Eslon? Parlyvous Englaise?"* I hopefully inquired.

"But of course! Please come in," he replied in perfect English.

I introduced myself and handed him the large sealed envelope Holmes had entrusted to me.

"You must excuse the absence of my servant. It is his day off." I acquiesced with a nod.

Professor D'Eslon motioned me into the study and indicated a chair by his desk. The professor sat down opposite me, reading Holmes letter for several minutes. Before me was a man in the prime of life with eyes that reflected inner vision. The sensitive curve of the brow was in contrast to the square jaw, which proclaimed determination. He spread the large ordinance map out upon the desk and quietly observed its details.

The study had a fireplace on the left with two large leather wing chairs facing it. A large set of French windows were to the right, which afforded a magnificent view of the mountains. The professor looked up. "It appears Mr. Holmes needs to locate a German naval establishment on the north German coast that manufactures submarines."

"That is what I understand," I answered somewhat indifferently.

"I detect a degree of doubt as to your belief in finding answers in an occult fashion."

It was strange that he perceived my skepticism so quickly. "Not at all," I stammered. "I simply rely on logic to solve whatever may be a problem."

"That is commendable, but extremely limited," was his strange reply. He looked keenly at me. "Although I am very much a child of the Victorian period, and regarding that last age as infinitely more civilised than the present, I do not view this strange idea as absurd." Again he regarded me closely. Then, as if making up his mind, he got up from the desk. "Let us sit over here by the fireplace, Doctor. I have some very fine cognac which is quite old."

We settled ourselves down in the large wing chairs opposite each other. I swirled and sniffed the cognac he handed me and tasted a small amount.

"Most excellent!" I proclaimed.

"Yes, I agree. Our family has kept a stock of it since the last century."

"Indeed, that is very old, as you say," I was beginning to exhaust my supply of small talk and wondered why the professor interrupted his work on the ordinance map.

"When I was a small boy in Marseille, I remember seeing a scientific exhibition in a museum which commenced a train of thought along the lines of the occult."

"How was that?" I asked, trying to show some interest.

"The exhibit was a human body chemically reduced to its original elements. They were labeled and capped in separate jars, such as sodium chloride, iron, phosphates, carbonate of lime, minerals and so on. I felt revulsion, for this was not my idea of myself. When I grew older I thought of this again. What about the spirit of man? Our terrestrial body is quite different from our celestial body. The chemist has never, nor will ever, bring the spiritual part of man to a chemical formula."

I considered Professor D'Eslon's earnest discourse and had to admit the logic of his contentions.

He continued, "From prehistoric times mankind has made use of supernatural powers in various forms. They were used in order to find direction, and much more vital, sources of fresh water. Years ago I experimented with this kind of power using a pendulum and was able to locate some old silver coins. I soon learned the procedure could be applied to a map and find lost items in that fashion."

Stuff and nonsense, I thought to myself. These people who think they have esoteric powers and know what could be and what could not seemed sadly disillusioned.

As if in answer to my unspoken opinion, he continued. "Of course, I do not believe in any of these things without convincing evidence. I was brought up and trained as a scientist and still retain an attitude toward them which is, I hope, more scientific than one of absolute incredulity. Mesmer had much the same problem in convincing the public that a person could be mesmerized. Of course, this is absurd to those who just dismiss such things as superstition or delusion. Don't you agree, Doctor?"

"As a matter of fact, I do not put much stock in any of it."

"So I thought," replied the professor. "Would you care to see a little demonstration of this power?"

"What kind of demonstration?" I asked hesitantly.

"Well, offhand I believe I could mesmerize you in less than two minutes."

"I rather doubt that, Professor D'Eslon. I pride myself in regard to my steadiness and logic."

"Good! Then let us try." He looked eagerly at me. I saw no way out of this and finally murmured my assent.

Rays of late afternoon sunlight filtered through the French windows. Professor D'Eslon held his glass of cognac in the center of the light. The glass sparkled and danced as he gently swirled its contents.

"You will concentrate on this glass. Doctor. You will watch the dancing light and you will become tired and weak." I saw his face behind the glass and it took on the appearance of a peculiar reptilian stare. "You are now feeling very tired and weak." The light beams radiated and sparkled as he continued to swirl the liquid. I tried to look away but could not. A feeling of physical weakness began to envelop me. I tried to fight it, but it pervaded my being more and more. I was sure if I tried to stand my legs would sag beneath me and I would fall to the floor.

"Now, Doctor, you are no longer tired and weak—you are becoming stronger. You feel as if you could float. You have formed a theory to counteract gravity." In an instant I felt quite light—then I felt my body slowly rising out of the chair. The feeling of euphoria surging through me was confirmation enough that the postulated theory was indeed correct. I remained suspended several feet above the chair for what seemed a rather long time.

Then suddenly, "Well, Doctor, it is time to come down." Immediately I began to descend and slowly sank back into the chair. "You shall remember everything that has happened." With a snap of his fingers he said, "Wake up, Doctor."

I stared in disbelief. "Great Scott! I had no idea such things could be done," I cried.

"Fortunately you were an easy subject."

"Really," I said sheepishly. "I must admit it was an extraordinary experience."

"Actually, my dear Doctor, it is a staggering picture of the unknown potential of the human mind in touch with forces beyond our total comprehension. Before I began my own experiments I knew little about the practical application of these inner abilities. Since then, through intensive experimentation and application, I have become intimately familiar with them. Through all this one develops an inner harmony that results in peace with the one universal force. This force can be identified by what religion calls God. Nowadays this concept of harmony has vanished; men tear up the earth with war."

Why was this interesting man telling me all this? There was no doubt as to his sincerity and logic, though I could not entirely find myself agreeing with all his ideas. Nevertheless, one could not help but admire and respect him for the courage of his convictions.

"Perhaps you may be wondering why I have spent so much time discussing these topics?"

Good Lord, it seems he is reading my mind again. "As a matter of fact I was," I replied, astonished.

"You must understand it is quite impossible to demonstrate some of these powers to a complete skeptic. If nothing else, I believe I have given you something to think about and it is not all nonsense, as you first surmised."

"How in the world did you know these were my exact thoughts before I arrived here?"

"We have not as yet discussed telepathy, my good Doctor, but perhaps you will visit me again and I will enlighten you. However, the hour grows late. Let me not deviate from the work at hand." He rose from his chair and motioned for me to sit across from him at this desk. Dusk was settling as the professor lit his desk lamp and spread Holmes' map out again.

From a desk drawer he took out an object that resembled a child's spinning top but much smaller. Attached to this pendulum was a thin gold chain. The professor put his elbow on the desk and held this strange instrument over the map. The pendulum oscillated back and forth. With his left hand he slowly moved a straight edge from left to right over the map.

It was as if he were dreaming with his eyes wide open, his concentration intense. Suddenly the pendulum took on the motion of an ellipse, then quickly formed a circle, gyrating rapidly. He stopped moving the straight edge, put the pendulum down and drew a line across the map.

Looking up at me, he said, "These forces are closely linked with the primordial energies that flow through the mind. I know this all sounds very difficult and possibly absurd, but these powers do exist."

I continued to watch closely and thought all this conundrum of invisible forces was something I could never hope to grasp. On the other hand, I saw manifested in front of my eyes that which my mind rejected. Altogether, I reluctantly had to admit at least a remote possibility that these powers somehow existed.

The professor continued with his pendulum, moving the straight edge from the top of the map toward the bottom. He again stopped when the pendulum gyrated, drawing a second line that crossed the first, giving him a reference point.

"It appears that what Mr. Holmes is seeking is located on the north German coast just south of the town of…"

Suddenly an explosion from the windows on my right shattered the silence. Momentarily I was transfixed by the horror before me. Professor D'Eslon had slumped forward on the desk, blood jetting from a terrible wound. Dismay and disbelief surged through me as I looked at this man who just an instant before was animated and full of vitality. I sprang up, drawing my Luger pistol. At the same time a dark figure rushed upon me. I fired my gun, then everything went blank as I felt the searing pain of a blow to my right temple.

CHAPTER SEVEN

▼

ALPINE MISADVENTURE

I awoke on the floor with the face of Major Saunders peering down at me.

"Easy, Doctor Watson. Drink this." I swallowed the proffered brandy. I was then helped to my feet.

"My God!" I cried suddenly, remembering the professor. "Is he...?"

"Yes, he is quite dead, and you are very fortunate—the bullet fired at you just grazed your right temple."

"The map! Is the map on the desk?"

"There is no map, Doctor."

"My God, what are we to do? What will Holmes do without that information?" I sat wearily down as I considered this shattering piece of news.

I looked at Major Saunders as if for the first time. "How on earth did you get here?"

"I was assigned to follow you just in case some sort of situation like this developed. I have been watching the house from the other side of the road, but I saw no one approach. When I heard the shots I rushed across and found you lying on the floor and the professor slumped over the desk."

"My God, what are we to do?" I repeated to myself grimly. "How can we recover the map? Its information is vital."

"The young man on the train, do you remember?"

"Great Scott, is he responsible for all this?"

"I am afraid so."

"But he stayed on the train," I protested.

"An old trick, I am also afraid. More than likely he jumped off before the train gained too much momentum. We were watching him on the train also. What name did he give you?"

"Helmut Stekel," I said in a hollow voice.

"We identified him as one of the agents in the employ of the Kaiser's special services. His name is Ernst Gunther."

"His name is of little importance to me," I said bitterly. "Retrieving the map is all that matters. Who is with you, Major?"

"I have an agent watching at the station. If by any chance Gunther showed up, he was to follow him."

"How would you know which direction he might take?"

"We have a signal set up for either circumstance of north or southbound along the rail line. I was about to warn you about Gunther, but decided against it when he did not leave the train. The fault is mine."

"No," I answered slowly. "I should have followed Holmes' injunction when I apprehended him going through my bag."

"We must leave here immediately. Are you up to it, Doctor?"

"Yes, yes, but what shall we do about poor D'Eslon?"

"There is no time now, but we will inform the authorities at Chamonix." A very resolute Major Saunders took command.

We went directly to the rail station. Major Saunders approached a man at the far end, sitting with his coat hugged around him as if asleep.

"Hans, has Gunther come through here?"

Hans sprang from his seat. "No, Sir, it's been very quiet."

Saunders' eyes narrowed in concentrated thought. "We can be sure he has not remained in Chamonix. There is only one other route leading out: The cog rail which heads south over the Petite St. Bernard Pass to Italy. If this proves to be the case, he will head to the largest city in northern Italy—Milan. Hans, you will take the next express to Milan. If you have the good fortune to spot him, keep him under surveillance until we arrive. Doctor Watson and I shall take the cog rail to verify if indeed that was his route."

After reporting the tragedy that occurred at Rue Des Moetieux to the authorities, we boarded the cog rail.

It was early in the evening as the train climbed the heights at a steady pace. I looked from the window at the tree line, which was receding rapidly as we approached barren rock. Further on it would be a snowy landscape.

I felt a reaction settling in from this bizarre series of experiences, which had left me nearly exhausted. There was little comfort realizing we still had a difficult task ahead of us. Difficult task, I repeated silently. More than likely, an impossible task. How could we hope to retrieve the map? What if this man Gunther had destroyed it? I turned to the major in panic.

"What if he has destroyed the map?" I cried.

"Easy, Doctor. Ernst Gunther won't do that. It is his only proof which will guarantee payment and, more than likely, a bonus to boot."

I tried in vain to relax, as we continued to climb.

I was in a high state of anxiety when we arrived at Entreves, a small mountain village. An official boarded the train. We learned there had been a spring avalanche of snow. The line was blocked near the pass. We could not go on until the next morning at the earliest. Then and there I despaired at ever seeing the map again.

"What can we do?" I asked, totally dejected.

"There is no way our man would risk returning to Chamonix," reflected the major. "Remain on the train, Doctor, while I make some inquiries in the village."

Nearly an hour later the major returned. "Gunther has taken the cable car up to the Rinderhorn Ski Lodge."

"How did you learn that?"

"I gave a detailed description of him at the small hotel restaurant and was directed to the local ski shop, where I learned he purchased a pair of skis and necessary equipment."

"Are you sure it was him?" I asked, fully alerted.

"He was carrying a curious attaché case covered with snake skin."

We stepped out into the snow and walked the short distance to the cable car station. As I boarded the car I felt a fleeting hope we could still overtake our adversary and recover the map.

Moving still higher, we approached the thin cold air of high altitude. A thousand feet above I could see strange wind sculptured snow leading to immense ice walls that were the beginning of a glacier.

At the ski lodge we were told by the desk clerk that a man of Gunther's description, a Herr Werner Schmeidler, had left to explore the upper ridge above the lodge to practice, as he said, for the next day's downhill event.

"Yes, he had a curious case with him. We expressed our concern to him as the light was beginning to fail, but he made light of the situation and insisted he needed the practice."

Outside the lodge we began to climb in dogged determination in the direction pointed out to us by the desk clerk. The night sky was clear and a full moon had risen giving an otherworldly somnolence to the treacherous landscape. Neither of us was dressed for the situation. I found myself perspiring profusely and completely out of breath as the way became steeper.

The face above the ridge was scalloped out in huge flutings and it was the most prominent of these we proposed to climb.

"Look there, Doctor!" cried the major. "Footprints!" He pointed down at the soft snow. By sheer luck we had stumbled onto Gunther's track.

At a point where the ice cliffs seemingly blocked our way, an alarmingly exposed strip of snow-covered rock allowed us to pass by and through the open snowfield beyond. We followed the track across the top of the ridge. I paused to get my breath and ease the suffocating beating of my heart. Going forward again, the tracks we followed became even more steep, winding in giant zigzags up the shoulder of the mountain. The tracks made a seemingly endless ascent. Mountain peaks were visible in all directions glinting in the moonlight.

I began to fall behind the major. My legs began to feel as if they were dissolving into a slowly draining liquid. The bones no longer felt solid, but bent and folded. I was losing control; I must stop; I must rest. I was about to call out to the major, when I saw him drop to his knees and motion me forward.

Was he in distress or had he spotted some danger? The thought made me press on. As I came closer, he put his finger to his lips and motioned for me to get down. I crawled to the base of a mound next to him.

"What is it?" I whispered.

"Crawl up and carefully peer over the mound," said he.

I did as he asked. Gunther's track led ever upward to an outcropping that was next to an Alpine hut on the right. I crawled down.

"Look, Doctor. For whatever reason he could very well be in that hut. He has the advantage of height. Furthermore, we can't approach in the open like this. We would be easy targets."

"What shall we do?" I asked uneasily.

"I propose that I go back down and around, then climb to the backside of the hut. If you could make it over to that far ledge and come across when I signal to cover me when I enter, we could very well take him by surprise."

My heart sank as I glanced at the ledge he indicated. It seemed the only feasible plan to gain access to the hut and remain unseen. I acquiesced feebly.

"You can rest a bit here while I go down. Then make your way to the ledge." I watched the major descend the way we came until he was out of sight.

I started forward. My feet felt blistered. Every muscle in my body cried out against further movement. I put my head down and trudged on, trying to think of something other than the utter weariness that engulfed me. I became hot from the exertion. The perspiration trickled down to the small of my back. It gathered in beads on my forehead, as sheer will power moved me slowly forward.

Below and to the right the snow fell away in a precipitous drop. My heart leapt as my footing began slipping on what was now ice. I felt the up draught of air as I slowly slid toward the edge. In total desperation I clawed at the ice and snow with my fingers and halted my slide, stopping short of dropping to infinity. I lay there momentarily and as God is my witness, I began to see my life pass before me. Was this the end? No, no, I could not let this happen. Too much was at stake: the war, Holmes was depending on me, the major was depending on me up above. I must get back.

Total fear lent strength to my limbs. With stoic resolve I inched my way up until I regained the ground I had lost. Finally I lay well away from the treacherous ice and tried to recover my breath. Then and there the realization struck me; mountain climbing was a young man's game. At sixty years of age it was no longer within my range of acceptable activities. I thanked God I was still alive.

I came to the ledge the major had indicated. Carefully looking out some fifty yards to the hut, I saw neither him nor any signs of Gunther. I watched and waited for what seemed an eternity. The perspiration of my body turned into an icy dampness. It was as if I had no clothes on at all and was simply wrapped in a clammy blanket. I began shivering with the cold. Was the major all right? Was it possible for him to approach in the manner he suggested? The thought of waiting much longer in this God-forsaken place was maddening.

Suddenly I saw a figure far in back of the hut on a jagged outcrop moving slowly forward. It was the major. He was a good ten years younger than I but his movements indicated he was extremely exhausted. He rested a few moments, then came forward again. Now he was above the hut and signaled me by waving his arm. Shortly thereafter he was at the side of the hut, motioning me forward.

I had great difficulty in struggling to my feet. While I had waited, I seemed to have stiffened up so that every joint seemed rusted and immovable. I took out my Luger and forced myself with every fibre of my being to go the fifty yards that looked like a thousand. By dint of considerable labor, I came to the door of the hut just as the major kicked it in and rushed forward with his gun raised.

I caught a tone of bitterness in the major's voice as he called to me from inside the hut. "Well, Doctor, our bird has flown the nest."

My heart sank as I came to the doorway. Was there no relationship between effort and reward?

"Come in Doctor. Here, take a drink from my flask. You look completely done in."

I accepted the flask as I entered and swallowed a long draught of brandy. I looked about and saw that it was a wretched place. The odor was overwhelming; something akin to the secretion of musk ox intermingled with droppings found in chicken coops. I was too overwrought and exhausted to mind very much.

I sat down on a crude bench and a few moments later I found the brandy gave a small measure of restoration. The major sat down next to me.

"It was touch and go climbing back up here," he said hoarsely.

"Likewise for me, getting to that infernal ledge."

"There is no doubt Gunther was here. His tracks verify that much. I'd best go out and see what direction he has taken."

"What good will that do?" I said bitterly. "We cannot follow him."

"That is true."

"Then you consider this a hopeless situation?"

"Not by any means."

"But what can we possibly do?"

"For the moment, nothing. But in the long run, possibly everything."

With that he left me to rummage around the outside of the hut.

I looked out the doorway. The moonlight shone a silvery tracing on the silhouettes of countless peaks, hard and crystal white with snow and ice. Far off in the distance there was a thunderous roar—another spring avalanche, I reflected. Could Gunther and the map be under tons of snow? I cast the thought from my mind.

The major stood in the doorway. "We have been fools, Doctor. This man is more clever and resourceful than I ever suspected, or for that matter, ever experienced. I found his ski tracks to the far left of the hut. There is but one direction to go from here, and that is northwest. Every other way is impassable. He waited here for the moon to rise before attempting to leave."

"But why should he do such a thing? He could have waited for the train tomorrow morning. The man must be mad attempting a flight like this," I postulated.

"Or there is something extremely important driving him—possibly a rendezvous somewhere that would account for this nonstop flight," answered the major. "At any rate, this is the way I see it: First, I believe his initial southward direction was a diversionary ploy."

"But for what reason?" I interjected.

"His strategy could have been to throw off any potential pursuers by appearing to go south toward Italy, but in reality, when he arrives at Aosta, he could swing back over the Grand St. Bernard and head for the Rhone valley, pick up the railway at Martigny for Montreux, then to Lausanne and onto the express for Bern.

"Second, this unexpected avalanche situation has only detoured and slowed him down. But he seems to show a talent for seeing situations from every perspective. Only someone with a thorough knowledge of these mountains would dare to do what he is doing. It would be hazardous to ski in this terrain in daylight, let alone in moonlight, which is infinitely more dangerous."

I listened intently while the major spoke. It was not an unreasonable inference. "Escape is one thing," I said, "but this mad dash across these mountains—what could prompt it?"

"I have the same question, Doctor, but until we can get close on his heels, we shall not know."

"Is there any hope of catching him?"

"We shall make every effort to overtake him. As I see it, he will spend the greater part of the night in these mountains, which will give us a small advantage."

"It would be a slim advantage," I agreed.

"In the morning we will take the cog rail to Aosta, then a ferry that crosses Lake Leman to Lausanne. With a bit of luck we could join him on the express to Bern."

"Are you certain Bern will be his ultimate destination?"

"We have certain facts by working outward from them. They, in turn, lead to other apparent facts, and so the snowball grows. But in simpler terms, Bern is the closest large city with a German embassy. It is second only to Zurich with regard to agents working there. I shall send a wire in cipher to Mr. Holmes asking for reinforcements to meet us at Bern."

CHAPTER EIGHT

▼

RENDEZVOUS IN BERN

The Italo-Swiss Espress looked as its name suggested with a cargo of travelling Italians on board. It left Milan early in the morning and rumbled through the day with only three stops on its way to reach Martigny. We caught it at Aosta, where Major Saunders wired for reinforcements.

The nightmare of last night shall be forever etched in my memory. Our descent from the Alpine hut had been infinitely more arduous than our climb to it. The few hours of fitful sleep at the Rinderhorn Lodge still left me feeling exhausted, but the weakness I had experienced from the high altitude was subsiding.

With the Great St. Bernard Pass behind us and the Pennine Alps receding, we steadily descended to the Rhone valley.

The compartment door opened. Major Saunders came in and sat across from me.

"Well, Doctor, I must say you look much better."

"Anything would be better than last night," I remonstrated. "But I was thinking before you came in; all these bizarre events we have been experiencing must be the work of the Mannings. My God, the cunning devils saw through me completely—it's incredible!"

"The fact that you were followed after leaving Lauterbrunnen suggests some development took place which confirmed your true identity. I really don't like it Doctor, but I must confess I haven't the vaguest idea what it all means. If we can lay our hands on Ernst Gunther, we shall learn the truth."

We fell silent as the train continued its downward course. Far down in the valley rain clouds were sweeping along the course of the Rhone River. By one o'clock we were in the valley racing beside the river, as the rain lashed against the windows. Again I felt I was not dressed for this contingency. My suitcase was still at the Albert Hotel in Chamonix.

Lord Byron and Percy Shelly came to mind as we quickly sped past the Chateau of Chillon on the east side of the lake. Shortly thereafter we arrived in Montreux. Major Saunders promptly hurried us off to the ferry landing where we embarked for Lausanne.

The afternoon was stormy but the rain-laden wind blew in our direction.

"We should make good time, Doctor. The train makes three stops before arriving at Lausanne, whereas we have a nonstop run."

"It will be a miracle if we can intercept Gunther," I said rather doubtfully, as the little steamer plodded sturdily through the choppy waters of the lake. We passed the tedious time in silence on the deck while the afternoon grew darker.

We arrived in Lausanne precisely at five o'clock. Our inquiries informed us the express for Bern would leave at six and arrive one hour later, leaving us just enough time for a quick repast in the station restaurant. Major Saunders insisted I board the train early while he waited inside the station for the incoming connection from Montreux. It was a moment of truth: Either Ernst Gunther would arrive on the five forty-five or he was ahead of us on an earlier train.

A short time later the major came into our compartment smiling. "You could hardly mistake that waxed moustache and attaché case."

"Thank God," I breathed.

"With our reinforcements, we will have that culprit in handcuffs by seven o'clock." The major had the air of a chess master who has just stated "Check and mate."

"You have my most profound congratulations," I said with enthusiasm. "I frankly considered it a hopeless situation. Your calm logic has been superb." My words had a soothing effect on my companion and we both relaxed for the first time in forty-eight hours. We drew the shades and napped during the uneventful hour's trip to Bern.

Shortly after seven o'clock we perceived Gunther moving across the far side of the Bahnhoff toward an exit.

"I don't see our agents," said the major in a concerned voice.

"I'll keep Gunther in sight while you locate your men."

"It's risky business, Doctor. If he identifies you, all will be lost."

"I shall be careful," I replied. "Come to the exit as soon as possible. If Gunther takes a taxi, I'll take the number and we can trace his destination."

The major left me as I watched Gunther go through the exit. I quickly moved in that direction and carefully stepped out onto the street. there was no sign of him. In a state of nervous excitement, I looked left and right. Further down the street, a hundred yards or so from the station was a tall, rather grim eighteenth century building that looked somewhat official. There was a small courtyard in front of it with tall, wrought iron railings. I caught sight of Gunther's short figure holding his attaché case tightly. He was in animated conversation with a much taller man who somehow seemed vaguely familiar.

The major came to my side. "I can't understand it," he cried. "Our agents are nowhere in sight. We have no alternative but to follow Gunther ourselves, reinforcements or not."

"He is down the street in that courtyard," I replied.

At that moment, the two men came out into the street and entered a taxi. We hailed a taxi and followed at a discrete distance.

"I never have been in Bern before," I said.

"Fortunately I have," answered the major. "Their taxi is heading east toward the old quarter of the city. We are approaching the Kirchenfeld Bridge. If they cross, we could have a long drive to some outlying area."

"No," I said, "look. Their taxi is turning left."

"They're going toward the bottom of the hill of St. Vincent's Cathedral," remarked the major anxiously.

We were now steadily going down hill, running parallel with the Aare River. The buildings were ancient riverside structures with wet, red tiled roofs.

"You know, Doctor, if nothing else, Gunther's meeting with that individual substantiates my deduction of a rendezvous."

"Yes, but without reinforcements it could prove difficult to apprehend Gunther, especially if the second man is armed."

"Time enough to worry about that when we know their destination."

A short time later the taxi we were following pulled up to a large building. We were about two hundred yards behind and instructed our driver to stop. Night was approaching, but there still was enough light to see the building down the street, wet with rain, foreboding and distinctly ominous. My impression was that it was nigh impossible to force an entry.

The two men had dismissed their taxi and entered the building. Again I had the nagging feeling of familiarity with the taller man, but at that distance it was impossible to identify him.

"How shall we get in?" I asked.

"Look, Doctor, this is not your responsibility. Of course I realize your concern, but this is a job for a professional."

I protested in vain. Nothing I could say would change his mind; he remained adamant.

"If I do not return within one half hour, you must seek help from our embassy. Is that clear, Doctor?" I acquiesced reluctantly.

We stepped out into the rain and dismissed our taxi. "I should imagine you would be less conspicuous if you stood in that doorway across the street. Remember, one half hour, Doctor."

I checked my watch as the major disappeared down an alleyway. I noticed the grey walls of the building where the two men had entered. It looked almost like an institution with forbidding black blinds drawn. Two immense zinc gutters, one on either side of the roof, were gushing water. The decorative imbrications of tiled roofs seemed incongruous against the storm-racked sky, somber and disquieting.

The other side of the street was a sea of terraced roofs. Some had cupolas shaped like beehives. Down the street I could see scattered lights of houses, and the clock tower of St. Vincent's tolling the quarter hour came faintly to my ears. there was no other sound but the rain falling on the tiled roofs. The minutes wore on as if each were an hour. It was a melancholy vigil.

Was Ernst Gunther handing the map to someone at this very moment? God forbid, we had endured too much. The major must succeed.

I checked my watch. There were still five minutes left. Here again was a dilemma. I did not want to go against the major's instructions, but on the other hand, I had a strong feeling he needed assistance. I resolved then and there if he did not return, I should go in after him. It possibly could be too late for Embassy help. At any rate, I was not going to chance it.

The half hour was up. There was no sign of the major. I quickly moved down the side alley he had taken. Judging the distance to be about right, I came to the back of a building that appeared to be the same as I had observed from the street. I entered the yard quietly and approached the back of the house. There were cellar window wells and I clearly saw one had been broken recently. I lowered myself carefully down into the well and crawled through the window.

It was pitch dark. I had no alternative but to strike a match and look for a stairway. In the flickering light I saw a stairway to my immediate left. With the light out, I slowly felt my way over and ascended to the top where there was a thin line of light from under the door. I listened carefully for a minute or so before opening the door an inch. Through the crack I could see a well-lit passageway floored with colored tiles. I cautiously went through the door and made my way down the hall. At the far end, another door confronted me. Again I listened, then slowly turned the handle and opened it just enough to look in.

It was a large empty sitting room decorated in a Gothic style with stag horns adorning the walls. A side door across the room was slightly ajar. I could hear a man's muffled voice speaking. I crept over to the door and listened intently.

In a voice of unabashed crassness the speaker bragged how he tricked the great man, how he knew he would come.

"You who think yourself so clever and so great. All your efforts have been in vain. You have failed, just like your stupid agent lying on the floor. You shall die for all your infernal interferences."

"I really think a dead body on your premises could prove rather embarrassing." Great Scott, that was Holmes speaking!

"Never fear, the Aare River shall be a convenient disposal for your body."

"Which, I presume, would not be the first."

"Enough of this idle chatter. It is time to say farewell, Mr. Sherlock Holmes. Revenge is truly sweet, as the saying goes. Are you ready Ernst?"

I quickly pushed the door open and took in the situation at a glance. Ernst Gunther was to the left, holding a strange looking weapon on Holmes. His antenna-like moustache was quivering with lust for the kill. Major Saunders lay on the floor next to the desk. The man who was speaking had his back to me. He was short and squat. His fat, hairless head sat on a slug-like neck, which was wet with perspiration.

I leveled the Luger pistol and took aim directly at Gunther's right temple. Momentarily I saw D'Eslon's face before me. I quickly pulled the trigger. Gunther slumped forward and sank to the floor. The weapon in his hand fired by a nervous jerk of his finger, shattering the plaster on the wall across the study.

At the same instant Holmes sprang at the short, squat man. I rushed forward and struck the bald head with the butt of my gun. He went down at once.

"Holmes, is the major dead?" I cried.

"No, just unconscious"

"Thank God!"

Gunther's body had fallen next to the desk. Blood was spreading over the carpet. His antenna-like moustache was very still.

"What shall we do with him, Holmes?"

"We have no alternative but to leave him here."

Major Saunders was coming around. Holmes poured some cognac from a decanter on the desk and handed it to me. "Here, drink this, Major." He took the glass from, me a little dazed, but recovered enough to say, "Well, Doctor, we certainly reversed the situation of Chamonix."

"Quite so," I answered, smiling.

"I'm also grateful you do not follow instructions."

Holmes came around from the side of the desk and grasped my shoulder in a spontaneous gesture of affection. "In this instance, I, too, am glad you did not follow instructions. Major, do you think you could manage to take this man to our embassy when you're fully recovered?"

"One more drink and I shall be as recovered as I shall ever be."

"Capital. Guard him well. He has caused enough trouble over the years. Take him to Ambassador Pearson. He will know what to do with him."

There was a stirring on the floor from where the short squat man lay. Major Saunders quietly slipped a pair of handcuffs onto him. As he awoke and took in the situation, he lashed out with German invectives.

"*Was ist los? Donner wetter! Ich Krige sie noch. Schweinehundt!*"

"That will do," said Holmes sternly. "You may take him away, Major."

At the doorway the prisoner turned and spoke in a biting tone of scorn. "You think you have won. I tell you, you have not. You will be dead before ever you leave Europe!"

"I have heard all that many times before and yet I am still here. Carry on, Major."

As they left the room, I remembered the map. "Holmes, the map!" I cried. "He may have it!"

"Tut, tut, Watson, have no fear. The map is right here in my pocket. I felt a wave of relief, when suddenly my eyes fell upon the curious snake-skin attaché case lying open on the desk. "Yes, Watson, the case contains a small shoulder stock and telescopic sight attachment, part of the ingenious equipment of Gunther's Mauser automatic pistol. With it he could kill at close range or at a far distance. Conveniently packaged with its small case, it could be easily transported. This man is a well-known and highly paid assassin in the employ of the Kaiser's special services. If I had not come here, he surely would have come to me with this equipment."

"But why did you come here? I was astounded when I heard your voice from behind the door. Why did you fail to send reinforcements as Major Saunders requested?"

"In answer to the latter question, its really quite elementary, since I never received the request. But I did receive this."

Holmes handed me a note: "We have your blundering friend Dr. Watson. If you wish to see him alive, take the seven o'clock express to Bern. You will be met in the Administrative building across the station."

"Good Lord," I cried. "That must have been from that wretched Von Strada woman."

Holmes had filled two more glasses of cognac and handed one to me. He sat down in a large chair next to the desk, lit a cigarette and watched the smoke curl up into the air. Looking up at me he said, "Watson, I owe my life to you."

"Not at all," said I. "You risked your own life coming here on my behalf."

Holmes reflected a moment. "Not after first endangering your own. Of course I realized it was a trap, but I believed they held you hostage. I came hoping to negotiate your release. When they laughed and told me you were dead...well, I must confess, old chap, I was prepared to go down, providing I could take them with me." Holmes had taken an object from his pocket, which appeared to be a cigar. "Yes, it is a bomb. It's an interesting device that more than likely could take this building down. If you had not appeared when you did—well, at any rate, I had considered my career was at an end."

Great Scott, what a near thing the whole affair had been, I reflected, and sat down weakly.

"Soon after you left on your mission, I had regrets about sending you."

"Why was that?"

"I had returned to Berlin and found, inexplicably, so and so was unavailable, or the highly noticeable fact that some officials simply refused to speak to me altogether. I was summoned to Koeniggratzer Strasse. Von Reichter questioned me closely with regard to my trips to the north coast. It was not hard to see that his attitude was definitely hostile. In any case, I sensed these incidents aroused his mistrust of me and I had the distinct impression of the danger I had placed you in, not withstanding my own. I quickly slipped out of Berlin, knowing full well they would be on my trail. By the way, have you any idea whose villa and cognac this is?"

"I haven't the slightest," I answered.

"Herr Oberstein lives here when he is in Bern, although I am afraid he will not be requiring the facilities any longer."

"Not Oberstein of the 'Bruce Partington' case?" I said incredulously.

"You may recall earlier I mentioned a name I observed in the door attendant's book at Koeniggratzer Strasse which, in all probability, would terminate my work in Germany."

"Yes, I recall."

"That name was Herr Oswald Oberstein. In the German spy hierarchy I found he was better known as simply the 'Double O.' Whenever he first recognized my presence in Germany he began to orchestrate my complete destruction, first by informing Frederica Von Strada, whose intuition immediately focused on you as Dr. Watson and not as Mr. Waterford."

"But Oberstein went to jail years ago," I protested.

"That is correct, but through a great deal of cunning on the part of the German government, he was exchanged for one of our own agents. Oberstein simply was too valuable to be allowed to languish in a British prison."

"What will happen to him now?"

"Oh, I imagine he will be taken to the Swiss border and shot. By the way, how did you enter this building?"

"Through a cellar window well." I answered.

"We shall leave the same way and go to my apartment—rather, I should say, the bookseller, Herr Brandt's apartment. a circumspect route is advisable under the circumstances. It will not take the German Secret Service very long to be cognizant of the demise of two of their top agents. From here on, we must take every precaution."

CHAPTER NINE

▼

G. S. S. REVENGE

We crawled out of the cellar window. The rain had ceased and was now a dismal mugginess. Holmes led the way as we moved down small alleys into smaller lanes and finally stopped in front of an ancient building with three floors. The River Aare was immediately to the rear.

I followed and climbed the steps to the third floor where Holmes unlocked a massive door. I was surprised to enter a very modern apartment that was incongruous with the building's outside appearance.

"All the comforts of home," exclaimed Holmes. "This has been my headquarters for coordinating and relaying all major information back to Whitehall."

As I sat down, Holmes was already setting up a small portable wireless that had been secreted in a false panel of the sideboard. He ran a long wire from the set, which he attached to a lightning rod outside on the window ledge.

"You realized, of course, the logistics to move men and machines are of immense proportions. One's information must be extremely accurate or untold lives are jeopardized. Our past intelligence work revealed that three, possibly four locations could be the center of U boat manufacture. According to D'Eslon's map, Kiel is our target. There is, of course, no way to substantiate that fact. We must take a calculated risk. It is the last card we can play in the game."

Having readied all his equipment, Holmes turned and faced me. His expression took on a concerned look. "My dear fellow, you look positively done in. Please forgive my neglecting your comforts. I would suggest a hot bath while I contact Whitehall."

Whitehall, I thought to myself; the heart of London. It seemed like a million miles away at the moment. "I am in need of comforts," I answered wearily.

"You will find a change of clothing in the wardrobe…brandy and cigars in the cupboard."

As I soaked in the hot tub, I heard the clicking of the wireless key relaying the vital information.

Having found great relief from my bath and a change of clothing, I returned to the sitting room.

"We are to leave here tomorrow morning at six from the Bahnhoff. We are instructed to return to England," said he, as I sat down with a glass of brandy in one hand and a cigar in the other.

"I shall be glad to leave," I replied. "I have just informed Whitehall regarding Kiel—the Royal Navy will strike within the next few hours. They will accomplish their task by sinking ships at the western entrance of the Kiel Canal, which will severely hamper their U-boat operations.

"Incidentally, Major Saunders is to accompany us on our journey, a journey that would not have been possible without your complete loyalty and bravery. Again, I am compelled to say I am truly indebted to you, Watson."

"Holmes, I must tell you in all honesty, the greater part of your escape from Oberstein was due to Major Saunders. Without his superb grip on the situation, we never would have arrived in Bern in time."

"I have already taken that fact into consideration and will report his valor to his superiors. I am sure a promotion will be in order."

"He really is an excellent chap," I remarked. "Thinks the world of you—considers his career successful due to studying your methods over the years."

"Studying my methods, you say? Yes, yes, a bright fellow indeed. Now, Watson, tell me everything that has taken place since we last spoke in Zurich."

I related my misadventure quickly, but deliberated at length on my encounter with Professor D'Eslon and his regrettable fate at the hands of Ernst Gunther. Holmes' brow deepened as I retold the horror I experienced with regard to D'Eslon's murder.

"I knew him primarily on a professional level and on occasion had consulted with him on psychic matters. He seemed a basically solid, rather decent sort of chap," said Holmes thoughtfully.

"I was," said I, "a complete skeptic in these matters of the psychic until I met him. In that short period of time he gained my respect, and what I experienced with him was truly awesome. It will take me some time to grasp the implications. I still cannot fathom how I was followed to Lauterbrunnen."

"That is to be expected when the Germans become highly suspicious."

"But I saw no one, and I was on guard ever since my experience with the Mannings."

"Well, it is just another example of German thoroughness. They were not convinced you were just an innocent traveler. Therefore they kept you under observation. When Oberstein alerted Koeniggratzer Strasse of my true identity, Von Strada immediately put our association in proper perspective. Her intuition is keen. She firmly did not believe your story and put Ernst Gunther on your trail. I have to admit, it was all cleverly done."

"That wretched woman," I said bitterly. "She could even look beautiful in her absurd knee breeches."

"Beautiful, but deadly," reflected Holmes.

"I was thinking, Holmes, since you have survived their attempt to stop you, is it not possible to carry on in some other capacity, especially with all your knowledge of the German high command?"

"When that note arrived, speaking of your confinement, I realized the game was up. My usefulness as a field agent was over. I was trapped in an untenable position."

"But who could take your place?"

"Whitehall is sending a Captain Sidney Reilly to take up the reins."

"I have never heard the name. Who on earth is he?"

"As I understand it, he has had a remarkable success in the Russo-Japanese conflict, and from all accounts, he is hampered by no scruples—totally disinterested in the war except for the making of large sums of money which makes him, as I understand, utterly ruthless. If all this is true, he should give the Germans a good run for their money."

"Well, let us hope so," I reflected. "In any event, it is all quite out of our hands now, and I must confess I am looking forward to my return to the South Downs."

It was very early the following morning when Holmes awoke me. Standing at the side of my bed I could see he was in a state of nervous excitement.

"Watson, I have just heard from Whitehall. We have scored a bull's-eye at the Kiel Canal entrance."

I sat up, wide-awake. "Then D'Eslon was correct?"

"Yes, yes. The blockade of England shall soon end, and our sea lanes will be free of the U boat menace."

"That is wonderful news," I said elatedly.

"Yes Watson, but now you must put these clothes on quickly. Tie this pillow around your waist."

"Holmes, what in the world? This is a priest's robe!"

"Yes, yes, but you must hurry. We have a good distance to go. I have tea and biscuits waiting."

After dressing I entered the sitting room feeling absolutely ridiculous.

"Ah, there you are. You make an admirable Friar Tuck," chuckled Holmes. "Here, use this black dye on your moustache, my dear fellow—it will make you look ten years younger."

"My God!" I exclaimed. "Is all this necessary? I feel like a participant in a Guy Fawkes celebration."

In answer to my protests he simply said, "Nothing more than simple precautions. But never mind, drink your tea and eat your biscuits."

Holmes retired to his dressing room and returned shortly as Herr Brandt the bookseller. "Now Watson, this is our plan of action: We shall walk together to the top of the hill to the cathedral. I will leave you at the cathedral and you will make your way to the Bahnhoff. Here is a first class ticket for the seven o'clock express to Geneva. Our compartment is in the forward section. At the entrance of the Bahnhoff, take the shortest route you can find to this section. Is all that clear?"

"Yes, but where will you be?"

"I shall meet you in the compartment. Speak to no one and under no circumstances speak to me until the train is well out of the station."

With our preparations finished we left the apartment. Outside the air was clear with the promise of a bright sunny day. The Aare River was already shimmering in the early light.

I followed Holmes closely as we wound our way from street to street up the hill. Always looming ahead of us was the imposing structure of St. Vincent. Flowers were everywhere along the streets, even in flower boxes attached to the lampposts.

After some time we approached the cathedral from the rear on a street lined with ancient sycamore trees. At the end of the street Holmes followed an extremely old and crenulated wall to a gate that led us into the Cloisters with antiquated tombs on either side of the walk, then through a garden to a massive carved door that led directly into the rear narthex of St. Vincent's.

Inside Holmes turned to me, "As you can hear, the morning mass is in progress. As soon as it is finished, go through this door to our left and join the people and follow them out through the front of the cathedral. Stay with them until you reach the main thoroughfare. Then take a taxi to the Bahnhoff."

I followed Holmes' instructions to the letter, feeling very self-conscious as I moved along with the crowd. I felt a wave of relief as I hailed and entered a taxi.

A clumsy dullard collided into me at the entrance to the Bahnhoff, almost toppling me to the ground.

"Confound your stu—!" I stopped short, remembering I was supposed to be a priest.

"A thousand pardons, Father. I did not see you.

Standing and blocking my way was an apparition that looked something of a beggar and somewhat a wandering minstrel. He must have been a gypsy. His oily curling hair fell over his shoulders. He was carrying a very large bag. "Begging your pardon, Father, could you direct me to the Geneva Express?"

"That is the Geneva Express," I said quickly. "Please let me pass." Holmes injunction to speak to no one was already broken.

"But of course. Please forgive me, Father."

I moved quickly by this creature and went toward the forward section of the train. My God, that man was following right behind me. Thoughts of the German Secret Service gripped my heart. I must be on my guard. The sooner I get to my compartment, the better.

I had no sooner sat down when the compartment door opened and standing there, looking about, was the gypsy.

"Here, my good man, you cannot sit in this compartment."

"Why not, Father? I have a ticket just as you do."

I rechecked my ticket. Compartment #5 was clearly marked on it. "Does your ticket indicate Compartment #5?" I asked, highly annoyed.

"That's right, Father."

My God, I thought, must I travel all the way to Geneva with this person? He put his large bag on the floor near the window and sat down heavily. I saw no alternative but to tolerate this seemingly noxious person until Holmes arrived.

To my utter revolt, he began laying his breakfast out on the seat. The smell of sausage with garlic and olive oil soon permeated the compartment.

"Look," I said testily, "this is not the dining car. You cannot eat in here."

His greasy face turned to me and he spoke with a dialect that sounded Hungarian. "But who can afford the dining car, Father? You would not deny me, would you? One must eat—one must keep up one's strength—is that not so, Father?"

I gave up in disgust. Where was Holmes? The train gave a lurch and began to move.

The compartment door opened. Holmes, as Herr Brandt, stepped in. I silently thanked God he had arrived and resolved to speak to him in private and tell him of my suspicions.

Holmes came forward, but did not return my gaze. Rather, he stooped over the other passenger, and spoke in a thin, wistful voice. "Ah, how wonderful that sausage smells.

The decrepit man looked up as if only at this instant was aware of another person in the compartment. "Here, try some."

"Oh, thank you sir. How kind you are."

What in the world is going on, I wondered angrily.

Pushing the sausage toward me and smiling broadly, the greasy man said, "And what about you, Dr. Watson? Would you like a piece of my sausage?"

Great Scott! That voice! I staggered at its familiarity. "Is that really you, Major Saunders?"

Pulling off his curly locked wig, he answered with a laugh, "Yes, it is I."

"Well, of all the…"

Holmes broke out laughing. Spontaneously, all three of us laughed uncontrollably.

"I just could not resist," said the Major, still laughing.

"My word, you certainly had me fooled. For a moment I thought you were from the German Secret Service. The stage has lost a great performer," I chuckled.

Holmes removed his grey beard. "I must also compliment you, Major. Your disguise was superb."

"Thank you, Mr. Holmes. As I have told Dr. Watson, I owe it all to you. Your methods are masterful."

"Yes, yes. So the good doctor has relayed to me. Beside all that, I am delighted to see you again. Your backup work has been invaluable. Do you have our change of clothing in that bag?"

"Yes, sir."

"Then I suggest we all make ourselves more comfortable."

Some thirty minutes or so later, we were all sitting comfortably, smoking cigars.

Holmes was speaking, "Earlier, my dear Watson, you were somewhat upset with your disguise as a priest. However, I am quite certain you now can see its importance. We have all boarded this train and the G.S.S. has no knowledge of that fact."

"How can you be sure?" I asked, remembering Ernst Gunther.

"Because I arrived ahead of you and watched the station carefully. I was not disappointed. Hans Bender from German Intelligence was observing every passenger at the entrance gate. German agents are required to immediately report by telegraph any foreign agents they may encounter, and, if possible, to follow them. Hans Bender did neither of these things. From that fact, we can assume Ernst Gunther's body has not yet been discovered, which gives us a slight advantage for the time being. We cannot, however, allow ourselves to be lulled into any sense of false security—we have stirred up a gigantic hornets' nest."

"What hornets' nest?" asked an inquisitive Major Saunders.

Holmes related the news of the morning: the complete blockade of the Kiel Canal and ultimate cessation of the U-boat menace. "This, coupled with the arrival of the Americans, hopefully in the next few months, may well be the turning point of the war—totally in our favor."

From what I have seen of this war," said I, "which is comparatively little, the turning point cannot be soon enough. It seems impossible to understand this carnage. It seems to vary in barbaric degree."

The major had grown reflective after hearing the news of the canal. Finally he said, "I presume this blockade had something to do with Professor D'Eslon?"

I looked at Holmes. "Go ahead, Watson. Tell the major."

"Indeed it did," and I proceeded to relate my experience with the professor in Chamonix.

When I had finished, the major, who had listened intently, remarked, "You mean to say this man using a pendulum over a map determined that information?"

"Exactly," I retorted.

"I have never heard of such a thing."

"Yes, of course it sounds like so much witless blather and I haven't the faintest idea why or how this should be so, but I saw it with my own eyes and it does occur. It is therefore far more than absurd theory."

There was a low chortle from Holmes. "Is this really my pragmatic Watson speaking?"

"I make no attempt to draw a conclusion, but the fact remains, Professor D'Eslon did pinpoint the target from a map."

"The entire matter strikes me as inexplicable," said the major.

"On the contrary, from my experiences in Tibet, the workings of the infinite really defy all logic as we know it. I am also sure you know the line between vision and illusion is thin, extremely thin. All that Dr. Watson has reported is not just another darkened parlour room trick that has been so rampant earlier this century. No, Major, it cuts deeper, much deeper."

"Well, Mr. Holmes, at the moment the subject strikes me as bordering on the outré. All things considered, the total evidence is persuasive, though by no means conclusive."

"Perhaps, Major, perhaps."

We had been moving across the landscape at a rapid rate. The Jura Mountains were visible in the far distance. Our arrival in Geneva would be within the hour. Holmes had remained silent for some time as Major Saunders and I continued the conversation.

"You know, Major, I have not had the opportunity to ask you exactly what happened in Bern."

"I don't mind telling you, Doctor, I was completely taken by surprise. As you know, it was necessary to break that window to gain access. I muffled the sound with my coat wrapped around a rock from the garden, but apparently I was heard. I made my way to the first floor passageway and looked down the muzzle of Ernst Gunther's automatic. He marched me into the study where he struck me from behind."

"At least," said I, "you certainly will have something to tell your grandchildren some day—that is, if you married that young woman. Hmm, let me see—Miss Montgomery, was it not?"

"Correct, Doctor, and if it were not for you, I would not be anticipating our thirty third wedding anniversary."

"Thirty third anniversary! My word! It seems like yesterday when we met on Salisbury Plain," I said, somewhat wistfully.

"Just a sign of growing older, my dear Watson," smiled Holmes whimsically.

Our conversation came back to the war.

"You spoke earlier of a turning point, Mr. Holmes. From your experience, can you shed any light when the hostilities will cease?"

"If it is as it seems on the face of it, we possibly could see the last great battle taking place this year. Then hopefully the end would come shortly thereafter. On the other hand, no one completely understands the dogmatic perseverance of the German Army."

"Then, I take it, you really cannot say with any exactitude when the end shall come."

"I am afraid not, Major. When one considers a nation like Germany, which chooses leaders who are beset with uncontrollable tendencies to bear arms, we can easily see the results."

"Are you referring to the political ramifications?"

"No, I am thinking of the ancient Chinese practice of foot binding."

"Foot binding, Mr. Holmes!"

"Yes, Major, a grotesque distortion of natural growth."

CHAPTER TEN

▼

DELAYED EXIT

It happened as we approached the environs of Geneva. Our train had slowed down considerably as we neared a large bridge, then suddenly it halted altogether.

"This is highly unusual," I exclaimed.

There was a shattering of window glass. "Get down, get down!' cried Holmes, his voice rising and his face a mask of pain and revulsion.

"Holmes, what is it?" I cried as we all slid to the compartment floor.

There was a trickling of blood on his right temple as I moved next to him. A nasty looking wound, but I thankfully noticed it was just a grazing as I examined him closely.

"It's a nasty cut, but another inch or so could have been fatal. That broken glass must have struck you."

"We are moving again. Are you all right, Mr. Holmes?"

"Yes, Major, but they have employed the use of an air gun," said Holmes acidly.

"Air gun," I repeated.

"Yes, yes, Watson, not the crude air gun of Von Herder, employed by the late Colonel Sebastian Moran. No, this is a highly sophisticated air rifle with telescopic sight and a velocity approaching a modern rifle. I have been aware of the existence of these arms since the assassination of Ambassador Henderson."

Once we had arrived in the station Holmes recovered his composure.

"Holmes, that wound will need some attention."

"No time, Watson. If one may judge by this incident, I fear we shall have to alter our plans drastically."

"This was not a precipitated journey. How did these cunning devils trace us?" asked a perplexed Major Saunders

"They have an infinite capacity for painstaking detail. The fact that this train has been halted (more than likely a misdirected signal) suggests a confederate. The fact that the assassin knew exactly which compartment I was in also suggests a whole contingency of information has been relayed. But above all, the fact that I could have been easily murdered just now suggests only one man who operates in such a fashion, Baron Von Oswald Bodenheim of the G.S.S. His trademark is a cat and mouse game with his intended prey—it is a subtle process of wearing down the nerves until, invariably, one's guard comes down and the victim is swept into the very vortex of terror. Then the fatal mistake is made, which results in extermination. It is a well-known fact that fear of death is a distressing blend of instinctual memory and anticipatory imagination. Von Bodenheim capitalizes on this premise extremely well."

"You horrify me!" I cried.

"Oh, incidentally, Von Bodenheim works directly for Von Strada, as did the late Ernst Gunther."

"That abominable woman again," said I bitterly. "What are we to do, Holmes?"

"To begin with, it is advisable to bear in mind that Von Bodenheim is a lone assassin. In this instance, however, we know he has an assistant, but I can assure you, he will have no knowledge of Von Bodenheim's plans. It is that fact which I plan to put to our advantage. In the meantime, we all must return to our disguises and spend some time in Geneva."

Inwardly I groaned at the prospect of donning my priestly robes again. Holmes, catching my look of discomfiture, wryly said, "Contingencies, my dear Watson, contingencies."

Upon leaving the Gare De Cornavin Station, once again in our disguises, Holmes instructed Major Saunders and myself to take rooms at the Dumont Blanc Hotel. He in turn would reside at the Hotel Beau-Rivage and contact us by telephone. I felt a sense of foreboding at the prospect of separating, but Holmes was insistent on our following his every injunction.

"Under no circumstances try to communicate with me. Believe me, Watson, when I tell you it is of capital importance this measure be taken. I shall make everything clear later. In the interim I want you to take a daily walk to the Cathedral St. Pierre and also visit the nearby museums.

"Major Saunders, you are to follow Dr. Watson and observe if he is being followed. Take every precaution not to be observed yourself."

"But what of yourself?" I asked, alarmed.

"There is a rule for safe guidance which is well to remember. It is the basic principal of reversing the disposition of the prey to that of the hunter. It calls for a play of the intuition coupled with a mental capacity to out-think your opponent."

"But Holmes, that sounds suicidal under these circumstances."

"On the contrary, in this situation I wish to be observed and watched closely, and this I must do alone."

I began to protest but he admonished me, saying, "No Watson, we must keep open minds and evaluate probabilities and hypotheses on the basis of their possible validity, and not on other more emotional considerations. Have no fear, I shall be safe enough until the critical moment and then I assure you, you will be at my side."

He would say no more and left the Major and I in complete ignorance as to his plans. The years had not deprived Holmes of his enigmatic desire to dramatize his results until the very last moment.

Major Saunders and I carried out Holmes' instructions for the next two days without anyone observing our movements. Holmes contacted us each evening and seemed relieved with our negative reports except for the curious incident that both the major and I received telegrams announcing the arrival of family members. We both felt this was simply a case of mistaken identity.

In the late spring Geneva is a very beautiful city, but I felt extremely preoccupied with our situation and excessively conscious of my priestly robes. I took my daily walks as per instructions but by the end of the third day, the Major and I were becoming more concerned with this delay to continue our journey back to England.

The following day I left the hotel shortly after one o'clock. The streets were wet and shining from a soft rain that had commenced earlier that morning. I took my same walk and crossed the Pont Dumont Blanc Bridge, where a hazy mist was rising from the Rhone River. Shortly thereafter I entered St. Pierre's Cathedral and observed the medieval stained glass, whose radiant brilliance was severely impeded by today's rain and overcast skies.

As a consequence, I did not stay very long. Leaving by a side narthex door, I distinctly heard another door open as I stepped out into the enjoining cathedral garden. I thought no more of the incident as I passed the reformation monument on my way to the art and history museum.

The museum was very large and housed one of Europe's finest collections of medieval armour. I spent the better part of the afternoon engrossed in the study of engraved breastplates by the Spanish masters of Toledo. The past two afternoons were spent in the German and French schools of armour making.

As I moved from one glass case to another, I caught the reflection of a person at the far end of the room. The museum was comparatively empty as most people were drawn to the historical paintings on the second floor.

I moved to the next room and again caught the same reflection in another glass case. An alarming thought crossed my mind: Was I being followed? I determined to put the situation to a test. I walked quickly toward the rear of the building, which had an exit to the street. I opened the door and closed it loudly without stepping outside. I then quickly moved to a small gallery on the left and secreted myself behind a large exhibit case. I carefully watched the exit. A moment or so later a dark clad figure rushed to the exit and left the building. I in turn moved to the front entrance and left the building to hail a taxi.

So it was true, the G.S.S. was aware of our presence. I had the taxi stop several blocks from our hotel. I entered a doorway and watched the street for several minutes before stepping forward to walk in a circumspect route back to our hotel. Uppermost in my mind was to inform Holmes of this development later in the evening when he telephoned.

Several minutes after I entered our hotel, Major Saunders knocked at my door. As he entered I could clearly see he was in a state of considerable excitement.

"You were followed today, Doctor."

"I know," I replied, "but I shook them off at the museum."

"Not so. I watched a man pursue you in a taxi and of course I followed that taxi."

"But I did not come to the hotel directly. I walked the remaining three blocks and saw no one."

"He was a good distance behind you and carefully recorded some information into a notebook as you entered the hotel; more than likely, the hotel address."

"Those clever devils! I shall be glad to leave this place," I said bitterly.

At precisely seven that evening Holmes telephoned. I related our new development. This information seemed to galvanize him into instant action.

"Watson, you and the major come to the Cafe Le Goulet at nine. I will join you there. Leave your hotel by the back entrance and come in civilian clothes. Leave everything else, but bring your firearms."

"Will we leave Geneva tonight?" I inquired.

"If all goes well, yes. Make sure you are not followed and by all means be no later than nine o'clock."

Today's light rain had continued into the evening hours and as the major and I stepped out into the back hotel courtyard we were blanketed by shimmering droplets. We walked rapidly through the damp night to a side street and took a succession of back ways to the main thoroughfare. The major was constantly directing me into doorways as he took the utmost pains to insure that we were not being followed. Apparently satisfied, he hailed a taxi.

A short time later we arrived at the cafe. We descended a staircase to the brightly lit cafe below. The major stopped me from entering.

"Let us wait a bit and see if any one comes after us."

I heard music and loud talking from within. No one came and we entered the cafe. We looked about us somewhat blinded by the bright light. To the immediate right was a bar crowded with patrons. To the rear was large room filled with people sitting at tables, smoking and drinking. I looked for Holmes either as himself or Herr Brandt.

"I don't see him, Major. I hope nothing has gone wrong."

"I suppose all we can do is sit down at that table near the door and wait," replied the major.

We had been waiting some ten minutes or so when suddenly a stooped, shabbily dressed man came forward from the bar. I was startled when he addressed us.

"Gentlemen, Mr. Holmes is waiting for you in the next room."

Incredulously I looked at this person with swollen jowls, bushy eyebrows and flared nostrils. In a soft, raspy voice that I could barely hear over the noise of the barroom, he motioned us forward.

"This way, gentlemen, if you will be so kind."

The major and I exchanged glances, then rose and followed this apparition.

We moved through the crowded room behind the bar and entered a small room at the rear. A table with three glasses and a bottle of Calvados were the only occupants in the empty room. As I closed the door behind me I demanded to know where Mr. Holmes was.

"Why, my dear Watson, I am right here." With a deft movement this obnoxious individual straightened up, removed one ring from each nostril, pulled off his bushy eyebrows, and took from his mouth two clumps of rolled cotton.

"Rather difficult to speak with these in one's mouth," said Holmes, smiling.

"Holmes, is there no end to your tricks?" said I, testily.

"It was no trick, Watson, but rather a vital necessity if we are to succeed tonight."

"But why let us wait when you were right here?"

"Elementary. I simply had to ascertain whether you gentlemen had been followed tonight. I had an excellent vantage point from the bar to observe if anyone was especially interested in you."

"I took every precaution against such a possibility, Mr. Holmes."

"And you did well, Major, for if you had been followed, three days' work would have been to no avail."

"I certainly would have never known you tonight. Your disguise was masterly, Mr. Holmes."

"Thank you, Major. A flared nostril, a bushy eyebrow can change one's appearance immensely. I shall write a monograph on the subject, hopefully in the near future."

"But Holmes, if we are to leave Geneva, what are we doing here?"

"Yes, Mr. Holmes, can you not tell us what your plans are?"

"Dr. Watson here can tell you I am generally reticent about such things. All will be clear in good time, but first let us partake in a toast to assure our success tonight."

We all sat down at the table. Holmes poured a small amount of Calvados into each glass and handed one to the major and I. He raised his glass.

"For King and country."

The major and I repeated the toast. This libation was formidable indeed. I felt the penetrating effect immediately.

"I can tell you this much, gentlemen. With a bit of luck we shall dispatch Von Bodenheim to the French border and leave Geneva tonight. We have some time before we leave. I suggest we partake in one more toast as our vigil could possibly be a long one."

"Mr. Holmes, was it not possible to elude Von Bodenheim instead of spending all this time in Geneva?"

"I am afraid not, Major. It took him exactly twenty-four hours to ascertain we had not left Geneva. His agent was extremely thorough in checking all hotel guest lists for the names of recent arrivals. I would hazard his field of inquiry was less than twenty-five or so. By an ingenious ruse of sending his agent to deliver telegrams to all these individuals in person, he quickly narrowed my presence to the Hotel Beau-Rivage Of course, I helped the situation by rubbing my Herr Brandt beard slightly askew, which the messenger quickly caught and reported."

"At least that explains that curious telegram we received with regard to a family member arriving on Friday," said I.

"In my case the telegram was addressed to the wrong man, but the correct room number. The following day Bodenheim made his second attempt on my life while strolling in the Jardin Anglais, all, of course, designed to break my nerves. The third and final attack will come tonight, but I see our time has come." Holmes rose and indicated a side door by which we should leave.

Mist and rain greeted us as we stepped into the street.

"Ah, for once," cried Holmes looking about him, "the weather is beneficial to our cause."

"I find it most inconvenient considering we may have to stand around in it," I said, somewhat disgruntled.

"You shall see soon enough, Watson."

Holmes led us down several side streets, then up stairs to adjoining streets, and finally to a side door to what appeared to be a very old apartment building. We climbed three flights of stairs to a hallway, which ended at a small door leading to an attic. From the attic we climbed through a trap door onto the roof.

"We are directly across from my rooms," said Holmes.

Earlier I have described the rooftops of Bern. In the same fashion, Geneva had identical beehive cupolas. We followed Holmes to the far side of the roof and stood behind a cupola. From this vantage point we could see the trap door on the right and the building across the street. There were no lights on in the three windows that were in view from this point.

The situation was reminiscent of "The Case of the Empty House" of so many years ago. I half suspected Major Saunders was thinking the same thing. Somehow Holmes succeeded in reverting our disposition of the prey to that of the hunters. A state of considerable anticipation was apparent in all of us.

The air was redolent with the cool misty rain that continued to fall. I looked to the rear of the building and saw the somnolent glow of the street lamps from down below silhouetting the rooftop in the distance. The time passed slowly. I judged we had been standing behind the cupolas nearly an hour but there was no way to verify this. I could see impatience spreading over Holmes' features. The strain began to wear heavily on all of us. Would Von Bodenheim come tonight?

Suddenly Holmes stiffened and listened intently. Then I heard what had alerted him: A slight noise from the trap door reached my ears. Holmes put his fingers to his lips as we watched intently.

A very lithe man clad in black came through the trap door. Carefully he looked about him in a crouched position, then reached down and brought forth what looked to be a violin case. Catlike, he stealthily moved to the edge of the roof, which had ornamental ironwork at its edge. Very quickly he opened his case and began to assemble his weapon. The shoulder stock was screwed into the main barrel housing. A telescope sight was attached by clamp and screw. The forearm of the rifle functioned as a lever, which he began to pump with methodical precision. As he finished, he turned slightly and I saw his pallid face from the soft argent lights below. Diabolic cunning was written over his features. Von Bodenheim appeared to be the very embodiment of all that was malefic.

As we watched him, he lay down in a prone position to wait for his prey. Holmes quietly took a handkerchief from his coat pocket and fluttered it several times from the left side of the cupola, hidden from Von Bodenheim's view. As if in response, lights from the three windows across the street went on. A figure came into view and sat down in an easy chair, picked up a newspaper and began to read. I looked keenly at the seated figure through the misty haze. Great Scott, it was Herr Brandt, the bookseller. How could this be? Holmes was right here. Major Saunders and I looked at each other in astonishment while Holmes wore the expression of a performer taking his bow before the footlights.

There was no time to speculate on this seemingly bizarre situation. Panic swept over me as Von Bodenheim took careful aim and fired his weapon. A muffled detonation from the air gun was simultaneous with the sound of breaking window glass, as Herr Brandt slumped forward in his chair.

"Now!" cried Holmes. "Now!"

We rushed forward. Von Bodenheim's rifle crashed to the street below as we attempted to hold him in restraint. Holmes was about to slip on a pair of handcuffs when Von Bodenheim, with a burst of super-human strength, broke free. He bounded across the roof to the rear of the building, and was over the parapet before we gained our feet or could aim our guns.

"Quick," cried Holmes, "we cannot let him escape!"

We rushed to the rear of the building and looked over the edge. Bodenheim was moving quickly and lithely toward a window ledge with an open window.

"Stop or we shall shoot," shouted Holmes.

The major and I had our guns trained onto him and were about to fire, when Bodenheim missed his footing as he tried to reach the window ledge. He fell, screaming, to the courtyard below.

Holmes looked at the sprawled body of Bodenheim below and quietly remarked, "Again, as we have seen so many times in the past, retribution has come from a higher power."

A vociferous alarm was raised as lights came on throughout the courtyard. Holmes motioned for us to leave quickly. We followed him back the way we had come and made our way to a main thoroughfare where he hailed a taxi, instructing the driver to take us to the Gare De Conavin Station.

We spent the night travelling in a northwesterly direction across France to Paris. The following morning we left Paris and took a circuitous route to the seaport of Cherbourg. Holmes had arranged baggage and various necessities for us. My own baggage was still in Chamonix with one of my favorite briar pipes. However, it was out of all question to return for it.

Holmes had slept a great deal as we crossed France. By late the following afternoon we were all fully refreshed and met in the smoking car for cigars and a bit of whiskey. Major Saunders posed a question: After all our adventures can we really be out of their grasp?

"I assume any efforts on their part to find us would lead them to follow the shortest route to the coast, namely the port of Calais. While they attempt to verify our departure from Calais we should in all probability be safely on our way back to England. I might add, however, past experience suggests optimism should be tempered with caution. So by all means, let us stay on our guard."

"You don't suppose they could send another assassin?" I inquired.

"I hardly think so, Watson. Frederica Von Strada has lost two of her most professional assassins. I feel quite certain she will have much to answer for to her superiors. The war is not going well for her department. She shall have much to occupy her fanatical energies. It is an amusing thought. She may even face charges for her failed missions. The G.S.S. is hard pressed to admit failure and therefore they may have her quietly shot."

"I for one would relish the thought," said I bitterly.

Major Saunders, again with a look of inquiry over his features, posed another question, "Why did Bodenheim elect such an extraordinary and difficult escape? Why did he not flee through the trap door?"

"There are probably a number of reasons why Bodenheim acted as he did. When we attempted to apprehend him on the roof, he immediately realized his miscalculation. As I am sure you know, a man who is surprised is already half beaten. In the usual sense of the word, assassination connotes terror and death. With regard to Von Bodenheim, we could easily say he turned assassination into a fine art."

"Apart from that," said I, "I think he was a lunatic, extremely cunning and sadistic."

Holmes looked up reflectively. "As to the last point, there can hardly be any doubt. What I mean precisely is this: He displayed such ingenuity and imagination in the pursuit of his unworthy ends that we are forced to admire his skill, however much we may abhor and disapprove of his motives."

Despite the considerable light shed upon our recent experiences, I was still puzzled by a number of questions. "Who was that unfortunate chap who was impersonating Herr Brandt?"

"Oh, that was Geoffrey Hodson from our British Embassy in Geneva. An excellent fellow in every way."

There was a coldness about Holmes that I had never sensed before, almost a blase indifference about the demise of one of our British representatives who had apparently sacrificed his life. I could not leave it at that.

"But Holmes, it all seemed so cold blooded," I remonstrated.

"Not at all," answered Holmes with nonchalance I was about to protest in earnest when Holmes interjected, "Geoffrey Hodson is not dead."

"But we saw him die," cried Major Saunders.

"Yes Holmes, we all saw this poor fellow die."

"On the contrary, you both thought you saw him die."

The major and I looked at each other, perplexed.

"As you know, Mr. Holmes, I have the highest regard for your methods, but this is uncanny. For the life of me, I cannot comprehend how you accomplished this."

"My dear Major, abstract theories of problems always look well on paper, but do not amount to anything without practice and more practice. If perhaps a student forces himself to examine all the facts, however absurd they may look at first glance, he is then on his way to becoming proficient at reaching a successful conclusion."

"I grant you all that, Mr. Holmes, but how did you accomplish this?"

"Well, the Greeks have a saying, 'Illusion is more real than reality.' Of course, you must understand I had the advantage of knowing Bodenheim's murderous habits, and as I said when we arrived in Geneva, we must reverse the situation and become the hunters."

"As I made my arrangements the first day, a far more important element revealed itself."

"Which was?" I quickly asked.

"It was a particular move in the game of chess,"

"Chess!" I said, aghast. "What has…"

Holmes held up his hand. "There is a term in chess, if memory serves me, called the 'Skewer.'"

As if just realizing what Holmes had stated, the major repeated, "Chess."

"Yes, gentlemen, the 'Skewer' attack operates by piercing through a piece in order to transfix another on the same line. It is the second piece, therefore, which is the real target. However, the real target was unknown to Bodenheim, as he was actually viewing a reflection of Herr Brandt. I had a polished metal wardrobe mirror arranged in such a manner as to allow Bodenheim to see just enough of his victim to convince himself of its reality."

Major Saunders face took on an aura of admiration. "It's simply masterful, Mr. Holmes."

"Thank you, Major, but as Dr. Watson can attest, art in the blood is liable to take the strangest forms. During my lifetime, it has only needed expression."

EPILOGUE

---▼---

The entire great war could be investigated on an infinitely wider scale than I could ever think about, much less ever hope to do. Likewise, this entire narrative is not meant to be, indeed could never be a comprehensive survey of the propriety or impropriety of that conflict. Rather, it is hopefully representative of Holmes' activities and work after 1903. His contribution to the war effort was immense and as questions and problems come to light by our present knowledge, his inestimable presence becomes considerably more apparent.

During the interim of the Great War, Holmes' old housekeeper, Martha Hudson, passed away. He was profoundly attached to the old lady, and her passing was a link with Baker St. that was no more. Holmes is less emotional than any man I have ever known, but it was plain to see he was affected in such a way that he felt impelled to re-establish the link by extending an invitation to me to reside with him as long as I wished. After the marriage of my niece Catherine, which took place just after the end of the hostilities, I left London and accepted Holmes' kind offer.

By the end of 1919, our lives had settled down to a simple routine. Mornings, when weather permitted, we took our walks along the chalk cliffs. Afternoons were generally taken up with our own private pursuits. Holmes divided his time between bee keeping, work on his ponderous tome ("**The Whole Art of Detection**") and chemical experiments. These noxious experiments, which were necessary to supplement his income in the early years of his career, gave way by the turn of the century to an intellectual pursuit that he sometimes applied to the solving of crime. However, after 1914, it was an abstract passion, such as one who plays a game of chess for the challenge of the problem. I am relieved to say the well-known chemical corner of years past was absent from our sitting room. I had prevailed upon him to install his chemical apparatus in an adjoining outbuilding. This, in turn, guaranteed Mrs. Murphy, our new housekeeper, and myself that we would not be exposed to his virulent fumes.

As for myself, a great deal of my time was spent researching a multitude of notes of past cases for possible future publication. In addition, I was slowly gaining more information from Holmes regarding his wartime activities, which could possibly be a book in itself at some later date. However, he cautioned that a great deal of the information was of such high sensitivity and still classified as secret by the British government, that it would necessitate a long interim before the public at large could be informed.

For a good portion of the year mist, rain and low clouds dwell over the South Downs. It was on just such a morning that Holmes and I were caught unprepared by a sudden downpour while walking near the cliffs. This, with accelerating winds, made the walk increasingly hazardous. We elected to return to the farmhouse earlier than usual as the inclement weather increased in its ferocity.

By early afternoon we were snugly sequestered in our sitting room, while outside the northeastern gales began to lash at our humble abode. I had settled down into my easy chair with the London Times in hand.

There seemed to be little of interest until an article on the third page caught my attention. The article read:

LIFE AFTER DEATH CLAIMED BY WELL- KNOWN AUTHOR

LONDON. Sir Arthur Donan Doyle, world-renowned author and lecturer has been keeping records of classifying reported happenings of a psychic nature that will eventually be incorporated into a book entitled *The Vital Message.* Sir Arthur has been a member of The Society of Psychic Research since 1893.

The article continued about the research of the society and gave several examples of some of the mysterious events that had occurred over the years. It went on to comment:

> Though the scientific community generally does not recognize aspects of the psychic, this phenomenon has been under-stood and practiced since pre-historic times.

It is pleasant to find someone expressing views that are similar to one's own, especially when that individual has the high achievement and repu-tation as does Sir Arthur. Ever since my astounding experience with Professor D'Eslon, I have taken a profound interest in these matters and never miss an opportunity to study them further.

I turned to address Holmes, who was sitting near the window working on his manuscript. I related the contents of the article.

"I really have a mind to correspond with this society with regard to Professor D'Eslon's psychic abilities."

Holmes looked up with a degree of concern over his features. "I would not do that if I were you."

"But we know beyond any doubt what D'Eslon achieved. It was certainly enough to convince me that the pendulum gives useful information and is not a worthless bauble."

"I grant you all that, Watson, but you must understand the scientific community will demand proof and there is no possible way you can produce such proof."

I reflected a moment. "Surely some of them, amongst all their test tubes, have experienced some of this phenomenon."

"That is possibly so, but if we look at psychic phenomenon from the scientific viewpoint, I am sure we would be disappointed."

"Disappointed?" I reflected. "How so?"

"Simply because so much of these experiences are inspired and not repeatable. Hence, they are in most cases inconclusive."

"If this is so, then all in all one has the impression there is a large residuum which clearly needs an explanation."

"Well, in all probability that is correct, but we must also realize the scientific community at this point in time is very slowly coming to agreement that the observable physical world is in reality very different from what it has so long assumed. But be that as it may, I would rather redirect your attention to a far greater problem.

"In 1914 on Von Bork's terrace I spoke of a cleaner, better and stronger land that would lie in the sunshine."

"I remember it clearly."

"None the less I believe the British Empire is an endangered species."

"But the war is over," I remonstrated.

"You look askance, Watson. It is true we have terminated the hostilities, the storm has cleared, but the winds of change are blowing and the reality of that fact is so thoroughly confused, it is impossible to draw a line—the war was nothing more than an illusion of glory."

Holmes had left his chair and went to the window where he held the curtain aside and looked out. From where I was sitting I could see he was looking out over the windswept downs and the sea beyond.

His voice took on a grave tone. "We find ourselves living in a culture that is collapsing with enormous speed."

I found my friend's somber discourse rather disconcerting. "Can we not trust that, given time, this problem will work itself out?"

"I am afraid not, old friend. As surely as the sun rises in the east, European powers will rise again. There is a lesson of recent years that we may not have learned well."

"What lesson?" I asked, perplexed.

"We should look into the heart of mankind and hope that he may learn in time that he acts in his own best interest when he helps others."

Holmes continued to gaze at the storm laden clouds rolling over the downs. I looked keenly at this man I had known for so many years. It was as if he were looking down the corridors of time and foresaw yet another struggle of titanic proportions in a future era. Suddenly the words I wrote so long ago came to mind: "He was whom I shall ever regard as the best and the wisest man I have ever known."